THE TERMS

Part Two

Ruby Rowe

ISBN-13: 978-1548462284
ISBN-10: 1548462284

Contents

NOTES

The Terms: Part Two is told from the points of view of
Camilla, Ellis, Greyson and Sasha.

The Terms: Part One must be read prior.
This novel contains explicit language and graphic sex,
including aspects of BDSM.

DEDICATION

The Terms: Part two is dedicated to the amazing book bloggers who share about my writing. Your help is making my dream come true.

CHAPTER ONE

Ellis

"What the hell did you say?"

"Sasha claims you met Camilla years ago," Rusty replies.

"You're full of shit. I'd remember talking to her; she's unforgettable."

He gives a half-hearted shrug. "I don't see what the big deal is if you had met her before. All I know is Sasha said there would be hell to pay if you remembered."

I shake my head, knowing damn well the prick's only trying to mess with it.

"Like I said before, get the fuck off my property, and I better never see or hear from you again."

He sneers, evidently pleased with my irritation. He accomplished his goal, which was to plant a seed of doubt in my mind.

"It was a pleasure doing business with you." Once he's in his truck, he drives around the circled pavement to head back the direction he came. Raising his hand toward the passenger window, he flips me the bird and takes off.

Smoke billows from the tailpipe, and his bumper rattles like he's rattled my mind. He had to have made up that story, but of all the lies he could've chosen to make me angry at Camilla, why choose that one?

Walking back to my office, I swipe the paper from my printer and stare at it. It figures the lab would screw this up. I take a seat and call Greyson.

"Douchebag," he says, "way to leave me hanging like that. What does it say?"

"It says I'm the sperm donor," I reply before chuckling.

"Wait—what?"

"Apparently the lab I chose was incompetent. Supposedly, I'm 99.9% Liam's father. It wouldn't show that high of a percentage, right?"

"I don't see how, especially with you and Tony only being half-siblings."

"Do you think we should retake it?"

"Call and ask, and chew the person's ass while you're at it."

Camilla peeks her head inside my doorway and smiles.

"Greyson, I'll talk to you later. Camilla's home."

"OK, man. Let me know what they tell you."

"Sure thing, bye." Ending the call, I walk around the desk with the test results. "Hi."

"Hi. I wasn't sure if I should interrupt or not. Were you able to get some work finished today?"

"A little. Look at this..." I hand her the paper. "The lab managed to fuck up the DNA test."

Camilla

"Camilla, wake up. Camilla." My eyes gradually open, and Ellis is staring down at me with a panicked gaze while clutching my shoulders.

"What happened?"

"You fainted. Do you feel like you could sit up?"

"I think so." He hooks his arm around mine and assists me in sitting up. After a quick stride to his desk, he picks up his cell phone and pushes buttons.

"Irene, could you please hurry up to my office with a wet washcloth and a glass of water?" Once he hangs up, he surveys my face. "Are you sure you're feeling OK? Maybe I should call an ambulance and have you checked out."

I shake my head. "No, I'm fine." My voice is raspy, and my mouth is dry, the roof of it a fly trap for my tongue. "I don't know why I passed out."

"I'm not sure, either. One minute I'm telling you about the incompetency of the lab"—he picks up a paper off the floor and glances to it—"and the next thing I know, you're falling to the floor."

His words stir and thicken the nausea in my gut, reminding me of what transpired moments ago. I put my hand over my stomach.

"Oh, right. The results of the DNA test."

"Have you eaten today?"

How should I handle this situation? I missed lunch before I left for my gynecologist's appointment, but that's not the reason I passed out.

"You know, now that you mention it, I did skip lunch. I got caught up in one of my assignments and didn't have time to eat before I left." I give him a faint smile of reassurance.

"My blood sugar must've dropped. That happens on occasion if I forget to eat." Irene briskly rounds the corner with worry creasing her forehead.

"Ms. Rose, are you all right?" She glances between Ellis and me, unsure of who to give the items to. Ellis swipes the washcloth from her hand, so she gives me the glass of water.

After folding the damp cloth, Ellis presses it to my forehead, but I feel smothered and start to get up.

"I'm fine, really. You can go, Irene, and thank you." Ellis is on his feet first and helps me to a chair by his desk.

"If you need anything at all, you call me again," Irene says before leaving. I take a sip of water, hoping it will rehydrate my mouth, and wishing it was a magic potion to wake me from this terrifying dream.

Kissing the top of my head, Ellis strolls around to his chair. He stares at the paper in his hand again.

"I guess I'll call the lab to see if we need to redo the test. Of course, I still believe Tony's Liam's father, but obviously I need to question them about the results. Did a technician transpose a number or something?"

"I don't know," I mumble as I stare past Ellis and out the window behind him.

"It's obvious they screwed up the test since the results say I'm the perfect match for Liam's father. It wouldn't show that close of a relation. I swear no one can do their job right anymore."

I drag my gaze back to him, and even that takes a great deal of effort.

"I'm sorry, what did you say?"

Pulling his eyebrows together, he examines me.

"No, I'm sorry. I should be focusing on you instead of going on and on about this. I'm sure we'll get it sorted out. Are you feeling any better? We should go downstairs and find you something to eat. I'll have Irene start dinner, as well."

Ellis continues talking, rambling really, and I don't know how to regain composure to form a sentence. He's Liam's father.

Ellis is my son's father.

Not Tony ... Ellis.

"Baby, you're worrying me," he says. His endearing term snaps me back to the present.

"I'm fine, but you seem overly anxious."

Glancing down at his desk, he sets the paper aside.

"It's been a strange, hectic day, and I'm concerned about you."

I tilt my head to the side and sigh. "I'm sorry. In the future, I'll make sure not to stretch out my mealtimes." What I should say is that I'm sorry for doing what Tony asked of me that night over four years ago.

I'm sorry you've been robbed of knowing Liam ... your son, a boy I can already tell you love. That's what I should say....

Before I can stop them, tears drop to my cheeks. Ellis shoves his chair back and walks around the desk. Squatting next to me, he cradles my face and brushes the tears away with his thumbs.

"Why are you crying?"

"I think I'm overwhelmed and tired." Needing to change the subject, I frown. "I got all the way to the gynecologist's office today, only to be told that I wasn't in the system for an appointment. It's like I'm not supposed to get birth control.

"They felt bad that they goofed, so they're going to fit me in first thing in the morning." I smile against his hands. "Since pot was legalized in this state, I'm wondering if people are smoking it for more than recreation. I think they're high on the job."

"I have to agree, and it's nice to see you smile again."

Covering his hand with mine, I lean in and kiss his lips.

"I'll go grab a bite to eat, and then if you don't mind, I'm going to lie down for a bit before Emma leaves."

"That's probably wise after your fainting spell. I'll wake you up for dinner." Ellis's forehead scrunches, and his eyes roam over my face, his expression intense.

"Is everything OK?" I ask.

"You just ... you've always reminded me of someone, but I've never been able to place who that someone is." His thumb skims over my bottom lip. "I also enjoy admiring you since you're so beautiful."

Giving him a nervous smile, I grip his dress shirt at his chest.

"Well, I hope that's not the only reason you're attracted to me."

"Hardly, Camilla. Yes, you're stunning, but you possess many other qualities that draw me to you. You're smart, kind and an amazing mother. You're also strong and genuine ... always wanting to do what's right."

Like my gaze, my mind strays, recalling negative memories.

"That's good to hear. After having to lie all these years about my identity, I wasn't sure I knew that girl anymore. I had to become someone distant and untrusting, but I'm working on changing that."

Squinting, Ellis takes a step back. "What did you say? Repeat what you just said."

"I said I had to become someone distant and untrusting, but I'm working on changing that. You're so kind to Liam and me, and I believe you when you say you won't hurt me with my past. I'm learning to trust wholeheartedly for the first time in my life, and I owe that to you."

Swallowing, Ellis walks back to his chair. He runs a hand down the front of his dress shirt and sits.

"You should eat something and rest before Liam demands your attention."

"That was too deep, wasn't it?"

"No, it was fine. I just remembered a call I need to make for work. It's important."

"OK. I guess I'll see you at dinner then."

Shuffling papers around, he doesn't look up, so I leave his office. Maybe our conversations will continue to deepen, and I'll find the nerve and strength to tell him everything. It must happen, and I'm terrified of that realization.

CHAPTER TWO

One Week Later

Ellis

"I figured Fletcher would drive us," Greyson says as we're about to exit his parking garage.

"I need to be in control tonight." I tug on my lower lip as I watch for a break in traffic to pull out onto the road. I get my chance but cut it close, so I hammer it, shifting my BMW Z4 fast. I get on it, hitting seventy in seconds, and Greyson grabs the handle above the passenger door.

"Damn, you know I love it when you cut loose, but you don't have that much practice at it, so be a little more cautious please."

I roll my eyes. "I'm not that uptight." Recalling a memory from our college days, I glance at him and grin. "And you're one to talk about not having practice.

"Have you forgotten that first weekend you were at Stanford? Ignorant about mixing different alcohols, you downed shots and beer all night long.

"You acted like a tool in front of my friends, and I thought you were going to suffocate on your vomit from how much you drank. Of course, that wasn't until after you threw up on that Theta sorority chick while hitting on her."

"Yeah, yeah, I've heard that story a million times, but I got it together and became cooler than your sorry ass in no time." As he chuckles, I grip the steering wheel tighter.

"There was a time I would've agreed. Now, I know the truth. You were only louder and obnoxious, not cooler." My tone is sharp–cold even. I sense his eyes on me in the silence.

"Damn. I was only joking, Ellis. You're right, I *was* obnoxious ... more reckless, too. Both Tony and I were handfuls, and you know I'm indebted to you for helping me get my shit together."

I shake my head. *I swear I'm losing my damn mind.*

"I shouldn't have said that. I apologize. I guess I am uptight most of the time, especially tonight."

"Stop being hard on yourself. I don't get why you always do that."

Neither of us speak again until I park at The Brown Palace. Greyson unbuckles and clasps my shoulder, giving it a squeeze.

"Come on, cuz. I'll let you buy the first round." He snickers since that means I'm buying two drinks for him, but you know what? I think I'm having a drink tonight.

"No, you can buy me a drink for a change. Just one."

"Wow, first you tear it up on my street, and now you're having a drink... What next? Are you going to tell me you knocked up some chick?"

"Ha ha, funny, man. I think the window for that joke expired."

"Oh, you got to admit those test results were funny."

"I called the lab again today to see if they figured out what went wrong, and they still insist they conducted the test properly.

"The whole thing was strange, like everything has been since Tony died. Let's go inside, and I'll tell you about it. I think I'm going crazy over something."

Greyson and I sit at a small table at Churchill Bar in the hotel. The few patrons are subdued, much like the dim lighting. It's how I prefer it. Actually, it's how I need it in order to keep a grasp on my social anxiety. My family members know better than to ask me to go to a nightclub or busy bar.

As I expected him to do, he orders us both a scotch. When it arrives, he takes a drink and sets it down on his napkin.

"Did you get the last email I sent you regarding Tony's trust? At least he did one thing right by setting that up before his death. It fast-tracked everything."

"I did. Thank you."

"So, what's going on that has you so worked up?"

As I think about how to proceed, I take a sip of my drink.

"Has anyone ever seemed familiar to you, but you're sure you haven't met them before?"

"Uh, yeah, sure. I usually realize they resemble someone else I know."

"Right, but what if you can't place who that someone is?"

"Where are you going with this?"

"It's Camilla... That first night I saw her at the funeral home, I thought I'd met her before, but she swore I hadn't."

"OK, so what's the big deal?"

"Last week, she said something, and it was like déjà vu. I could've sworn she'd said the same thing to me before, but not recently."

He shrugs. "Everyone experiences déjà vu occasionally."

"But this felt more real than that, and she seemed even more familiar to me." I take another drink of the gold liquid and look away. "Something else happened, too."

"I swear it's like pulling teeth to get information out of you. What happened?"

"The reason I hung up on you when I saw the test results was because Sasha's boyfriend showed up. He wanted money."

"You told him to fuck off, right?"

"No, I gave him ten grand. It was all he asked for."

He brushes back his blond hair. "Why would you give him a dime?"

"I needed him to disappear for good. I don't want him around Camilla, Liam or Sasha ever again."

"All right. What does that have to do with the other part of your story?"

"He claimed I had met Camilla before. He said she was keeping it a secret from me, but he didn't know why. Sasha supposedly told him while she was high."

Greyson arches a brow. "That's odd."

"Tell me about it. If he wanted me pissed at Camilla, which he did, you'd think he would've made up something more convincing. He could've said she was after my money or was seeing someone else. What he said made no sense."

"Yet you can't seem to wonder if he was telling the truth."

"I didn't say that."

"Not word for word, but it's obvious."

"OK, but it's ridiculous, right? That's what you're supposed to tell me. I mean, if it was only a casual meeting between us, say through Tony, what would be the reason for her to keep it from me? If it was more than a casual meeting, I'd remember. You can't forget a woman like Camilla."

Nodding, Greyson grabs his drink and downs it.

"That, I agree with. She's beautiful and stands out since she doesn't look or act like the snooty bitches in our circle."

"Exactly. Camilla didn't come from money. She still wears some of her old clothes and hates that Irene waits on her. She wouldn't have a nanny care for Liam if I didn't insist. Hell, she doesn't even get manicures. Her down-to-earth nature makes me want to give her everything."

"But you can't shake that she's hiding something." Glancing away, I take another drink. I can't look him in the eye and say I don't trust Camilla. It feels wrong. "Look, just point-blank ask her if you've met before."

"I did at the funeral home."

"Ask again. You two are closer now, so if it's true, maybe she'll admit it. If she's adamant you didn't meet until recently, you can move on and chalk it up as paranoia caused by Sasha's dick of a boyfriend. I should say *ex*-boyfriend. Speaking of which, how is Camilla's sister doing?"

"She's angry at us for putting her in rehab. I don't know if it will work out or not."

"It's only been a couple of weeks. That behavior is to be expected, but if she's not more receptive to treatment soon, I could go see her. Maybe it would help."

"Why would you do that? You barely know her."

He smiles. "She's Liam Burke's aunt. That makes her important to me."

Liam Burke...

"I want Liam's last name changed, but I'm trying to exercise patience with my demands—I mean requests."

Greyson's smile spreads wide like the Hoover Dam.

"Demands ... interesting. You know, I overheard you on the phone that night we went to Camilla's apartment. You mentioned a playroom. Care to elaborate?"

"It's private." I swallow the last of my drink, and our server is at our table in seconds. I cover the glass with my hand and shake my head. One is my limit. I won't tell Greyson, but I can already feel the damn drink.

"I shouldn't be surprised you're into kink; the quiet ones are always the freakiest."

I roll my eyes. "OK, so I'm into BDSM, but out of respect for Camilla, I'm not going to discuss the details."

"Damn. You've been full of surprises since Tony passed." Greyson's smile falls away. "I miss the arrogant bastard. He was the life of the party. I guess there'll be less drama at family gatherings now."

"I wouldn't count on it."

His grin returns full-scale. "Oh, right. You're going to lie to your family and announce that you have a kid. When is that happening, by the way? It's paining me to keep this secret."

"I'm thinking I'll spring it on them at the benefit gala they're hosting this weekend. They won't have the privacy or time to interrogate me until after they've processed the news."

"*Please* make sure I'm at the table when that happens." His eyes arc round, exuding excitement. While I may take life a little too seriously, Greyson doesn't enough.

He's avoiding what he believes is the inevitable: a wedding with Whitney Peterson. Their marriage was arranged once they were teenagers, and although he did love her then, he doesn't any longer. He feels trapped, but only he can change that.

He'll have to fight for what he desires, like I'm finally doing. The problem is, Greyson doesn't know who or what he wants, and he's running out of time.

CHAPTER THREE

Ellis

"Good morning," Camilla says at my office door.

"Hi." Rubbing my eyes, I lean back in my chair.

"Did you even go to bed last night?" She frowns and steps closer.

"Yes, about midnight, but then I woke up at four and couldn't go back to sleep, so I figured I'd work while the house was quiet."

"I thought I'd pop in and say hi before I left for my doctor's appointment. Irene is going to keep an eye on Liam until Emma gets here. I'm crossing my fingers that everything goes smoothly this time and I get my pills."

I glance to the clock. "Mitch is supposed to be here in ten minutes to ride with you."

She rolls her eyes. "Is that still necessary?"

"Don't roll your eyes at me, and yes, it's necessary. Christopher thinks Tony's death was due to his dealings with foreign intelligence.

"If so, then you shouldn't be out alone. I used my connections and formed the best security team. Mitch was a Delta Force operator, so he'll keep you safe."

Strolling around my desk, she leans over and kisses my cheek. I use the opportunity to take hold of her and give her a passionate kiss; it's one that conveys my desire for her and the need to keep her safe.

"OK, he can ride along. Thank you for looking out for me."

"You're welcome, and I always will."

Once Camilla leaves, I yawn and attempt to reengage in work but it's difficult. I'm tired after waking up early from a dream I had about a party I went to at Tony's house four or so years ago. I assume drinking last night with Greyson caused me to have the dream.

Attending my brother's party is why I seldom consume alcohol. I got drunk on only a few beers, and then I pulled a Greyson and added a bottle of champagne to the mix without any recollection.

I woke up the next morning in a spare bedroom, remembering little from the night before, and I'd never felt so hung over in all my life. I couldn't shake it for a couple of days. I only remembered the champagne since an empty bottle and glass were on the nightstand.

I believe I awoke from the dream this morning because of the lady in red. The one I frequently have of her merged with the one of me at Tony's party. Somehow, she was in the spare bed with me.

I need to get Camilla back to our hideaway. Time with her in the playroom stopped me from having the unsettling dreams. I have to regain my control again.

Camilla

Arriving home from my doctor's appointment, I go straight up the stairs. I bypass Ellis's office and resist the urge to stop at Liam's room when I hear him giggling with Emma.

Once in my bedroom, I set my purse on a chair and pull out the pharmacy bag with my birth control pills inside. I take them into the bathroom and put them in a drawer where Liam shouldn't find them. My little one...

Being at the gynecologist's office stirred up emotions I've so far managed to stuff. My doctor is an obstetrician, as well, so being in the company of pregnant women in the lobby was a reminder of my time carrying Liam in my belly.

Feeling weak, I shift around and lean back against the vanity. I lower my head and weep.

I was also reminded of how Ellis missed over three years of his son's life. The thing is, even if I'd suspected Ellis was the father, I wouldn't have changed a thing all those years because before I knew him and recalled everything about the night we spent together, I believed he was a dangerous human being.

One to be feared. A man capable of selling top-secret government information to the Chinese that could cripple our country.

When I agreed to assist Tony, I felt like I was the hero's lover in a spy movie, helping to save the day. It seemed right at the time.

I would distract Ellis while Tony went to his house, broke into his safe and stole pertinent information before it ended up in the wrong hands. In exchange for that, I would please the man I was in love with and receive twenty-five thousand dollars to pay for a longer rehab stay for Sasha.

I was so foolish. I can't believe I fell for Tony's bullshit. I thought doing what he asked of me would lead to a commitment from him, but instead, I woke up the next morning feeling more disposable and used than I ever had.

Sucking in a breath, I grab a tissue to wipe my eyes. There's a knock on my bathroom door that causes me to jump.

"Who is it?"

"It's me," Ellis says. "Are you OK?"

"Uh, yeah. I was going to take a quick shower and then come find you."

"OK..."

I cover my pounding heart as if my hand could quiet it. I fear the second Ellis gets a good look at me, he'll see the truth. He'll discover my secret.

***

After I shower, I put my hair into a neater bun and dress in jeans and a teal sweatshirt. I sit on a bench in my walk-in closet and put on my tennis shoes.

I need fresh air and time with Liam. I have to clear my head and decide when it's best to tell Ellis my news. Will he kick me out? Will he break his promise and take Liam from me? Will he tell Greyson not to pay Sasha's rehab bills?

All my life, I've done what was needed to protect myself and my family. As important as it is for him to know the truth, I feel incapable of stepping out of my survival mode.

Liam, along with the opportunity to raise him, must come before everything else, but Ellis is quickly moving up the priority list. His heart is special to me, and I don't want to break it. I can't win no matter what decision I choose.

Shaking off my frustration and fear, I grab my purse and walk to Liam's room.

"Momma!" he exclaims before he practically falls from the chair at his desk, trying to get out of it. He brings me the workbook in his hand and holds it up.

"Emma showed me how to make numbers." Grinning with pride, he points to the page so I can see his handwriting. "I drew this many." He holds up five fingers.

"I see. You did a great job."

"I want to show Boss." He slurs his letter *S*, and it sounds adorable.

"OK. We'll go find him in a minute." I point at the desk. "Pick up your pencils and crayons while I talk to Emma." He skips away but adds a huff of irritation.

"He's doing really well for his age, but I have noticed he squints often and has to look back at my examples more times than he probably should while he's writing."

"What are you saying?"

"Um, I wonder if he could be having trouble seeing."

"Oh ... OK. No one in my family has vision problems, so I'm not sure how to handle this at his age. I guess I'll call his pediatrician and see if there's an ophthalmologist they recommend. How long have you been in glasses?"

She pushes the black frames up her nose.

"Since I was about ten. I remember struggling to read things before that. I'd squint and lean forward a lot, and I've noticed the same habits with Liam. It seems like he has trouble seeing far away, so he holds everything close."

I think about his everyday activities, trying to recall if he's ever shown those signs, but I'm too stressed to focus.

"I came to tell you that you can leave for the day. I'm packing a picnic for Liam and myself, and then we're heading to the park. I mean, you're welcome to join us, but I thought you might prefer to start your weekend early."

Liam's head whips my way. "We're going to the park?"

"Yep. In just a little while."

Emma grins. "You really wouldn't mind if I leave?"

"I insist. I feel like I'm spending less time with Liam now that I have so much help with his care. I miss the little one."

"I'm not little; I'm big now." He scowls as he stares down at his crayon box, trying to push a blue one into its slot. He pulls the box up near his face, and I witness what Emma was talking about.

Only when he lifts it close to his eyes can he put the crayon inside. I feel terrible for not noticing before. Emma has barely been in his life and already picked up on his poor vision. At least, it appears she could be right in her observation.

"If you're sure, then I'll take off." Strolling back to Liam, Emma holds out her fist. "See you later, Mikey."

He gives her a fist bump and grins. "Bye, Em." After she leaves, I find a jacket in his closet, and we walk to Ellis's office. Liam's holding his preschool workbook, eager to show him how he traced the numbers.

I remind him to tap on Ellis's office door instead of barging in, and I can tell the simple act makes him feel older.

"Come in." Ellis hardly gets the last syllable out before Liam pushes through the door and runs to his desk. "Boss, look what I did."

It's as if Ellis's tired eyes refresh in seconds. They widen like his grin before he lifts Liam up and sets him on his lap.

"Let me see what you're working on here. Numbers..." His eyes examine the page. "Good work, kid. Next week, a new friend is coming over. He's going to teach you how to speak another language ... Italian."

Ellis looks over at me. "I wouldn't normally suggest starting with Italian, but seeing how he has it in his blood, I think we should give it a try. I also think he needs an evaluation by a speech therapist. Shouldn't he be pronouncing some of his letters more clearly?"

"Are you saying I should've noticed he needs speech therapy?"

He gives me a puzzled look. "I didn't say that, nor was I implying such a thing. *I'm* not even sure he needs it."

I exhale my frustration. "I'm sorry. Emma suggested Liam get his vision checked, so when you said he needed his speech evaluated, it made me feel like a bad mother." Tears wash over my irises.

"Momma, you're not bad."

"No, she's not. She's an awesome mother."

Squirming his way out of Ellis's lap, Liam runs over to me and wraps his arms around my legs. "Mother, you're awesome."

Ellis leans his head back in laughter, and I can't hide my smile.

"So, I'm mother now, huh?"

Giggling, Liam turns back to face him.

"Wanna come with us to the park?"

"Isn't it almost lunch time?"

"We're going to have a picnic at the park," I say. "You can join us if you'd like." I yearn for time alone with Liam, but I would never exclude Ellis. He glances to his watch and grumbles.

"I wish I could, but I have a conference call at one." He finds his smile for Liam. "I'll go to the park next time. OK, Mikey?"

"OK. Can we go now, Mother? Can we?" He jumps up and down.

"It's *Momma*, and yes we can go."

"Take Mitch to the park with you, too, and tonight we can discuss what a great mother you are."

Smiling, I try to convey through my gaze the affection I hold for him. He surprises me more every day.

"We'll talk tonight."

CHAPTER FOUR

Camilla

We're at City Park, about a mile east of downtown Denver. I shield my eyes from the sun as Liam goes down the green slide. He hops to his feet, stomping the brown mulch below.

"Momma, I wanna do it again, but all by myself."

"Sure, but I'm going to stand next to the ladder as you climb it." I watch as he carefully takes the steps to the wooden platform that leads him to the slide.

Once he's at the top, I recall we're not alone and glance to the tree close by that Mitch is leaning against. His arms are crossed, and he's eyeballing the area intently. Remembering Liam, I rush around to the front to watch him slide down.

"I'm gonna do it again by myself." He grins up at me but quickly looks to the ground because of the sun blinding his eyes.

"One more time, and then we're having our picnic." He's a little braver this time as he climbs the steps. He grabs a glimpse at me over his shoulder and gives a serious look.

"I have to be carefawl 'cause Boss isn't here to catch me."

"Yes, that's right, so look up at the steps." He slides for the tenth time before I take his hand and walk toward Mitch, where the picnic basket and blanket are resting next to his feet.

As we approach him, he uncrosses his arms and stands straight. His golden-blond hair couldn't get any shorter, yet he runs a hand over it, anyway.

"Is he worn out yet?" he asks. The earthy tones in his hazel eyes blend in with the scenery, and much like the trees, he's tall and stout.

"Not in the least, but I insisted on a break." Picking up the tan blanket, I spread it out and set the picnic basket on top of it. Liam drops to his knees, panting.

"I'm thirrssttyy." I open the wicker basket Irene loaned me and pull out a bottled water that's still cool from the ice pack it was pressed against.

"Here you go." Picking up another, I hold it out to Mitch. "I brought one for you, too, and a sandwich."

He holds a hand up like he's stopping me. "No, thank you."

"Please ... at least drink a water." Cracking a faint smile, he takes the plastic bottle from me.

"Thanks." I dig in the basket again to find our turkey sandwiches.

"Chris!" Liam exclaims. I look up, and Christopher is walking toward us, flaunting a grin. Mitch repositions his body to where we're directly behind him. Once Chris is closer and he recognizes him, his shoulders relax and he steps aside.

"Hi, Mitch."

"Hi," he replies in a protective tone.

"I came to see Camilla and my favorite buddy." Mitch watches his every move as Chris steps on the blanket. His hands are shoved in the pockets of his khakis.

"Is everything OK?" I ask.

"Irene told me where you were going, so since I had some errands to run, I thought I'd stop by."

"I went down the slide this many times." Liam holds both hands up and spreads his fingers open.

"Wow, I wish I'd seen that," Chris replies.

"Have you had lunch yet?" I ask.

"No."

"Then sit. I have an extra turkey sandwich." Christopher takes a seat on the blanket, and I hand him a sandwich and a bottled water.

Fishing out a container of grapes and carrot sticks, I open it and rest it between the three of us. It's awkward having Mitch stand guard, but I'm not sure what I could do about it.

"Did Ellis know you were stopping by?" I ask, already sure of the answer.

"No. I imagine he'll find out, but I don't care. I never get to talk to you anymore. I miss hanging out with you and Liam." He grabs the top of my kiddo's tennis shoe and shakes it.

"Yeah, things sure have changed," I mumble.

"How are you handling it?"

"Good, I guess."

"I heard about Tony's will."

"What did you hear?"

"That he left his estate to Ellis. I'm disappointed in Tony. Even if he didn't wish to see Liam, he should've left him money for his future. I never understood how he could sit by and allow you to struggle."

I want to ask him if he ever spoke up for me and Liam to get Tony to provide for his son, but I fear I'd be hurt by his answer.

29

I suspect Christopher had one motive only—to keep us to himself.

"What's done is done. He obviously wanted Ellis to have it instead."

Chris looks to Mitch and back at me. "Do you think we could have a minute alone?" he asks me under his breath. I weigh his question and look to Mitch.

"Mitch, I'm sorry to ask this, but could you give us some privacy for a few minutes?"

"Sure." His glare at Chris doesn't go unnoticed before he strolls off and scans the area again.

"We shouldn't be talking like this. Ellis wouldn't approve since he knows how you feel about..."

"How I feel about you?"

Staring at my sandwich, I pick at the corner of it, creating crumbs.

"Yeah, that."

"Momma, there are big birds over there." Liam points toward a few geese creeping closer to us.

"Yep. Those are geese. Maybe we can toss them a few pieces of our bread when we're finished."

"Have you thought about challenging the will?"

"It had crossed my mind, but I've decided against it."

I brave a look at Chris, and he scowls.

"Why would you do that? You should get that money for Liam. Ellis is unpredictable. He could suddenly move you out, and then what? You need to fight for it now before it's too late."

"Slow down, Chris, and watch what you're saying in front of Liam. He tends to repeat things, and he's understanding more every day." I look to Liam, but he's distracted by the geese.

"Tell me why you won't do it."

"I have my reasons, but I can't share them with you."

"You owe it to Liam to get that money."

"Please drop it. I'm trying to give my mind a break from all the drama."

"Have you forgiven me?"

Biting on my lip, I stare off at Mitch, who's roaming around nearby.

"I was angry with you in the beginning, but I'm not anymore. I've kept secrets of my own, and we know what Ellis did to me initially. None of us are perfect, so it doesn't seem fair to punish you when you were always good to Liam and me."

Grabbing my hand, he gives it a squeeze, so I look back at him.

"Thank you, Cammy. I can't tell you what that means to me. Please let me spend time with you and Liam. Ellis doesn't have to know about it. We could pick times to meet when he's busy."

"I can't hide it from him, and you say we'll hang out as friends, but we're already talking about personal stuff, like Tony's estate. I have a feeling you'll cross a line."

"I won't." He shakes his head, but his lack of eye contact isn't convincing.

"Ellis is never going to go for it when he knows how you feel."

"You say that like you need his permission."

"It's about respecting our relationship. I wouldn't want him spending alone time with a woman who had romantic feelings for him, so he deserves the same consideration in return."

"Did you ever consider that Ellis could be doing all this so you don't go after Tony's money? Caring for you and Liam is pocket change compared to Liam inheriting Tony's millions."

"No, that thought never crossed my mind, and it doesn't matter; Liam can't have the money."

My little one pats my leg. "I'm done and want to pway on the swings."

"OK, sweetie." I yank my hand away from Christopher.

"Why can't you get the money for Liam?" He's squinting in confusion, and he needs to drop it. I can't tell him it's because Tony isn't Liam's father.

"Look, I came here to spend time with my kid. You're welcome to stay and play with him, too, but we're done talking about this."

"Fine. Will you think about spending time with me?"

I sigh. "I'll talk to Ellis, but I guarantee it's futile."

"He's known you for five seconds in comparison to our years together. I deserve time with you."

"As friends..."

"Right." Sliding a hand along his dark hair, he brandishes a devilish smile, confirming why we can't spend time together. It's going to be hard enough to do damage control on the stunt he pulled today. My phone vibrates in my pocket from a text message, so I pull it out.

Ellis: *Do you think Liam would be afraid of climbing after our fall?*

Me: *Trust me, he's over his fear. Why?*

Ellis: *My maintenance guys are headed to the hardware store to buy a jungle gym kit for Liam. I'm having one built in the backyard, but I started wondering if he would be afraid of it.*

Me: *I can't get over your sweetness.*

Ellis: *You can get over it by getting under me—in my bed—tonight. I'm feeling all better and more than ready to fuck you hard.*

Blushing, I swallow and send the emoji that makes an *O* face. Fumbling with my phone, I shove it back in my pocket. Having gained some clarity, I sit up straight and look at Christopher.

"Since you want more than a friendship with me, I'm not hanging out with you unless Ellis is present. Now, if you want to go push Liam on the swing, I'm sure he'd love that. Then, I think you should go."

As if Mitch can sense the tension, he starts heading back toward us. Annoyed, Christopher shakes his head and stands.

"Come on, Liam. Want me to push you on the swing?" Clapping, Liam forgets about the geese he's been trying to throw crumbs at and jumps to his feet.

"Yay!" With the brightest grin on his face, he grabs Chris's hand and beams up at him. Even through his frustration, Christopher finds his smile, and their sweet moment leaves me once again conflicted. How do I find an appropriate compromise to this bizarre situation?

CHAPTER FIVE

Camilla

After using Ellis's ginormous bathroom, I trade places with him and sit on the side of his bed. Becoming fidgety, I play with the hem of my short red chemise and examine the dark mahogany frame surrounding me.

Like his bathroom, it's massive, and I feel it could swallow me whole as my mind dwells on the incident with Christopher at the park.

With the door open between Ellis and me, I hear the sink turn on, and my mind reaches the conclusion that if my confession is barely audible over the running water, the impact on him and the backlash on me will be less intense.

"I have something to tell you," I blurt out.

"What's that?" He starts brushing his teeth, so I feel as if the safety belt is buckled, protecting me from an oncoming collision.

"Christopher dropped by the park today to spend time with Liam ... and me."

Water off.

Spit next.

The sound of a ping as his toothbrush connects with the marble vanity.

Oh, damn. Brace for impact.

He appears at the doorway, so I take a glimpse at his blue eyes that are iced over with anger.

"What happened exactly?"

My gaze falls to his bare feet and roams upward. I see there's no barrier between his large cock and the thin cotton of his grey sweats. His slender hips do me a solid and barely hang on to his pants for my viewing pleasure.

I follow the sexy V up to his chiseled abs and on past them until I reach his shirtless chest, which has a spattering of hair. Oh, how I love this irresistible man.

"Camilla, answer my question." Reluctantly, I look at his eyes. Yep, still icy.

"He said he dropped by to hang out with us, so since Liam and I were having a picnic, I was polite and offered him a sandwich. He ate lunch before entertaining Liam on the playground. Then, he left."

I bite the corner of my lip, hoping this is the end of the conversation. Leaning against the doorframe, he crosses his arms and furrows his brow.

"What did you two discuss while *hanging out*? And your honesty decides whether you receive a reward or a punishment."

All his sexiness and the use of those two words cause my pelvic muscles to contract. My stomach flinches from the need and desire, and my breathing accelerates.

"Stop eye-fucking me. Even though it's working at getting my cock hard, it's not enough to take my mind off you and Christopher alone at the park."

I can't help but look at his rigid cock now. Removing the distance between us, he grasps the back of my hair and pulls it downward so I have no choice but to look up at him. This move of his is one of my favorites, so my desire mounts.

"Technically, Mitch was present also."

He purses his lips. "Stop stalling. I'm giving you one more chance to answer me."

"He asked if I would spend time with him on occasion. He said he missed us, and he also questioned whether I would be fighting for Tony's money ... you know, for Liam."

"And how did you respond?"

"I said I wasn't pursuing Tony's estate. I also told him I wouldn't hang out with him unless you were present. I handled it. I promise."

"And why did you tell him you wouldn't challenge the will?"

"I didn't share with him my reason, but it's because I want to say Liam's your child, Sir."

His eyes soften in an instant, and his lips twitch. His fingers delve deep inside my long tresses and massage my scalp.

"Mmm..." I hum.

"Since I'm so pleased with your good behavior, I'm going to reward you, my Rose."

Enraptured by his words, I gasp and feel my body stiffen. Beneath the surface, it's tingling with anticipation, ready for a hit of his delectable touch.

Putting a knee on the mattress, he slips his arm around my back and moves me up in bed. I stretch out in the center and stare up at his firm pack of abs. Unable to resist, I skim my fingers over each raised section.

"You seem rather turned on tonight."

Pulling my gaze away from his amazing body, I stare at his piercing eyes.

"When you're extra sweet to Liam, like you were today when you said you were building him a playset, it does something to me. Oh, and when I get a chance to gawk at your body, which looks like this, I can't help but get turned on."

Ducking his head to my neck, he nuzzles it with his nose before I hear his long inhale.

"I like when you're in the moment," he breathes in my ear. "You've seemed worried and in another place lately. I think I'll take your mind off things even more."

His mouth begins its journey down my neck, applying faint kisses, but they feel the furthest from faint. They're hot ashes to my skin, his wet tongue snuffing them out after, leaving a smoldering sensation in its wake.

I *need* to be in the present with Ellis to forget the painful past and scary future. I want to let go and feel the tingling pleasure he's delivering, so I clutch the sheet with both hands and tilt my head back to give him all the room he needs to take my mind off things.

His open mouth trails down my chest and sneaks beneath my silky chemise. He yanks a strap off my shoulder and pushes up my breast, freeing my nipple.

"It's ripe for me already." The tip of his tongue skims around the peak, and I buck beneath him, feeling the hardness through his sweats. I crave more of his mouth and his cock inside me. I yearn for Ellis in a way I've never craved another man.

He blankets me with his body, and I lose my breath from his powerful muscles. His thundering heart against mine is hypnotic, and I get lost in his magnetic presence.

Slithering his way down, he pushes my lingerie up to my chest to expose my skin. I experience a chill but only for a second before there's more wet kisses ... more heaven ... more promises. He provides a sense of protection I've never known before.

"Baby, you smell so good. I can't wait to taste you." His gruff voice and erotic words unfurl a moan from my lungs. I grab his hair and clutch it as he grazes his mouth farther south, giving my most sensitive spot a feel of his sizzling breath. "Hold the headboard and don't let go. No. Matter. What."

"Fuck," I mumble, aware of how difficult it will be. His headboard is a sleigh design, but I can reach the top where I grasp it with both hands.

"Fuck, *Sir*," he says before smirking at me. God, I love playful, sexy Ellis, and to think I'm about to get a cocktail of both playful and alpha male only makes me wetter for him.

"Fuck, Sir. Please taste me."

Ellis

Camilla begging for my tongue kills my humor, and I pierce her with a stare that emits my lustful thoughts—my torturous plan. Picking up her leg, I place it over my shoulder and slide two fingers right into her.

She's soaked more than usual, and damn it all to hell. I'm losing my control once again, growling and burying my face against her sweet cunt.

Her scent, already familiar, is only mine to breathe, her pussy only mine to taste, and this sensuous body was only made to tangle with mine.

Camilla is *mine*, and no weak and conniving man like Christopher is going to swoop in and take her from me. *No man is ever stealing her away.*

I lick her rough and hear the squeaky sounds of her hands grappling to hang on to the headboard. She's moaning excessively, so to further drive her wild, I pull away often and rake the stubble on my face along her inner thighs.

It's to mark her so she'll remember this tomorrow; the way I fucked her with my tongue until she unraveled against my face.

Removing my fingers from her, I slow it down, barely licking her clit with the tip of my tongue. I don't move from that spot, and ever so faintly, I graze my wet fingers down between her ass cheeks.

Her breath hitches, and she comes apart at the seams. My girl crumbles until she's leveled by a paralyzing orgasm.

Damn, if it were possible, I'd watch her for hours as she drowns in the pleasure only I can give her.

It's too brief of a moment where I get to relish in her orgasmic glow; a combination of her damp, flushed skin, tight nipples and parted swollen lips. Add her pounding heart and eyelids straining to stay open, and she's a sensual painting come to life.

"Ellis ... Ellis." Her words are longing whispers as her arms shake above her. "I need to feel you inside me."

"You're about to feel me all right. Let go of the headboard." Moving up over her, I prepare to stick my aching cock inside her, but her eyes open wide, and she grabs my biceps.

"I can't start my pills yet. *Please*, this time wear a condom." I scowl. No can do. "I don't ever want that barrier between us. You'll be the only woman..."

Reaching up, she traces my jawline. "That's sweet, but I told you I wasn't having another child out of wedlock."

"I want to make a little human as awesome as Liam. I want a child of my own ... with you." I look over her head. Why do I always tell her vulnerable shit? It's silent, so I glance down, and her eyes are swimming in tears.

"Camilla ... for fuck's sake, don't cry. I'll pull out if it's that important to you." Realizing I'm kind of being a jackass, I gradually lower myself on top of her and kiss her soft lips.

"You feel so good beneath me. Please, let me inside you."

She stiffens and gasps for breath. The next thing I know, she shoves against my chest.

"Oh, god. Marshmallow, marshmallow, marshmallow!" I move off of her, wondering what the fuck's happening. "I—I'm sorry. I have to go to my room."

She climbs off the bed at lightning speed, but once she reaches my door, she stops with her back to me. "Ellis, I'm so sorry. For everything."

Just like that, she's gone. I fall onto my back and rub my forehead. I'm a dick. She shouldn't have needed a safe word in that moment.

I pushed too much too soon, yet she's the one apologizing. She's afraid she's going to end up alone with another kid, but I'm not my brother.

CHAPTER SIX

Ellis

"Red's your color," I say as I glide my fingers along the bottom of her negligee. I touch her bare thigh, my knuckles grazing her silky panties. "It matches the auburn in your hair."

Unlike the rest of my body that's numb from the drinks Tony kept feeding me, my dick is at attention.

"Thank you." She rubs her temple. "Damn, the champagne seems stronger than usual."

"Probably because we drank the whole bottle." I hold it up before setting it on the nightstand, along with her glass. My lightheadedness increases, so I fall back on the bed. "Lie down with me. We can be dizzy together."

I wake up in a sweat, burning hot and experiencing the same lightheadedness I felt in my dream. That's fucking wonderful; my mind's making up new disturbing shit about the lady wearing red.

I glance to the clock. 1:00 a.m. Jerking off the sheet, I sit at the side of the bed and run a hand through my hair. I've got this nervous energy and a cock that's hard as nails.

Damn, the night took a turn I didn't see coming. First Camilla freaked out and now this. A cool shower–that's what I need. Stumbling to my bathroom, I adjust the knobs for the water.

I conjure up thoughts about public speaking, the IRS and my mother's parental tone to get my dick limp enough to take a piss. I manage to relieve myself before I step inside the stall.

Grabbing the bar of soap, I scrub my body briskly, determined to ease my anxiousness. My cock is semi-erect, but I refuse to jerk off when I have a gorgeous woman across the hall.

This isn't helping me in the least, so I rinse, grab a towel from the rack and stroll back to my bedroom.

"I'm sorry for earlier," Camilla says from my bed in the darkness. Her voice is timid and sweet, and I'm standing still, unsure of how to proceed.

Briefs. Yeah, underwear between us is necessary so I don't fuck this up again. I find my way to my dresser and pull open the drawer.

"No. Please come to bed and make love to me ... or fuck me hard. I'll leave it up to you."

My towel hits the floor, and I stalk over to her.

"I'm turning the light on," I say before I hit the switch to the one on my nightstand. Her arm covers her eyes, but as she slowly brings it down, her gaze lingers on my cock, making me harder than ever.

Moving over top of her, I cage her in with my arms. Her hair is a thick mess of waves, like I've already fucked her, and as she stares up at me all doe-eyed, I soak up the sight of her.

"Let's see if you're doing this for me or for the both of us." Lowering my body, I push her nighty up above her tits. As I skim my fingertips down her stomach, she squirms, her hips moving beneath me. "Stay. Still."

I slide them down her slit next and tease her nipple with my tongue. She taunts me back with an alluring whimper and starts to move again, but she stops herself in an instant. "Compliant"—I slip two fingers inside her pussy—"and wet. That means you want this, too."

Nodding, she brings her hand up and traces my jaw like she did earlier in the night. Her finger grazes the slope of my crooked nose before her thumb presses into the deep cleft of my chin.

She appraises my harsh features often, which is perplexing. I'm not the pretty boy my brother was, but Camilla seems to revel in my looks.

"Why the word marshmallow?" I move my fingers languidly in and out of her, drawing her closer to the brink. She pants to get her breath enough to speak.

"In the kitchen, the first night we had sex, I was watching you hold that fork and marshmallow. You were grinning and joking and had been so sweet to Liam, reading to him.

"I realized then how complicated this would become. How hurt I could end up." She closes her eyes and gasps from the feel of my fingers working her over.

"At that moment, I thought I should say stop and then flee as fast as possible, but you were mesmerizing. I couldn't run away then any more than I can now."

Grabbing my arms, she clenches them, her fingernails digging into my biceps. She's close to an orgasm, but I won't let her come. I want to feel her squeezing my cock first before I'm forced to pull it out of her.

Removing my fingers from her tight pussy, I push one of her legs up until her knee touches her chest. I drive into her, and she releases a trill of satisfaction, so I pull back and do it again.

"*Christ*, baby, I love being inside you." I move faster, deeper, harder until she cries out my name. "Come, my Rose."

My own release hits me without warning, so I drop her leg and manage to pull my cock out just in time to shoot my load onto her stomach.

Damn, seeing her flushed and sated with my cum all over her skin is erotic as hell. I'm still claiming her, only differently, and I can't say it's all that bad. Well, it won't be on occasion.

Pressing our bodies together, I kiss my way down her neck and inhale her sweet and addictive fragrance. I need the name of the perfume she wears so I can buy it in bulk. I envision the boxes being delivered now, and I'm wondering when I lost my damn mind.

This woman causes me to do illogical things. I forced her to live in my home, and I undermined her attempt at getting birth control. She and Liam turned my world upside down, so I'm blaming them.

I have a hideous child-proof gate a mile long at the top of my staircase, crumbs under my dining room table and sticky fingerprints all over my home.

I read bedtime stories to my brother's child who I want the world to think is mine. I want *Liam* to think he's mine. What happened to the Ellis I knew all my life?

"Your scent makes me irrational," I mumble as I skim my nose along her chest. "No, *everything* about you makes me irrational."

The satin fabric of her lingerie sticks to my damp skin, and I experience déjà vu again. I raise up to stare at her hazel eyes. She's relaxed and sleepy now, so they open and close ... open and close.

"So, what is your name, Lady in Red?"
"Let's keep this night a mystery," she mumbles.

Feeling as if I've been throat punched, I lose my breath while I'm teleported back in time. Like the beach at Normandy on D-Day, my mind is trampled with memories from the night at Tony's party: Camilla entering the room, her bashful smile, and her sensuous body in silky lingerie.

I recall her sitting next to me on the bed and handing me a bottle of champagne.

Fuck, I met her that night.

Camilla is the lady in red.

I blink several times, thinking it can't be true. Beneath me, her eyes are closed, her breathing slow but heavy. She's asleep.

Climbing off her and the bed, I find a pair of pajama pants and quietly leave my room. I head to my office, my place of reprieve, and shut the door.

As I pace, I try to summon more memories from that night, but I'm drawing a blank past the point of us drinking together. When was that party? The fall I believe. September or October three years ago. No, maybe it was four. *Dammit.* I rub my forehead.

Tony was celebrating a business deal he'd scored and insisted I come. I showed up to find strippers and way too many guests. The music was loud, alcohol and drugs were abundant, and I wanted the hell out of there.

My brother gave me several drinks to calm me, and before I knew it, I was hiding out in a spare bedroom, only because he begged me not to leave yet.

I know Camilla wasn't there the next morning. I stumbled to the bathroom and then left before finding Tony, figuring he was passed out with a woman in his bed, anyhow.

God, all this time Camilla has been sparing me the embarrassment of being drunk with her in that bedroom. I likely said stupid shit before I passed out. Wait—I know what I said. It's what I dreamed earlier last night....

I mentioned her looking good in red and how it matched her hair. We were both dizzy, so I think I suggested she lie down with me.

What happened after that? Did I pass out then? Shit, she was probably dating my brother at that point, and I was hitting on her ... feeling her up.

I bet she didn't tell me at the funeral home that we'd met because she didn't want me to find out about Liam. Then, after she moved in, I imagine she didn't want to admit she'd lied about that, too.

This is too much to process. Coming to a stop, I press my palms to my eyes. Meeting Camilla at that party is the reason I was drawn to her when I saw her again at the funeral visitation.

Somewhere in my mind, I held on to her beauty and kindness, and maybe I've had the dream all this time because the control freak in me needed to remember that night.

I strive to be aware of every aspect of my life, and at that party, I was the furthest from feeling in control.

Should I mention this to her? I'm humiliated she saw me in an inebriated state, but on the other hand, I want all the pieces to the puzzle.

I also don't want her to carry guilt for a secret she doesn't need to keep. The woman has class, sparing me the humiliation all this time. My Rose deserves another reward.

CHAPTER SEVEN

Camilla

I inhale the aroma of the wine-colored roses on my dresser. Vases of them are resting on every available spot in my bedroom.

I point to each and count. Eight dozen to be exact. If I had to guess, there are more on display throughout the house. I'm not sure what I did to deserve them, but they're lovely.

I can't wait to thank Ellis, but I need my earrings in first before I'm ready to attend the fundraising gala tonight. Once my ensemble's complete, I put my hand over my stomach.

I'm such a wreck, yet I'm excited, too. I love anything involving charity work, and this event is to raise money for Ellis's mother's literacy program.

The funding pays for teachers to work at after-school programs, where they help children learn to read while they're waiting to be picked up for the day.

Tony's finest collection of paintings will be auctioned. Like his brother, Ellis appreciates the arts and has paintings hung throughout the house.

There's a knock on my door, and I'm sure it's him.

"Come in." Upon opening it, he stops abruptly. His Adam's apple bobs as his eyes travel over my body.

"Shit," he utters through gritted teeth. I glance down at my dress before I take a glimpse of myself in the mirror above my dresser.

"I'm sorry. I know you wanted me to wear the scarlet dress, but this ivory one is more appropriate for spring, and I really don't wish to stand out in that bold color—"

"Camilla," he says slowly, hanging on to every syllable.

"What is it? Do I not look elegant enough?" I tug on the teardrop diamond earrings Ellis gave me this morning. "I'm already nervous and self-conscious, so say something."

Strolling over, he cups my cheeks and gives me a gentle kiss before he lowers his head to rest on mine.

"Shut up, you stunning woman. I said *shit* because I didn't think of the consequences of you appearing this gorgeous in the presence of males who will undoubtedly hit on you."

Exhaling the breath I was holding, I press my palms against his firm chest beneath a black tux.

"I could say the same about you."

He leans back and smiles. "I certainly hope no men hit on me, seeing how I'm straight."

"And taken." I blush from declaring he's mine.

"I like the sound of that."

"I do, too, Sir."

His lips land on mine again. "Sir ... that one word is all I need to hear to get hard for you," he mumbles against them. Reaching in his tux pocket, he pulls out the ruby necklace I wear in the playroom. "I have one request; I'd like you to wear this tonight. It still matches the gown you chose."

Nodding, I turn my back to him. He drapes it over my neck, and as he secures the clasp, my body trembles. His hands slide down my arms, and his mouth skirts along the bare skin of my neck and shoulder.

"If I didn't wish to admire you in this dress all evening, I'd take you to our hideaway this instant."

"I hope it happens soon, Sir."

"Oh, it will," he breathes in my ear. "That I promise you. And the pleasure I'm going to deliver will make you forget the word marshmallow."

***

"You're fidgety. I need you to be the calm one," Ellis says as Fletcher drives us to the gala.

"It's my first time at something like this, and I'm meeting your family. I'm sorry, but serenity is not at the forefront. What do I say if someone asks about my past or what I do for a living?"

Ellis grasps my hand between us. "Tell them you're from South Carolina and working on your master's. Give them some truth but not the whole truth. It's a game to them, so don't make it easy."

"OK, but I don't know the rules of the game. What if they ask where I live?"

"Tell them you live with me."

"You don't mind if I drop that bombshell?" Bringing my hand up, he kisses it.

"Take a deep breath, Camilla. Once my parents know they have a grandchild, everyone will find out, so it's fine to say we live together. I'd prefer people think I'm in Liam's life every day, as opposed to some every-other-weekend arrangement.

"I'll be right by your side, so I'll fill in the gaps. The guests will be so enthralled by your beauty, they'll be too busy building themselves up so as not to feel inferior. Trust me; they'll mostly talk about themselves."

I sigh with relief and lean my head against his shoulder in a way that won't mess up my updo. Once Ellis surprised me with my earrings this morning, I was whisked off to a salon where I was given the royal treatment from head to toe.

I was served champagne while I received a mani-pedi, and then my hair was pinned up into a loose style of curls and braids. I've never experienced such pampering.

"Thank you for everything today. I'm excited." I grin as I admire my evening gown. The empire dress reaches my ankles, yet the thin material leaves much to the imagination.

The entire ivory fabric is adorned with beading, lace and tiny pearls, especially the bodice that's more intricately detailed. The delicate cap sleeves and sweetheart neckline make me appear younger, and the dress has a romantic feel.

I love everything about it and wish so much that Sasha could see me in it. Although, I doubt she'd give me the response I'd like right now.

She's frustrated over her stay at Passages and is threatening to leave. It's not that she doesn't appreciate the generous help she was given, but the affluent environment is foreign to her.

I'm beginning to wonder if more isn't better in her case. She's not accustomed to receiving massages or having chefs prepare her meals.

She's never rubbed elbows with celebrities, yet she's hearing their darkest secrets and sharing with them her own.

I wouldn't be surprised if she showed up on our doorstep soon, but I don't want Ellis aggravated by the possibility, so I'll keep that worry to myself.

The Mercedes pulls up in front of the Denver Center for the Performing Arts. Releasing my hand, Ellis rubs his palms on his knees, leans his head back against the seat and begins breathing harshly.

"Fuck, I hate attending pretentious shit like this."

Brushing my fingers along his hair, I smile.

"Imagine you're taking me out on a lavish first date, and the others are simply guests we don't know."

Turning to me, he clasps my chin, and his warm breath comforts me.

"Damn, in all this time, I've not taken you anywhere."

"Ellis, you've brought more excitement to my life than I ever could've imagined. It doesn't matter the place. Besides, I think today makes up for our lack of outings."

"Let's do this. I want everyone to see how spectacular you are."

Ellis

I'm clutching Camilla's hand harder than I should be. How did I ever walk into one of these functions without her? I'm ashamed it's so difficult for me.

I'm a successful, wealthy man, who for reasons unbeknownst to me, women find attractive. I also have a gorgeous woman on my arm tonight, so why does it stress me out to be amongst this crowd?

Loosening my grip on Camilla's hand, I feel her fingers tremble against mine, so I slide my arm along her back and lead her in the direction of one of the bars. She's got to relax so I can. I'd love a drink right now, but I don't trust myself to stop at one.

While we wait for Camilla's glass of wine, my eyes canvass the room. I purposely arrived last minute so that we'll soon have to take our seats at the table. The less mingling the better.

Someone clasps my shoulder from behind, so I flinch.

"Relax, cuz, it's only me," Greyson says before he comes up beside me. "Although, I will say Aunt Estella has already cornered me twice regarding your whereabouts."

I roll my eyes. My mother would be waiting impatiently. Camilla turns and smiles.

"Greyson, it's so nice to see a familiar face."

"It's great to see you again. I wouldn't miss tonight for the world," he adds with a clipped laugh before he takes a drink from his glass.

"Why is that funny?" she asks.

"Uh, there's just a lot of entertainment at these functions."
Noticing who's walking toward us, I lean in to him. "Whitney
at one o'clock."

"*Dammit*, I haven't had enough drinks to tolerate her."

Whitney Peterson's perfectly plucked eyebrows lift as she
gets closer. She's long forgotten about Greyson as she sizes up
Camilla.

"Ellis ... Greyson," she says while smiling at my girl. "Who
do we have here?"

"Whitney, I'd like you to meet my girlfriend, Camilla Rose."
She holds her hand out like Camilla's supposed to kiss it. She
instead shakes it more than Whitney would like.

"Camilla, this is a family friend, Whitney Peterson."

"Soon to be family, once Greyson here makes an honest
woman out of me. It's nice to meet you. Hmm ..." She covers
her chest with her hand. "Oh, my gosh, are you related to the
late cellist Leonard Rose?" She's exuding excitement that's
genuine since this is an opener for her to brag.

"No, there's no relation."

Whitney's eyes dart between Greyson's and Camilla's.

"I don't know if Greyson told you, but I'm a gifted cello
player for the Colorado Symphony." Her fingers lightly brush
back her strawberry-blond hair. "Have you ever attended the
symphony at Boettcher Hall?"

"No, I'm sorry, I haven't."

Whitney swats my shoulder. "Ellis, you must take her." Not
waiting for my response, she taps Greyson's nose and frowns.

"Sweetie, my parents are insisting I sit with them this evening. I hope you don't mind."

"Nope." He stares her down until she's uncomfortable.

"Well, find me after. Camilla, it was nice meeting you, and make this recluse take you to the symphony to hear me play."

"Of course. Take care," Camilla replies. Once Whitney strolls off, Greyson shakes his head.

"Be sure Ellis points out the piranhas before they get the chance to sink their teeth in you. They're not only found in the Amazon basin and can now miraculously walk on land."

Looking puzzled, Camilla says, "But she implied you're a couple."

"The key word there–implied." Holding his glass up and discovering it's empty, he excuses himself.

"Wow, I suspect this evening will be interesting."

"You have no idea. Damn, my parents are approaching. I'll keep it brief."

Camilla

As Ellis's parents come closer, every neuron in my brain signals for me to run. I glance to the door we came in, emergency exits and a hall that I hope leads to a bathroom so I can vomit after this introduction.

"Ellis, sweetheart, I was beginning to think you weren't going to show." She kisses both his cheeks and then grants me a smile. Her eyes survey me as Ellis speaks to his father.

This woman is the epitome of classic elegance. Her blond hair is up in a tight twist, and her soft makeup gives her a youthful appearance. She's petite, whereas Ellis's father is tall and broad.

"Mother, Father, I'd like to introduce you to my girlfriend, Camilla Rose. Camilla, these are my parents, Estella and James Burke."

Upon hearing the word girlfriend, Estella's eyes sparkle with joy. I think that's a good sign. I reach out to shake her hand.

"Dear, you're absolutely radiant," she coos as she examines my face. James practically pushes her aside and takes my hand next.

"It's a pleasure to meet you, Camilla. Ellis, being the private man he is, has starved us of details, so we look forward to getting to know you."

"Thank you. I look forward to it, as well, and I'm touched to have the opportunity to attend such an important event."

Estella beams at me. "I love her already. Ellis says you're interested in philanthropy. We must have lunch soon to discuss it."

"Yes, I'm getting my master's now in Public Administration."

"Ohhh," she says in frustration. "I wish we could chat about it this instant, but I need to make sure everything's in order for the auction. It was lovely meeting you. Let's talk a bit over dinner."

While she leans up to give Ellis a peck on the cheek, his father smiles at me and takes a moment to give me a once-over.

"Ellis, son, you better not let this one out of your sight."

"I don't plan on it." He leans down and presses his lips to my temple, and I blush from his father watching.

As they speak about people I don't know, I take the time to admire the ballroom. Sections of white fabric draped from the ceiling meet in the center, where a lavish crystal chandelier shines with dozens of lit bulbs that reflect light off brilliant strands of multi-faceted glass prisms.

I thought the one hanging in Ellis's home was impressive, but it's not nearly this size. It's a centerpiece above tables blanketed in light grey linen cloths. The walls are draped with pale pink rippled fabric. The lighting is subdued, and I'm in awe.

"We better find our seats," Ellis says.

Estella points toward a stage. "Your father can direct you to our table. Naturally, it's front and center." I nod and smile as

Ellis nudges me forward. Taking my glass from me, he looks for a waiter passing by and sets it on a tray.

"Oh, do I have time to use the ladies' room?"

"Absolutely." Hooking my arm in his, he directs me to the restrooms. "I'll wait right here," he says next to the doorway, hesitating to let my arm go.

"I won't be long."

Once I'm in the stall, I discover it's anything but ladylike to hold up a gorgeous gown and pee, but I do my best to make it quick.

As I walk toward the sink, I see a gorgeous woman standing there, fooling with her lustrous raven hair. I wash my hands next to her, and as I touch up my makeup, I catch in my peripheral vision her staring at me.

I close the cap on my lipstick and take a glimpse of her. She smiles with her full lips and midnight eyes.

"Hi. I couldn't help but notice you're with Ellis Burke this evening," she says with a Middle Eastern accent, and I'm not pleased with the exotic, seductive way his name rolls off her tongue.

"Yes, and you are?"

Clasping her clutch purse, she shifts to face me.

"I'm Dalia." I stick my hand out to shake with the beautiful woman, but she only glances down at it and holds her purse tighter. "Ellis and I dated a couple of years ago."

I gulp and wish she hadn't noticed, but her smirk says otherwise.

"Oh, well, I'm sure he'll wish to say hello."

"Yes, I'd like that." She holds her hand out toward the door. "Shall we?"

Oh, she wants to do it now. Giving a weak smile, I head for the exit and hear her follow. Ellis is where I left him, speaking to a man, but the second his eyes catch the sight of us, he stops mid-sentence. His upper lip twitches, and he pulls on his bowtie to make room for more air.

"Ellis, how lovely to see you." Dalia takes hold of his bicep and leans up with her long legs to kiss his cheek. She lingers, and it stirs a jealousy I haven't felt before.

I hate knowing that when she steps back, he'll struggle not to look at the plunging neckline of her striking purple gown, which reveals an excessive amount of cleavage.

"Dalia," he says curtly.

"I was just getting to know your friend in the ladies' room."

He holds his arm out and nods for me to loop mine around it.

"*Girlfriend*. Camilla and I live together." I sidle up to him, pleased by his response.

She shoots me a wicked glare but quickly recovers and lifts her chin. She says something to him in another language, Arabic I believe, and Ellis furrows his brow.

"She moved in only recently. Now, keep it in English please so Camilla can understand you."

"I must admit, I'm intrigued as to how you got this man to want more from you than sex. Women have been trying to accomplish that for years."

Her eyes flit back to Ellis, and the anger emanates off him.

"That's precisely it, Dalia; Camilla didn't try. She's quite extraordinary and was above throwing herself at me."

"You're still brash as always, I see, and that's my cue to leave."

"I agree, and stay away from Lawrence and Aspen."

"Be careful, Camilla. This one holds grudges. I wouldn't cross him if I were you." As my stomach sinks over her warning, I watch her march away. Tugging on my arm, Ellis starts walking.

"Let's go. I'm calling Fletcher to pick us up. This is the exact bullshit I didn't want you to witness."

I come to a stop, pulling back on his arm.

"Ellis, please, let's stay. Your parents will be disappointed, and I need them to get to know me before they hear how they've lost time with Liam. They're going to be hurt."

Sighing, he rubs the back of his neck and shifts his jaw to loosen it.

"Fine, we'll stay, but let's take our seats so we only have my crazy family to deal with. That's a job in itself."

I raise up to kiss his lips. "Thank you." As we stroll toward the tables, I bite my lip and admire the affluent guests. "Can I ask who Lawrence and Aspen are?"

"Lawrence is my cousin, Greyson's older brother. After I'd been dating Dalia a few weeks—and I use the term *date* loosely—I found out Lawrence had slept with her not long before.

"He's married to Aspen, and she's an incredible woman. Greyson said Dalia made passes at him, too, so I knew then she was only trying to get her paws on any Burke she could. He confessed about Lawrence when he thought things might get serious between Dalia and me."

I steal a glimpse of him as we walk. "Do you believe you would've become serious if she hadn't slept with your married cousin?"

He smiles down at me, and seeing him lighten up is a relief.

"No, Camilla. She wasn't you. No woman could ever be you."

CHAPTER EIGHT

Ellis

I'm trying to keep it together for Camilla, but it's a struggle. I don't want her meeting women I've slept with for mere sexual gratification. She'll let one bitter partner slide, but more than that, and I'm going to lose the respect I've fought to gain.

We reach our assigned table without any more interference, and my uncle Rich, who's sitting to the right of my father, stands up from the other side of the round barrier. I say barrier because if it wasn't there, Camilla would already be on the inside of a bear hug. He grins broadly.

"My favorite nephew, how are you this evening? And who's this beautiful lady?"

"I'm good, Uncle Rich, and this is my girlfriend, Camilla. Camilla, this is Uncle Rich. He has that southern drawl, similar to yours, after years of working in Texas."

"But he's Ron to you, Camilla," Greyson quips. "Only the golden boy here gets to call him Rich."

Ignoring him, I introduce my aunt Mary Ann, who's sitting to the right of Rich, and then continue around the table. "That's my cousin Lawrence and his wife, Aspen."

I glance to Camilla, and she frowns for a fleeting moment, and I'm certain it's because she just heard about Aspen being cheated on. Thankfully, Aspen and Lawrence worked through it, and her forgiveness made her stellar in my book.

Everyone is welcoming to Camilla, but I expected no less. I smack Greyson on the shoulder next. "And you already know this annoying bastard."

"Greyson is a sweetheart," Camilla says before she sits in the seat I've pulled out for her next to him.

"Ellis secretly envies me, Camilla; he wishes to be me. It's why he resorts to name-calling." He brandishes a cocky grin and winks.

"Maybe I need to sit between the two of you," I say. My family laughs, and at least the introductions are out of the way.

"How do you already know Greyson?" Aspen asks. She looks elegant tonight in her yellow gown with her light brown hair resting over her shoulders.

"Oh, we've talked at the house. I mean, I've spoken with him at Ellis's home."

"*Our* home," I interject before I pick up my glass of water and take a much-needed drink.

"Excuse me?" my father asks in his curt voice, and suddenly I feel smaller as he waits for my response.

"I said it's *our* home. Camilla lives with me."

Her head shakes. "Ellis, this isn't the best time..." I squeeze her hand under the table.

"No worries, dear," my father says to her. "We're all aware this is how Ellis operates. He blurts his thoughts out at the most inopportune times.

"I think he enjoys his tactless behavior, but little does he know; this news makes my day. It's about time he settles down."

"Now who's choosing an inopportune time to speak their mind?"

"Damn, I love this family," Greyson says. There are two empty seats to the right of him, and I'm sure one is for Whitney, but I'm curious as to who the other is for.

My mother arrives at our table as we're being served our salads. She sits to my left, between my father and me, and smiles at everyone.

"Finally, everything is in place for the auction. Ellis, change seats with Camilla. I want to get to know her without yelling over you."

I roll my eyes. "Sure. I should probably keep her out of Greyson's reach, anyhow."

"Dad, why is Ellis your favorite in this family when he's so cruel to me?" he asks Uncle Rich.

"After what you've put me through over the years, it's a joy to see him torment you," he replies before nodding at me.

Camilla and I switch seats, and with the noise level in the room, it's hard to overhear her conversation with my mother, which cranks up my anxiety.

Greyson leans over to my ear. "As much as I'd enjoy the show, maybe tonight's not the best time to tell them about Liam."

"I want it over with."

"Or you wish to give your parents heart attacks."

"Fine, I'll wait." Out of nowhere, Christopher appears behind the empty seat next to Greyson. Staring up at him, I scowl.

66

"What the hell are you doing here?"

"Ellis!" my mother scolds.

"Your gracious mother invited me. May I?" he asks, smiling at Estella as he grasps the back of the empty chair.

"Of course, and Ellis, Christopher was your brother's closest friend and employee. He should be here to honor Tony. I don't know why you're surprised."

OK, so my comment was rude, but I haven't had a chance to address the stunt he pulled yesterday, when he went to see Camilla behind my back.

I grit my teeth. "I apologize, Christopher. I wasn't expecting to see you, so it caught me by surprise."

"It's all good, Ellis." After he sits, a waiter appears to take his drink order. Camilla squeezes my hand, and I watch her gnaw on her lip, giving away that she's uneasy, too.

Thousands of square feet close in around me. My throat thickens, so I take another drink of water. Penny, a woman who's stalking Greyson like prey, approaches our table and stands between us.

"Good evening, Burke family. Greyson, could I have a word with you?" she asks.

"Uh, sure." He lays his napkin on the table and stands.

"Hi, I'm Penny," she says, reaching across me to shake Camilla's hand. "Oh, and congratulations; my friend Dalia told me you two are living together. It's nice to hear Ellis is taking the plunge."

My mother gasps. "Excuse me?"

"My sentiments exactly," my father chimes in before he takes a drink of his scotch. Uncle Rich laughs, and I'm about to lose my shit.

"Oops, did I spill the beans?" Penny asks before she covers her mouth. Greyson grabs her arm and pulls her away.

"Come on. Let's get this over with."

"This family could be on one of those afternoon soap opera shows." Uncle Rich chuckles boisterously. "Not that I watch them or anything."

Aunt Mary Ann gives him a stern look, and Aspen giggles. Shaking his head in embarrassment, Lawrence tosses back his scotch. Maybe I need to reevaluate the drinking.

"Camilla," Christopher says out of nowhere, "it was nice running into you at the park yesterday." He flashes her a sly smile, and it couldn't be more obvious that he's instigating trouble.

Her eyes widen. "Right … it was a pretty day out."

The asshole sneers in my direction, and I'm about to climb across this table and beat the shit out of him. I pull on my bowtie, ready to rip it off.

"When did the two of you move in together?" Mother asks Camilla. Dammit, we still have this to address.

"Uh, I—"

"Last month," I say.

"You should've told us, Ellis. I shouldn't have to hear it through the gossip mill."

"You're right, Mother. I apologize."

"So, Camilla, how well do you know Christopher?" Lawrence asks with a cocked brow and thin lips that want to turn up into a smile.

Another asshole.

That's it.

I'm done.

Time to leave.

"I have to go." My alien family looks at me, so I lean over to Camilla. "*We* have to go," I whisper in her ear and slide my chair back.

"Um, OK." She gets up, chewing on that lip, and all I can think about is how I need a stiff drink and a hard fuck.

"Just take a breather outside," Lawrence orders, giving me a pointed look. He's relaying that I better pull my shit together and return to my seat like a grown-ass man, but if that's the case, then he shouldn't have stirred the damn pot only moments ago.

Unable to wait for Camilla, I tear off toward the exit. She calls my name, and I want her—need her, but my chest is caving in, much like the walls around me. She can't see me any weaker.

Saying my name again, she begs for me to stop. *Dammit.* It's unfair of me to do this to her, so I freeze in the lobby. Stepping in front of me, she cradles my face.

"Look at me. Let me help you through this." Reluctantly, I gaze down at her. "I had no idea it was this difficult for you." Tears rush to her eyes, and it pisses me off that I'm the cause of it.

"I don't want you to see me weak."

"You're not weak. You're simply not like them, so it makes sense you'd be uncomfortable here. I am, too."

"It's not that simple. You're not the one trying to leave."

"Only because I'm putting your and Liam's needs first. His grandparents, aunt, uncle, and cousins ... they're his family and in that ballroom, so I need to present my best self to them."

Inching closer to me, she presses her body to mine. "I want to make a good impression for you, too." She slides her hands from my cheeks to my neck and then down to my chest.

Her bedroom eyes, beneath heavy lashes, tilt up at me and stare as she licks her lips, her seduction intense and intimate, as if we're alone in the busy room.

"Let me ease your tension. Find somewhere in this place to fuck me."

Camilla

Panic had caused the flame that resides in Ellis's eyes to become only a flickering ember, but my daring words are the sparks that send it back up in flames.

I watch it roil with desire and domination until he clutches my hand and pulls me behind him. I struggle to keep up in my spiked heels, but I let him take charge. He's desperate for the control, and I need to feel safe.

His command gives me a sense of protection. Through his dominance, he's confidant and won't let me fall. It shows him he's not alone, and I'm beginning to see that Ellis has felt alone most of his life.

Far away from everyone, we reach a set of doors.

"Please don't be locked," he mutters before yanking on one of them. It pulls back, and he practically pushes me inside. No lights are on in the spacious room, but windows allow the setting sun to filter in.

Dragging me to a round table, he bends me over it and removes his tux jacket before tossing it on a chair. I realize we're in a much smaller venue, not rented out tonight, but there's still a sense of recklessness since I'm certain we shouldn't be here and anyone could walk in.

Lifting my long dress, he yanks my panties to the floor and taps my ankle, signaling for me to step out of them. He leans over my back and stuffs the ivory silk fabric inside my mouth.

"My dirty girl..." he whispers in my ear.

Holy shit, what if someone comes in? I whimper against the silk and squirm, so he squeezes the back of my neck to hold me still. This only incites a long moan, my body shocked to life by his authoritative touch.

"Put your palms and cheek down on the table." I hear his zipper and the rustling of his pants as he shoves them down. "This is going to be fast and rough until I come all over your gorgeous ass. You're *not* going to come this time. Do you understand me?"

I don't make a sound, so he swats my ass. "Nod that you understand." I don't move, so he hits me harder across both my cheeks, and I whimper from the sting and excitement it creates.

"Nod now, my Rose, because if someone walks in this room and see's your superb ass, your punishment when we get home will be unimaginable."

Panicking that someone could catch us, I nod.

"Good girl." Without another word, he drives his cock into me. It stings, so I cry out, my sounds muffled and erotic. Each thrust feels better than the last, and I relish in the buildup of pleasure.

With my torso pressed to the table, I hear the beading on my dress scraping against it, and my cheek shoves forward and back as he aggressively pounds into me.

He's still clasping my neck, and this fuck is rough like he warned … dirty, too, as he takes back the control he lost. I want this from him. I long for Ellis to use me to find that in himself.

I'll also give him my submission as restitution for the years he lost with his son. I yearn for him to punish me as much as he needs the power to do it.

Oh, god, I'm gonna come.

Moaning, I clench my muscles, squeezing his cock.

"Don't you dare fucking come." Two more thrusts, and Ellis pulls out of me. He digs his fingertips into my ass cheek and comes all over it. His legs jerk against mine, his grunts animalistic, only reaffirming the virile male that he is.

Stretching his arm around me, he pulls the panties from my mouth, and I suck in a taxing breath. I'm enthralled by the shameless way he fucked me, and how the lewdness of it turned me on. Even though I didn't orgasm, I feel satisfied knowing I gave him what he needed.

He fixes his pants and uses my underwear to clean up the mess. My dress is pulled down next, and grasping my waist and arm, he stands me up but doesn't turn me around.

As if he hasn't had enough, he clings to my body tighter and nips at the back of my neck, biting it in random places. We're sweaty and gasping for air, dizzy from the fog of passion we're so often lost in.

"Thank you," he whispers. Moving his arm from my waist to across my stomach, he pulls me back against him and hugs me snugly. "Every day you gain more of my trust." His lips kiss their way from my neck up to my ear, and I let my head fall back against him. "I love you, Camilla."

I stiffen. He loves me … trusts me. I can't hold this secret in another day. I'm telling him once we're home tonight. Twisting in his arms to face him, I wrap mine around his neck.

"I love you, too, Ellis, and I hope you'll hold on to that truth."

CHAPTER NINE

Camilla

Who knew that within an hour of arriving at this fundraiser I'd be fucked and pantiless? I think he shoved them in his tux pocket.

In the restroom, I scrutinize myself in the mirror, wishing my skin would change to a different shade other than the color of my auburn hair. I push a few wispy strands back and straighten my gown.

I also wish I had my purse, but I left it at the table when I ran after him. Since there's no way to make myself more presentable, I give up and head to the door.

Ellis is waiting for me again, but he's calmer this time. He smiles and kisses my head.

"What's with the frown?" he asks.

"I'm afraid people are going to know what we did."

"Good. They'll be jealous that someone's having fun tonight." Entwining our fingers, he leads me toward the ballroom again.

"Oh, I imagine there are people here who enjoy these events."

"Yes, and my mother is one of them." We return to the table, and everyone stares at us as we take our seats. Their eyes soften upon seeing Ellis more relaxed. Well, except for Christopher's. He's sullen like usual.

Glancing around, Estella waves at a server nearby, and he strides over. "Could you please bring their entrees out for them right away?" she asks, pointing to us.

"Of course, ma'am."

"You two can finish dinner while the other guests peruse the paintings one last time." As if nothing has happened, she smiles brightly.

Christopher wipes his mouth. "I think I'll check out the paintings before the auction begins." My eyes follow him as he walks across the room. He stands in front of the roped off area and admires them.

"Camilla, while you were away, Estella mentioned you're involved in public service," Aspen says.

"Oh, I haven't done anything yet. I'm still in school, but that's always been my dream, since I was an adult, anyway."

"What areas are you interested in?" Estella asks.

"Feeding our hungry is what I'd like to focus on, particularly among our youth. There are so many children whose only meals come from those they receive at school. It breaks my heart."

"Do you have any ideas as to how you'll help in that department?" Ron asks.

"I have a few ideas, but since I haven't been exposed to the ins and outs yet, and the politics of it all, I'm not sure if they're doable." I smile and look down. "Maybe my plans are foolish." Feeling my skin flush, I take a drink of champagne.

Ellis clasps my hand on the table. "There's nothing foolish about you." I look around and everyone at the table is eyeing him, instead of me.

"I love a lady who can make the impossible happen, so tell us one of your ideas," Ron adds with a hearty laugh. His wife, Mary Ann, rolls her eyes as if she's used to his flirting.

"OK... I know there are already programs at schools for children to take donated food home in their backpacks, so what I'd like to do is expand on that to educate children about healthy eating.

"My reasoning is that if they're knowledgeable about nutrition and the importance of it, or are at least familiar with the food groups, then they'll want better for their own children one day.

"Maybe that will make them strive for more in other areas of their lives to ensure their kids have proper nutrition. If this small change can break the cycle of poverty and hunger in a single family, then it's worth it to me."

Covering her heart, Estella releases a high-pitched gasp.

"Do you hear this delightful woman? She's full of hope and compassion, envisioning the much bigger picture. Ellis, do you hear her?"

"Yes, Mother, I'm sitting right here."

"That's surprising," James, Ellis's father, says.

"Why is that?" Ellis asks in a guarded tone.

"No offense, son, but you've never supported your mother's charity work, so it's surprising to see you with someone who's as equally passionate about it."

"You know I make charitable donations myself. Not actively participating in the organizations of such causes doesn't mean I'm against them."

"I didn't say you weren't generous. I said you've never shown interest in your mother's work, so I find it intriguing that you're listening so intently to Camilla."

"Boys, stop it. I was enjoying listening, so please, dear, tell me how you think we could educate the children," Estella says. Christopher sits back down at the table and directs his attention to me.

"I want to send home a cartoon activity kit with their food that would be informative but also fun for them so they might absorb the information.

"Did you know there are children who've never seen or tried common fruits and vegetables? You can show them an orange, and they honestly have no clue what it is. That's mind-boggling and sad to me.

"So, each kit would focus on a cartoon character of a specific food and would give facts about it. I'd include fun things like jokes, a coloring page and puzzles for them to do. Liam—I mean, a little boy, helped me come up with the cute cartoon characters."

"The boy's name is Liam," Ellis says.

I grab his shoulder. "Ellis, no, not now."

He turns to me. "Yes, now. He's not something to hide. Not ever. He's a Burke, and they need to know it."

"What are we missing here?" Lawrence asks.

I might die right now.

"I have an announcement." Ellis clasps my hand again on the table.

"Holy shit, you never listen," Greyson exclaims before he scratches the back of his head.

"Camilla and I have a child together. His name is Liam, and he'll turn four this summer."

Mouths fall open around the table.

"What the fuck?" Christopher asks. Ellis shoots him a glare.

"Liam is mine," he says, and the underlying threat for Christopher to keep his mouth shut isn't mistaken by either of us.

"Whatever. I need some fresh air," Chris replies before he storms off.

"Well, I'll be damned," Ron says before bursting into laughter.

James grits his teeth, "What are you doing, Ellis? You know this event is not the time or place for such nonsense."

"It's not nonsense. Camilla and I shared a night together and then lost touch with one another. We only realized recently that Liam is mine, so we're together now, and they're both living with me."

I steal a peek at Estella. She's covering her chest, and I'm praying she doesn't have a heart attack. There's snickering from across the table, and Lawrence is failing at hiding his grin.

He's a Burke through and through. He has the same stark blue eyes, and like his father and uncle, he's tall. Greyson is a tad shorter, maybe taking after his mother. Lord, I wish Estella would say something.

"I have a grandchild?" she asks, dabbing at the sweat on her forehead. Please don't stroke out.

"Yes, Mother, you have a grandson, and he's smart, inquisitive, and well-behaved. He looks just like us. Oh, and he has our odd sense of humor, too. The kid's a riot sometimes."

My heart melts from Ellis's grin, the pride shining around him like a yellow aura of excitement and warmth. It's as if he truly believes Liam is his own.

"This is unreal," Estella says before she grabs her glass of champagne.

"I swear, Ellis"—James scowls and points—"if you weren't too old for it, I'd lay you over my knee for choosing this time and place to tell us this news."

"Wow, this is wonderful," Aspen says, attempting to lighten the mood. "I'm happy for you guys."

Lawrence smirks. "Ditto."

"What a night. I'm a great-uncle," Ron declares with his glass held high.

"Don't make this about you, Ronald." Mary Ann gives him a sideways glance.

"I'm proud is all. Now, someone show me a damn picture of him." I begin fumbling with the clasp on my purse, but Ellis pulls out his phone, beating me to it.

"You have photos of him?" I ask quietly.

"Of course, and I think my parents should see them first." Ellis hands the phone over to Estella, and she begins to weep.

"He's so precious and is most definitely a Burke." Sniffling, she regains her composure. "He has your hair and eyes, Ellis. This is such a blessing, especially after the loss this family has suffered. Tony would've been thrilled."

Hmph, if she only knew.

Turning to me, she pushes back her shoulders and lifts her chin.

"Why would you wait so long to tell Ellis he has a child?"

"It's complicated, Mother, and is not Camilla's fault. That's all I'll say about the subject. She's an astounding mother, and I'm grateful to finally have them both in my life."

Relaxing her body, Estella passes the phone to James.

"Did you hear that, honey? Ellis is happy. Camilla, I must know everything about you and your family. What's your mother's maiden name? What's your heritage? Ellis, didn't you say she's from the north? A Yankee?"

"Lord, Mother, I said she's from the south. And who even uses that term anymore?"

"You wouldn't know my family. As far as my heritage, my maternal grandmother is Italian, and still lives in Italy, and I believe I have English and Irish ancestors, as well."

"I can't wait to hear more. We're acquaintances to several southerners, so we're bound to be connected in some way."

"Let's get to know Camilla and our *apparent* grandchild first," James says.

"We've already taken a paternity test, Father," Ellis replies. "He's mine."

Grabbing my hand, Estella beams. "This calls for a party; a welcoming celebration for you and Liam. We'll have cake and clowns—"

"Kids hate clowns, Estella. They're scary fuckers," Ron says.

The family laughs, minus Mary Ann who replies, "Watch your language, Ron."

Greyson tips his glass toward me. "I think it's Camilla who should be concerned about what's in the gene pool on this side of the family."

"OK, so no clowns, but we can have one of those jumpy things kids love to play in." She fiddles with her diamond necklace. "Ellis, you have me so frazzled with this news and right before I have to give a speech in front of five hundred people."

"You'll do fine, my love," James says to her. "You always do." They seem to possess a strong love for one another, and it's comforting to know Ellis has witnessed more than one couple work through their indiscretions, troubles and loss.

Maybe seeing that forgiveness in his family will spur his ability to forgive me, too.

CHAPTER TEN

Ellis

My parents handled that better than I expected, but I'm certain James will give me an ass-chewing later. We have what I call a loving, dysfunctional relationship. It's a pleasure to get a rise out of him, but it's my defense mechanism. I strike before he has a chance to.

Ever since I became a hacker, my father has treated me differently, but my brother and I wouldn't have spent every waking hour on computers if we'd had parents who weren't so wrapped up in their own careers.

His notion of an esteemed profession is what he desires for me, and it's yet another situation he doesn't understand. What I do is vital to our existence and something for him to be proud of, even if he can't share all the gritty details with his friends and associates.

Since I'm private and anti-social, he worries others will think I'm a hermit freak, playing on a laptop while hidden away in my mansion.

Maybe I have been the beast in hiding, but now I have a beauty to heal me and a nephew who makes me want to be a better man.

Damn, Camilla and I need to figure out what to tell Liam, and since we haven't settled that, I'm surprised she's not pissed at me for what I told my family tonight.

I gaze at her as she touches the pink peonies and ivory roses at the center of our table. She's in awe of her surroundings: the very things I take for granted from being exposed to luxury all my life.

She picks up her fork, and it's cute how she checks to see if anyone is watching before she shoves a bite of food in her mouth. I think she's barely eaten today, so she's likely starved.

My mother takes the stage, and everyone applauds. Greyson scoots his chair closer and leans in.

"Did you not get enough of her when you slipped away?" His breath reeks of liquor, so I point to his glass.

"How many of those have you had?"

"Don't change the subject. Admit you fucked her in this building. I can recognize that look on a woman anywhere. Rosy skin and mussed-up hair. Swollen wine-colored lips." He gawks at her, and I may stab his eyes out with my fork.

Since my mother is speaking, I lower my voice and say, "Stop before it's too late, asshole. You need to slow it down on the scotch, too."

"It's Pappy, actually. He's my only friend tonight."

"You get hammered on bourbon."

He scowls. "Blame it on the bitches here. They're all up on my junk, and not in a good way."

Shaking my head, I shift back toward Camilla and the stage. Estella praises my brother, telling lies I wish were truths, until I'm forced to exile my brain to keep my panic at bay.

Camilla's body becomes rigid as my mother speaks of Tony, so I scoot away from Greyson and closer to her, moving my hand around to rest on her thigh.

Threading our fingers, she relaxes her shoulders, and for once it looks like I'll get through an entire gala without running ... well, maybe.

My girl's not wearing panties, and the thought keeps running through my head. My cum is all over them as they rest in my pocket. *Damn*, I might ditch this event yet to have a taste of her.

As the paintings are auctioned, my mind drifts back to Tony and some of the times we visited art galleries. One interest we did share was an appreciation for the arts, particularly paintings.

I tend to choose pieces that express deep emotions, and maybe that's because I have trouble expressing my own.

The auctioneer pointing straight at our table brings me back to the present. I look to my right, and Christopher is holding up his paddle, bidding twenty thousand dollars.

A woman a few tables to our left outbids him at twenty-one, but Christopher holds his paddle up again at twenty-two.

What the hell is he doing?

My eyes dart to the current painting. It's a Johan Jongkind marine oil painting of a ship and sea. Hmm...

"We have twenty-two," the auctioneer says. "Can we get twenty-three?" He points to the back of the room before Chris can get his paddle raised. "You there, for twenty-three. Can we get twenty-four?"

Christopher outbids, and I recall a conversation we had after Tony died. He claimed my brother wanted him to have the painting, but since there was no proof of that, I told him no.

He seemed desperate after I refused, asking if he could buy it, but I'd already agreed to this deal with my mother. I never dreamed he'd be willing to spend what we could get for it at auction.

Making more bids, he catches Camilla's attention, too, and she stares at him in disbelief as he wipes a bead of sweat from his forehead. I lean over to whisper to Greyson.

"Bid against him."

"Why? I don't want it."

"Do it. I'll pay you back."

"But the painting was left to you. Why would you buy it?"

"Dammit, just do it."

"Fine," he snaps. With the bid now at twenty-six, Greyson holds up his paddle. I glance to Christopher, and his lips purse as he takes a glimpse at Greyson.

The two of them, a female to our left, and the person behind us continue to bid. I look back and see it's a friend of my father's, Mason Gerard.

The female yields at forty, but Greyson, Christopher and Mason go at it, outbidding one another quickly. The tension builds, and all eyes are on our table now.

"Chris," Camilla says in a harsh whisper after he lifts his paddle at forty-eight grand. He ignores her, forging on, and at this point, it's become a game for Greyson.

He's enjoying the attention, throwing caution to the wind, especially since the money's not coming from his wallet. At fifty, Mason drops out, and after a bid of fifty-six thousand by my cousin, Christopher throws his paddle on the table in the most undignified way.

"Can we get fifty-seven? Anyone? Fifty-seven?" The auctioneer is scouring the room, but no one else raises their paddle. "Going once, going twice..." He brings his hammer down. "Sold for fifty-six thousand to the gentleman in the front."

Good thing this is for a worthy cause since I highly suspect we overbid the value of this painting. The guests applaud, and Greyson leans over to me, losing his fake grin.

"You need therapy, and you owe me one. As soon as I have a need, I'll collect on it."

My teeth grind. "Thank you."

Getting up from the table, Christopher storms toward the exit, so Camilla turns her head and glowers at both Greyson and me.

"I'm going to go talk to him for a minute." As she starts to stand, I grab her wrist.

"If you go after him, you better be prepared for a painful punishment." My jaw is set tight, and my heart is hammering.

"He's my *friend.*"

"And you're *mine.*" Having a showdown of wills, she huffs a breath, turns her chair to face the stage, and crosses her arms.

"That might've backfired on you there, cuz," Greyson says with slurred speech.

"Shut up, asshole."

Camilla

For all the excitement Ellis incites, it's accompanied by a great deal of stress. I'm pissed that I'm turned on by his threat and grasp of my wrist.

I'm angry and confused as to why he had Greyson bid against Christopher. I saw Ellis whispering to him, so I have no doubt he was behind it.

Maybe Christopher has more money saved than I thought he did if he'd bid such an outrageous amount on a painting. It doesn't make sense when all I've heard is how disappointed and angry he is with Tony.

Taking a drink of my third glass of champagne, I blow out a long, slow breath. I'm losing my resolve to get through this night, especially when I think of the confession I'll make in mere hours.

***

"We have to take Greyson home with us and keep an eye on him tonight," I say to Ellis as we wait in the lobby for Fletcher to pick us up.

Grabbing my waist, he brings me close and kisses my ear.

"But I owe you multiple orgasms for your good behavior this evening, and I plan to deliver."

"He's already stumbled to the bathroom three times to vomit. What if while he's alone, he chokes on it and dies?"

Ellis growls in my ear. "OK, if you insist."

Pulling away, I look at the floor and bite my lip.

"Besides, we need to have a discussion tonight. There's something I need to tell you … about the past, and it can't wait another day. It's been weighing on me heavily." Lifting my chin, Ellis lowers his head and fastens his gaze to mine.

"I think I know what it pertains to, and we probably should discuss it so we can stop dwelling on the past and get on with our life together."

I shake my head. "No, I don't think you know what this is about." Greyson stumbles back from the restroom, and he's in rough shape. His tux jacket is open, bowtie hanging from his collar. His skin is ashen, and his textured blond hair that's longer on top is now drooping over his face.

Ellis gets the call that Fletcher has pulled up out front, so we help Greyson to the car. The guys lug him into the front passenger seat before Ellis and I take the back.

On the drive home, I decide to make small talk to distract me from what lies ahead.

"What type of work does your father and Ron do? I was afraid I'd insult them if I asked, but you've never told me."

Ellis's eyebrows pinch together, and he smiles.

"They would've had belly laughs over that one, especially Uncle Rich. You seriously don't know? They've been in the paper often, and our name is well-known."

"I'm sorry. I've been too busy over the years to follow much of the news. I was struggling to make a living to care for Sasha and Liam."

Bringing my hand up, Ellis frowns and kisses it.

"My Burke ancestors bought up land parcels throughout the west, and most of those were sold off over the years, so that's how my family first acquired wealth.

"Then, my father developed business management software, and Microsoft purchased it in 1996. Needless to say, he was able to retire."

"Ah, I see now where your interest in technology came from."

"Yes, and my father feels I've wasted my talent and the use of our name." Uncomfortable by his admission, he clears his throat. "Uncle Rich chose a different path. He married Mary Ann Gant, whose late father was half owner of Gant-Peterson Oil Company. Rich worked for him."

"Isn't Peterson Whitney's last name?" I ask quietly.

"You pay attention. Yes, and her late grandfather owned the other half of the company. Now, her father runs it with Rich." Ellis looks to the front seat and back to me. "Greyson was already supposed to marry Whitney," he whispers.

"What? Like some arranged marriage?"

"I guess you could call it that. He keeps putting it off. I shouldn't discuss it, especially now."

I sigh as I think about how miserable Greyson seemed tonight. Getting to know the Burke family has reaffirmed my belief that although money can ease some burdens, it doesn't buy happiness.

"Why did you have Greyson outbid Christopher for the painting?"

"I want to examine it. I don't believe Christopher would spend that kind of money to have a keepsake of Tony's."

"You really don't trust him."

"No, I don't, and it's not only because of you. There's something else about him that doesn't sit right with me, and I've decided to get to the bottom of it so I can finally put his ass on the road."

"I think you're overreacting."

"And I think you need to be less trusting of him."

Sighing, I recall the times I've misjudged someone's character.

"Maybe you're right. My track record for trusting people stinks."

CHAPTER ELEVEN

Ellis

Fletcher helps me haul Greyson to my family room. We remove his jacket and drop him on the sofa. I'm not about to drag his limp ass upstairs.

"Thank you, Fletcher. I won't need you tomorrow, so rest assured you'll have the day off."

"Thank you, sir. Have a good night." He nods his head at me, and his silver hair shines off the top of it. I consider his age and when he might retire, and I hope that's not happening any time soon. His wife died about seven years ago, so he hasn't minded my erratic schedule.

He lets himself out, and as I remove Greyson's shoes, his legs slide off the sofa. I shove them back onto it and attempt to straighten his body.

Camilla's in the kitchen, getting a glass of water and a wastebasket to set beside him. He's a lucky man tonight. If it wasn't for her, he'd be on his own couch, fending for himself.

It's been a long time since he's been this blitzed, and it concerns me since he's a recovered addict, to drugs that is. He never stopped drinking, but he usually knows his limitations.

"Ellis," he mumbles.

"What?"

Opening his eyes, he works at bringing me into focus.

"I don't want to marry her."

"Then don't."

"I have to or … or Dad and Lawrence will hate me." His eyes close again, and his mouth is agape.

"I don't believe that." As I shove a pillow beneath his head, he grabs my arm.

"Whit … she's not the one. Why don't they want me to be happy?"

I sit down on the coffee table in front of the sofa and rest my arms on my knees.

"Greyson, I don't know why they're different with you. All I know is you have to fix it before you're looking for something stronger to numb your pain."

Hearing a noise, I look up, and Camilla is at the doorway. She clears her throat and brings over the items for him.

"I'm gonna go change," she says.

"I'll be up in a few minutes."

Before leaving the room, she looks at Greyson with sympathy in her eyes. She heard too much. If my cousin doesn't have a talk with his father soon, I'll be the one to do it.

I watch him until he drifts off to sleep, which doesn't take long. Camilla isn't in my room, so after I change out of my dress clothes into a pair of black sweats, I search for her. She's sitting on her bed, staring at Liam on the video monitor.

"I thought we agreed you weren't sleeping in here any longer."

She doesn't take her eyes off the screen.

"Sorry, I got sidetracked. I wasn't able to spend much time with him today."

"Yeah, I missed the little guy, too. Is he OK?"

"Yes, but I'm wondering if Beatrice had trouble getting him to sleep since she's on the cot." She peels her eyes off the screen to glance at me. "Do you think I should wake her and send her home?"

"It's late. If she gets uncomfortable, she'll go to the spare bedroom."

Leaning her head back, Camilla stares at the ceiling and takes a deep breath. Her boobs push outward in the thin tank top she changed into, and it's turning me on. I stroll over and hold my hand out.

"Come. It's time for me to have a taste ... or maybe a feast. And don't worry, I'll gag you so your screams don't wake our guests." Expecting a coy smile from her, I'm surprised when she lowers her head and frowns.

"I think one of us should sleep downstairs in the family room so we can keep an eye on Greyson."

"He hasn't thrown up since we left the gala, and he was snoring when I headed up. I think he's out for the night."

"Then have a seat so we can talk."

Grabbing my hips, I tilt my head to the side.

"Baby, going down on you seems way more exciting for the both of us. We can talk tomorrow."

"Ellis, please... I know it's poor timing, but this can't wait." Bringing my arm across my chest, I grab my shoulder and contemplate whether I want to cooperate.

She's so stressed out. I guess the sooner we talk, the sooner I can get her in my bed, even if it's only to sleep.

"All right." I sit down next to her. "Let's talk."

She touches her forehead, palms her cheeks and then wrings her hands in her lap.

"I don't know how to do this."

"Don't be nervous." I rest my hand on her thigh. "Maybe I can help. Is this about the night we met at Tony's party years ago?"

Her head swings toward me. "You remember that night?"

"Some of it came back to me recently. I've had this recurring dream for a few years now, and I thought it was just that—a dream, but I guess the time we've spent together triggered the memories."

"Um, so you know we were in Tony's spare bedroom together?"

"Yeah, and I remember we were drinking champagne." Falling back on the bed, I scratch my stomach. "I figured you were keeping it a secret to spare me the humiliation. I know I was drunk, and that's never a pretty sight."

"That's not why I hadn't said anything." She turns back to look at me. "What's the last thing you remember?"

"Let's see ... I was on the bed like this and asked you to lie with me. I said something about us being dizzy together."

She rubs her forehead. "God."

"Camilla, just tell me the whole story." I graze my fingers along her lower back.

"I didn't just happen upon you that night. Tony asked me to spend time with you."

My hand drops to the bed. "Why would he do that?"

96

"Remember how I said he made you out to be evil and dangerous? Well, he told me he needed to get inside your safe to retrieve a flash drive that held top-secret documents."

I sit up. "What?" As I try to make sense of her words, I shake my head.

"Tony said the classified information on the flash drive was about our country's power grids. He claimed you were going to sell the information to the Chinese government. I know it seems so stupid now, but I believed him. He was convincing and persuasive—"

"What the fuck, Camilla?"

"Ellis, I didn't feel I had a choice at the time. He said he'd pay me to do it. I was broke, and Sasha was strung out. I was going to use the money to get her clean. He offered me twenty-five thousand dollars to distract you while he broke in and stole the flash drive.

"He said he had to get his hands on the documents before you sold them, but after getting to know you and hearing the truth about him, I now wonder if *he* wanted to sell the information."

"So, you got me drunk on champagne while he snuck into my home?"

"Yes, but there's more to it than that."

I stand and pace in front of her. "What else?"

"Tony gave me the impression you would pass out right away since you had already consumed a few drinks, but that's not what happened. We drank the champagne, and then I didn't feel right. Not at all. It was like something had been added to the bottle.

"You were flirting and touching me a little, and then you asked me to lie down next to you, like you said earlier. And then ..." Camilla presses her palms to her eyes and struggles to take a breath.

"Finish now. Tell me the rest," I demand coldly.

"I can't say it."

"Tell me, dammit!" Flinching, she begins to cry, so I drop to my knees in front of her and grasp her hands. "I have a right to know what happened that night and what my brother did to me."

"I didn't remember everything, either, Ellis. I swear I only recently recalled the entire night."

"OK, then tell me what I don't remember."

Slinging her head back, she blows out a breath and stares above us. Tears streak her cheeks and drop to her pajama pants.

"The next thing I knew, you were on top of me. We could hardly hold our eyes open, but you were kissing on my neck and breasts, and then—and then you begged me to let you inside of me."

"No ... no, that didn't happen." As I jerk away, her cry becomes a wail, and the sound is like a fast-moving train. The crash is imminent, and there'll be casualties for sure. This, I'm certain of.

"Shit, Camilla, tell me I didn't force myself on you." With desperation in her puffy eyes, she grabs for my arms, but I step back.

"You didn't hurt me. You asked … and I said yes." Her tears spill as her head drops to her chest.

"We slept together?" I squint in astonishment. Nodding, she sucks in air to catch her breath and stop her cries. How could I not remember? How? I fall to the floor and pull my knees up to rest my arms on them.

"Is that it? Is that everything?"

"No. The next morning, I woke up face down on the floor between the bed and the wall. I'm guessing I tried to get up in the night but fell and passed out again. When I finally woke up, no one was in the room.

"All I remembered at that time was us sitting on the bed and talking, so I knew I'd blacked out at some point. I looked for Tony in the house."

She shakes her head as if she wants to erase a bad memory. "I won't say how I found him, but he did confess to drugging us with GHB.

"He said he wanted to be sure neither of us left that room, and he implied he might be killed for not finding what he needed. I didn't take the money, Ellis. I couldn't do it."

Grabbing my head, I tug on my hair. How could my own brother drug me? That flash drive wasn't in my safe, so what he orchestrated was for nothing. He risked our lives for not a goddamn thing.

"You lied to me. You kept this huge secret even after I bared my soul to you about my relationship with Tony and our careers. Even after I forgave you for the secret you kept about Christopher."

"I'm sorry, but I was terrified you'd take Liam from me if you knew the truth, and after discovering you were the good guy and loved your brother, I couldn't find it in myself to break your heart."

"You mean not until now." I stand up and charge toward the door.

"Wait, there's something else. The most important detail of them all."

Gripping my hips, I hang my head.

"What's that, Camilla?"

She sniffles and hiccups a breath.

"The paternity test ... it said you're Liam's father. It's true, Ellis. Liam's your son."

With my back to her, I press my hand against the door in front of me to brace myself. From the shock, my head spins as it falls against it. My blood pounds in my veins hard enough to feel it in my neck, and I could vomit.

"Please say something." She sobs again, and I'm trapped in a cramped, dark space where strobe lights flash and speakers blast metal music I can't decipher. What I wished for with Liam has now blinded me and knocked the air from my lungs.

"Ellis, all my life I've had to protect those I love. It's all I've known, so that's what I did. By the time I remembered we'd slept together and believed I could trust you, it seemed too late to confess, but I never meant to hurt you."

"I thought I could trust you, too, but I was wrong. It's over, and I wish I never fucking met you."

I hear her come off the bed. "You take that back." Jerking open the door, I storm out. "I mean it!" she shouts. "For Liam, you take it back right now!"

In the middle of the hallway, I fall to my knees. I sit back on my legs and struggle to take one agonizing breath. She steps in front of me, and I stare at her balled fists.

"You can be furious with Tony and me, but don't you dare think of taking it out on that sweet boy."

"Get out of my face, Camilla. You're no longer the only one who'll make decisions where he's concerned."

"What does that mean?"

"Go back to your room."

"You're going to take him from me. I knew it. It's another reason I couldn't tell you the truth."

"I can't believe you still think that. Get out of my face." Wailing again, she stomps back to her room and slams the door behind her. Another door opens, and I look up to see Beatrice leaving Liam's room.

"Mr. Burke, is everything OK?"

"Go to bed, Beatrice. I'm sorry we woke you."

Nodding, her head lowers as she scurries into the spare room across from Liam's. I stand and walk down to his bedroom. Pressing my palm to his door, I listen in the silence to hear if he's awake. There's not a sound other than the thundering in my ears.

"I don't regret you, Liam. I could never regret you."

CHAPTER TWELVE

Camilla

As I open and close my dry mouth to moisten it, I place a hand on the bed and work my way up to a standing position. I'm alone in the room, one that's spinning, and I'm about to hurl, so I look for a door to a bathroom and run there fast, just making it to the toilet in time.

After vomiting, I drop to the floor in front of the commode and rest my head against the cool porcelain. It's a gross thing to do, but I'm too sick to care.

Once I throw up two more times, I drag myself up off the floor and pee. While washing my hands, I stare at death in the mirror and try to remember what happened last night, but I can only recall bits and pieces.

Why did I think I could help Tony without consequences? Dishonesty brings Karma, and the choice I made must be the definition for rock-bottom desperation. It was made from an urgency to save my sister.

Cupping my hand, I catch water from the sink to rinse out my mouth, and after pulling up the straps to my chemise, I leave to find Tony. I know the lunatic drugged Ellis and me, and he better be in this house somewhere so I can confront him.

I amble to the family room first and roll my eyes over the number of people passed out on the floor and furniture. There are strippers, who Tony likely has on his payroll, and I only recognize one from Octavia. Hell, for all I know, they may be prostitutes.

Since the house is quiet, I stumble back down the hallway to Tony's bedroom, where I left my purse and dress last night. I crack open the door and see from a shape under the covers that he's in bed.

Anger festers as I think about how he left me drugged in one of his spare bedrooms all night. What if he had killed Ellis and me? Would he even care?

Walking to his bed, I spot his brown hair peeking out, so I yank back the comforter.

"You son of a bitch," I breathe. Rolling from his stomach to his side, he opens one eye and looks up at me. "I wouldn't roll over any farther unless you want to squish the bitch next to you, which would be fine with me."

Like it's no big deal, he glances behind him and moves his leg around to feel for another set. "Seriously?" I ask.

"This is nothing," he replies through a yawn.

"Wow, you having sex with someone else means nothing?" The blonde whimpers and rolls away from him.

"I don't recall us ever saying we were exclusive, and besides, when I opened the door to the spare bedroom late last night, you were sleeping pretty damn close to my brother."

"That was because we were drugged, you asshole. Admit that you put something in our champagne."

Sitting up at the side of his bed, he sighs. He's naked, and for the first time ever, it repulses me.

"OK, I did it, but it was necessary. I couldn't take a chance of you letting him out of that room. Although, a lot of good it did me. I couldn't find what I wanted, and I'll probably end up dead because of it."

Wrapping an arm around my stomach, I inhale slowly to ward off the sadness and shame setting in. It was all for nothing.

"I can't believe you did this."

"I didn't think you'd realize it, so I didn't see the harm."

"You could've killed us by mixing a drug with our alcohol."

Looking to the floor, he ruffles his hair.

"It was just a little GHB. A bad hangover and possibly memory loss was all I was shooting for."

I smack him hard across the cheek, and his head slings to his right. He brings it back to face me, along with a glare. The slut next to him sits up, and her ginormous fake boobs bounce in the process.

"What's going on?" she asks.

"Nothing, baby."

"Baby?" I snarl. "Has he slept with you before?" I ask her, with my hand firmly planted on my hip.

"Don't answer that," Tony interjects.

"I hate you, and I don't want one cent of your goddamn money." Stomping to the bench at the foot of his bed, I grab my burgundy dress and pull it over my head, not bothering to remove my lingerie. I pick up my purse and spot the envelope that I already know is full of cash.

I stare down at it and think about Sasha. It's so tempting. I could take it right out of this room and never look back ... but I would look back and often. I'd think even worse of myself for the sick scheme I partook in.

"Take it," he says. "I know you need it."

Pulling out the envelope, I toss it on his bed.

"I need my dignity more."

"You're a stripper, Camilla. I think you lost your dignity a long time ago."

"Heyyyyy," the blonde whines, "I strip, too." God, I want to rip those pouty lips right off her face.

"Fuck you, Tony." I say.

He shakes his head. "If you breathe a damn word about this to anyone, you'll pay for it."

"Don't worry, I'm going to forget you ever existed."

***

My throbbing head wakes me from a dreadful dream, but then I revisit reality, which is much more devastating. I open my eyes, but strands of hair block my view, so I try to move them. A chunk is stuck to my cheek from crying myself to sleep.

My alarm clock reads 7:00 a.m., which means Liam will be up soon since his internal clock couldn't care less that it's a Sunday.

From thinking about him and Ellis, tears rush to the surface, but I can't break down again, fearing I'll never get out of this bed if I do.

Instead, I trudge to the bathroom and take a shower. Tears come again, and I can't combat them this time, so while I weep, I let the water rain on my head.

My heart is broken, and knowing I shattered Ellis's makes it ache worse. What will he do now? Will he make us leave? Make only me leave? He implied he wouldn't, but he still holds the power.

I dry off and pad to my bedroom. Spotting a note resting on the comforter, I freeze. I'm sure it's from him, and I'm terrified of what it could say. Biting down on the inside of my cheek, I will my feet to step forward.

Camilla,

      I want you to leave this morning. I booked a room for you and Liam at Embassy Suites and paid for an early check-in. They have an indoor pool Liam would enjoy, so pack him some swim trunks.

      I'm leaving town at 9:00 a.m. tomorrow, and you can return to the house after that. Don't even think about running, or the promise I made to not take Liam will be void. I WILL find you if you try anything stupid.

Crumpling the note in my hand, I fall over on the bed and bury my face against it. Hearing his cold tone through his callous words springs forth heavy tears. He's done with me—with us.

Maybe he'll find it in himself to forgive me, or maybe he won't, but in the meantime, I'll do what I do best; I'll pick myself up and take care of my child. I'll go through the motions of surviving like I've done all my life.

I was foolish to think I deserved a better life, but Liam deserves greatness and then some. He's the innocent one in all this, and at least I know Ellis will be a good father and provide for him. I'll never have to worry as to how I'll put food on the table. Not for him, anyway.

I dress and pack an overnight bag before I walk down the quiet hallway. The door to the room Beatrice sleeps in is open, and the bed is neatly made, so I assume she already left this morning.

I slip into Liam's room, and as I rummage through his dresser drawers, I hear him stirring.

"Momma..."

"Hi, sweetie." Turning to him, I force a smile. "I have a surprise for you. We're going on an adventure."

He rubs his eyes with his small fists and grins.

"Where we going?"

"To a hotel. It's this great big building where people have sleepovers, and there's even a swimming pool inside. Would you like to go swimming like we do in the summer?"

Clapping, he jumps off his bed. "I wanna wear my superhero swim trunks Boss got me."

"Sure, you can wear them." Swallowing down the hurt, I escape to his closet, where I find one of his backpacks and stuff his clothes inside.

When I come out, I hear him in his bathroom, peeing like a fire hose, and I can't help but snicker. I stroll inside to ensure he brushes his teeth and to gather some items for our short trip.

He stomps his feet onto the bench in front of his sink and turns the water on for a whole two seconds to wash his hands. While I'm squirting toothpaste on the bristles, he holds up a small container of dental floss.

"Boss says I have to fwoss when I wake up, before bed and after I eat. He's gonna take me to the dentist." Pulling out a foot-long string of floss, he holds it over his front teeth and moves it back and forth. Leave it to Ellis to teach him the benefits of good oral hygiene.

"OK, let's finish up so we can go." Dropping the floss, he says, "Hooray," and I hand him his toothbrush.

Once we're packed, we walk downstairs, and I don't see anyone, but I hear snoring coming from the family room. Crap, from all that happened, I forgot Greyson was here. At least he's still breathing.

Needing to be quiet, I decide we should eat breakfast in the car, so I pour milk in a travel cup for Liam and find some fruit and breakfast bars. I think about our stay in the hotel and pack a small cooler of snacks and drinks so I don't have to waste money on junk food from a vending machine.

After shushing Liam a half-dozen times, we make it to the front door, where I grab my purse and keys off the table.

"No, Momma, I forgot my Ninja Turtles and my truck."

I sigh, aware that I need to let him take some toys. We can only swim and watch movies for so long. Setting our stuff down by the door, I walk Liam back up the staircase. Reaching the top, I wait at the gate while my little one trots to his room.

A minute has passed when Ellis steps out of his office to my right and freezes. Liam darts from his room next and is coming toward us with his toys piled up in his arms. Ellis quickly turns his back on us and starts walking to his office.

"Boss, want to go to the hotel wif us? They have a pool."

Ellis's head lowers to his chest, and he stops again.

"I can't today, Liam. You have fun for me."

"Ellis, please ... turn around," I beg.

"I can't." In a heartbeat, he's out of sight, retreating to his safe place, where he works too much so he's not forced to face his troubles and pain.

He can't run from this and be a good parent at the same time. I hope he realizes it and doesn't punish Liam for my and Tony's poor decisions.

I'll give him a day, a few even, but then we're talking about the future. I'm not giving up on us that easily. I love him and will fight for him, and even if he rejects me, I'll still be in Liam's corner, ensuring that Ellis shows him the love he deserves. I'll never stop protecting my child. Never.

CHAPTER THIRTEEN

Greyson

"Go awayyyy," I yell and groan after the doorbell rings twice. *Fuck*, my head might combust. The bell rings again. Who's at my door on a Sunday morning?

I sit up, and shit, I'm not at home. Right ... Ellis's ... gala of bitches ... Pappy Van Winkle ... drunkfest. There's a pounding on the door next, so I get up and stumble my way to it. I swing it open and *dammit*.

"Why the hell aren't you in rehab?" I ask Sasha. Her gaze averts in an instant.

"I didn't expect to see you here."

"Answer the question." Recalling the physical state I'm in, I run a hand through my messed-up hair.

"I can't talk about it with you." Lifting her eyes, she stares into mine, and I'm surprised by their brightness. She looks a hell of a lot better than she did the last time I saw her. Pretty even.

Her brown hair's back in a ponytail, and thin strands of it are shaping her filled-out cheeks. It's good to see less of that hollow look I stared down at the night I carried her out of her apartment. She lifts her eyebrows. "Can I come in? I need to speak to my sister. She's not answering her cell."

I step aside so she can enter. "Of course, but this conversation isn't over." I raise my eyebrows back at her as she sets down her two suitcases. "Understood?"

"I found out you're the one who paid for my rehab stay, and thank you for that. It was extremely generous, but it was crazy, too, especially when you don't even know me. I couldn't run up a higher bill."

"Who the fuck's here?" Ellis shouts, his voice booming throughout the hall. Sasha jumps and recoils, so I scowl and turn around to find out what his problem is. He's coming down the staircase, and is that a bottle of booze in his hand?

"Ellis, what are you doing? Where's Camilla and Liam?"

"I sent them away."

Shit, this isn't good. Stumbling, he grabs the railing about eight steps from the bottom. He's in only a pair of sweats, and this is too much for me to deal with while I have a killer hangover.

"Be careful before you injure yourself again."

"Where's Camilla?" Sasha asks, sounding panicked.

"Who is that?" Ellis replies, stretching his head out to see, and before I know why the hell I'm doing it, I shield Sasha behind me. Maybe it's because I haven't seen Ellis drunk in a long damn time and never drunk and angry simultaneously.

"Stay put," I whisper to her. "Where's Camilla, cuz?"

"At a hotel." Holding up his bottle, he points it toward the door beside me. His eyes stare off like they could show me the way.

"Why is that?" He's in front of me now, trying to focus on my face. He looks like shit. We're a goddamn pair, and Sasha's going to wonder why she's the one who was sent to rehab.

"You haven't heard the news?" he asks, slurring every word.

112

"No, tell me."

"Even dead in the cold ground, my brother's a dick. The fucking bastard." Damn, and like always with Ellis, this is going to take a while. I turn to face Sasha.

"Can you wait in the kitchen or living room?"

She crosses her arms and steps around me.

"I want to know where Camilla and Liam are."

Ellis's eyes widen for a second before he glowers.

"How did you get through the gate?"

"I'm Camilla's sister, so of course they let me in. Now, where is she?"

"Why did you—you leave rehab? Did you come to tell me lies, too?"

"What are you talking about?"

"I found out the life-altering secret." Struggling to bring the bottle up to his face, Ellis takes a long drink, so I jerk it from his hands.

"Tell us, Ellis. What news?"

"Tony drugged me a long, long time ago. He drugged Camilla, too."

"You know?" Sasha asks before she covers her mouth.

I grab the back of my neck. "Somebody tell me what's happening."

"Long story short—Liam's my kid."

Sasha gasps. "I told her I thought you could be the father." Pointing at her, Ellis squints.

"She knew all along, didn't she? Camilla's nothing but a liar."

"Ellis, she didn't remember you had slept together until right before I left for rehab, and she didn't think it was possible that you were Liam's father. She always believed it was Tony."

"You *had* met Camilla before?" I ask, shaking my head.

"Yes. She was always the lady in red; the woman from my dreams."

Shit, this is gettin' weird and personal. "Sasha, can you give us a minute? I'll find out where Camilla is."

"Fine. Um, I'm really tired after the long bus ride. Could I lie down for a while?"

"No, she can't," Ellis spouts, so I give him a shove.

"Stop being a dick. Kitchen now. I'll make us some coffee. Sasha, there are spare bedrooms upstairs. Just pick one." Ellis wanders off, mumbling shit, so I rub my hand over my hair.

"This is exactly what Camilla worried he'd do … push her away," Sasha says. "She never meant to hurt him. Tony was the mastermind behind it all."

"I still have no clue what happened, but I can tell you that Ellis is never trashed like this. He was the one taking care of my drunk ass last night, and he'd never hurt Camilla or Liam. I'll find out where they're at for you."

Cocking her head to the side, a smile branches from her lips.

"You're being nice to me, and I sense it's genuine. Why is that?"

"Do you ask every person who's nice to you that question?"

"Aside from Camilla and Liam, people aren't kind to me unless they have something to gain."

"Were the people at rehab not kind to you? Because I donate a shit ton of money to that place, and I'll call—"

"Stop, they were kind, but they also needed their jobs."

"Maybe they were being *genuinely nice.*"

Her forehead scrunches in this cute way, causing her golden-brown eyes to squint, but then she shakes her head.

"No, I don't give people a reason to be nice to me."

"Yet you're sensing I'm being nice to you."

Her gaze flits to the wall. "Well, yes, and that's why I'm confused." I grab hold of her shoulder, but she pulls away. "Please don't touch me."

"Sorry, my bad." I bring my hands up in front of me. "I was just going to say that you're Liam's aunt. That means something to me."

"Right ... I get it now."

I clench my eyes shut. "No, you're not getting it. Liam's not the only reason I helped you. Look, I haven't had coffee yet, and you need sleep. Come down later, and we'll talk then."

She stares at me like I've grown two more heads for being nice.

"OK..." Walking over to the staircase, she looks up it. "Wow," she mumbles before taking a step.

Wow is right. She's different, and I don't like how I can't read her. It's usually so easy for me with women. Shaking the frustration off, I head to the kitchen to face the other person who's striking a nerve with me today.

Sasha

Making it to the top of the floating staircase, I come to a stop and look around. I'm blown away by the size of this mansion. There's one room to my right, and I hope it's a spare bedroom so I don't have to snoop down the long hallway to my left.

I walk over to the doorway, and as soon as I peek inside, I see it's an office and quickly turn back. I guess I'll be exploring this place.

I head the other direction and discover Liam's room on the right. I stare inside, amazed by how perfect it is. He's never had his own space. Reality is, neither Camilla or I have ever had a bedroom that looked like this.

His toys and furniture are new and shiny, and seeing items he loves makes me miss him. I took his presence for granted when we lived together, treating him more like a nuisance when he loved me like no other person had besides my sister.

Suddenly sad, I yearn for sleep. It's my only form of escape if I don't use drugs, and I don't want to. I mean, I do want to, but I won't. Not this time.

Too much money was spent for only the short time I was in rehab to ever use again. I have to find a way to recover. I owe that much to Camilla and Liam ... and now Greyson and Ellis.

I bet they feel obligated to help me because of Camilla, but regardless of the reason, I owe them my life. I don't know the details, but Camilla got me out of that apartment where I'd reached an all-time low with Rusty.

The door across from Liam's is closed, so I crack it open. The room is beautiful, but I don't notice any personal belongings, so I stroll inside.

There's a queen-size bed, dresser and nightstand. A lone chair sits off to the side, but otherwise, there's nothing else. Spotting a couple of doors, I go to them and look inside. One's a closet and the other a spacious bathroom.

It's awkward being here, especially without Camilla, but it's not as strange as it was to be in that lavish rehab facility where I didn't fit in. I roam around the room, and Greyson steps inside the doorway.

"Here are your suitcases. I thought you might need them."

"Oh, thanks. If you think it's OK, I'll probably shower after I rest."

"It's no problem. I'm going to be a while with Ellis, anyway. He has to sober up before we can talk."

"I hope Camilla's OK. It's not like her to ignore my calls."

"I'm sure Ellis put her and Liam in a suite at their hotel."

"Her physical safety isn't what I'm worried about."

Greyson scratches the back of his head, and now that I have a good look at him, I smile. There's a black bowtie hanging around his neck over his wrinkled and untucked white shirt. He's in black dress pants and socks, and his hair is a hot mess. What's unnerving is how sexy he looks like this.

"What's with the smile?" he asks, wearing one himself.

"You have a bowtie hanging around your neck. I don't see that every day, and I assume you slept in it?"

He yanks it off and looks down at it. His skin is pink and smile broader, revealing adorable dimples.

"Yeah, we were at this obnoxious benefit gala last night." He pushes back the top of his hair that's wavy and longer than the rest. "I guess I should go shower, too. Uh, just come down later. I'll have answers, and we'll get you something to eat."

"Thank you … for everything."

"No problem." He strolls to the door, and I try not to look at his firm butt. Stopping, he turns, and I hurry to bring my gaze up. "Why did you take a bus here? I can't imagine how long that took."

I shrug. "It's all I could afford."

Nodding slowly, he looks as if he's trying to wrap his brain around that concept. He leaves me alone with my humiliation, and I try to wrap my brain around *this* lifestyle.

CHAPTER FOURTEEN

Ellis

I've been staring at the TV for some time now after waking up from the nap Greyson forced me to take. I'm sitting on the sofa where he was passed out only hours ago. What a role reversal. My coffee mug is cold in my hand, so I set it on the table in front of me.

"Are you sober enough to talk now?" he asks after strolling into the family room.

"I guess." He's wearing a pair of my athletic shorts and one of my t-shirts, and his hair is damp.

"I see you snooped around my closet and helped yourself to my shower."

"Yeah, and if you hadn't been a drunken ass this morning, I could've gone home to my own shower." He glances down at his attire. "I would've preferred jeans, but you and your long giraffe legs made that impossible."

I fall back against the sofa. "Thanks for handling Sasha. Where is she?"

"Upstairs." He takes a seat in the chair to my right. "Did you confront Camilla last night about having met her before?"

"She brought it up. I guess the guilt was eating at her."

"When did you meet?"

"Tony hosted a party over four years ago for the sole purpose of drugging me so that he could come here and get into my safe to steal a flash drive. It had classified government documents on it. He and Camilla were dating at the time, and he used her to distract me."

"Are you kidding me?"

"No, I'm not. He offered her twenty-five grand, Greyson, which she said she was going to use to help Sasha. She claimed she didn't keep the cash after she discovered he'd drugged us by adding GHB to our bottle of champagne. It fucked us up, and we had sex.

"I've been having dreams about it since after the party, but I couldn't see Camilla's face in the dreams, so I thought it wasn't a real occurrence."

"Why are you so angry?"

"Are you serious right now?"

"You already love that kid. I figured you'd be thrilled to know he's yours, and Sasha said Camilla didn't know, so you can't be pissed at her over that."

"She should've told me what Tony did a hell of a lot sooner."

"Maybe, but it sounds like she was a victim, too. It had to suck to find out the man she was dating drugged her and didn't care if she spent time with his brother."

"None of it changes that our relationship started from a bunch of lies and deceit. I'm not entirely innocent. I hurt her, too, threatening to take Liam after Tony died, but we can't keep starting over. There's too much baggage between us."

"Maybe your stupid move is why she kept shit from you. Did you ever consider that?"

I glare at him. "This isn't my fault."

"No. Your brother definitely gets the credit for that. What was on the flash drive?"

"All I can tell you is it was something that could've destroyed the U.S. if it landed in the wrong hands. I suspect he planned to sell the information.

"It was always about money with him, and he was willing to risk everyone's lives for more of it. I'm sure he would've moved to some island afterward, knowing him."

"He wasn't always law-abiding. Maybe he got himself into some trouble and was forced to get the information."

"There's no proof of that."

"No, but I can't see your brother doing something that could harm you or Camilla, either. Hell, maybe he even suspected Liam wasn't his. That could explain why he never saw him and didn't leave him anything from his estate."

"Trying to make him out to be a saint doesn't change the fact that he drugged Camilla and me. It doesn't change that she kept it from me for as long as possible."

"Was she regretful?"

"Yes. She was a mess."

"Do you love her?"

"It doesn't matter."

"Cuz, you told me she was different from any other woman you'd met. The way you looked at her last night ... damn, man. Unlike me, you get to choose the life you want, and you can either stay bitter all your life, living alone and seeing your son only part-time, or you can forgive her and have the family I know you've always wanted."

"Rehab made you such a fucking girl."

"Shut up, dickwad. This isn't comfortable for me, either, but I'm trying to save you from your self-destructive ways."

"I don't know if I can forgive her that easily. I couldn't even look at Liam this morning. He's not my nephew, and I don't know how I'll react once I see him as my son."

"You react however you need to, but you step up and do it. I can't believe you sent them away." He shakes his head, making me more ashamed.

"I told her she could come back tomorrow. I'm leaving town for a while to think."

"No, you're going to stay here and be a father to Liam, and while you're doing that, you can work on repairing your relationship with Camilla."

I scrub my face with my hands. "Life was so much easier before Tony died."

"Your life was depressing as fuck, cuz. Just sayin'."

"Yeah, and now I'm overrun with house guests. Sasha will be living here next. I had their apartment emptied out last week, and I doubt she knows it."

"Let's worry about one thing at a time. Rest up today, and tomorrow ... meet your son."

Sasha

After I shower and dress in jeans and a black t-shirt that has a cute rainbow and unicorn on the front, I leave my hair down and straighten my brown waves.

Thinking about Camilla, I decide to call her one more time before I head downstairs. I'm nervous about facing Greyson and Ellis. I just want to be with my sister.

I press the button on my phone and pray she answers this time.

"Hello," she says on the third ring.

"Sis, I've been trying to reach you."

"I'm sorry. I had a lot going on this morning and didn't take my phone out of my purse."

"Uh, I have some news; I'm at Ellis's."

"Sasha! What are doing out of rehab?"

"I know, and I'm sorry, but I couldn't stay at that place another day. It was helping, but I didn't fit in. Do you know the kind of money the other patients, or whatever they call them, have or were raised with?"

"I can guess, but it's about the treatment. You had a chance to stay for as long as you needed."

"But I can't relate to them. We might all share the same issues as addicts, but our lives are too different in every other way.

"On top of that, word got to me about what the place costs, so I went to their office and found out Greyson was paying

123

instead of Ellis. I totally flipped and left. There was no way in hell I was staying and running up a bill like that."

"What now? How are you going to stay clean?"

"I swear I'll go to NA. I'll find a sponsor, and I won't hang around any of the lowlifes I used to associate with. I won't tell them I'm back at the apartment."

"Sis, we closed out the apartment last week. I didn't want you living there again."

"Then where am I supposed to go?"

"I don't know. I thought we had time to figure that out, and now I'm unsure if I even have a place to live since Ellis is furious with me. He knows everything. Did he talk to you about it?"

"He was so trashed when I got here. Greyson's downstairs trying to sober him up."

"He doesn't drink."

"Well, he's drinking today. He was rude to me, too, but Greyson put him in his place."

"If he's drunk, then he's more upset with me than I thought."

"Where are you staying? I'll have Greyson give me a ride there, and we'll figure everything out."

"Embassy Suites. If Ellis talks to you, please tell him I'm sorry."

"I will, sis. I love you."

"I love you, too, but I'm still mad at you. I just want you well, Sasha."

"I know, and I promise to do good this time."

Ending the call, I put on my red converse tennis shoes and walk down the quiet hallway. I hope Ellis doesn't yell at me, and I hope Greyson doesn't come across any sexier or kinder than he already has today.

The last thing I need is a crush on a guy I can't have. I might as well join a nunnery since I can only be with a man when I'm under the influence, and I'm staying clean this time.

Halfway down the stairs, I smell food. Having not eaten since yesterday, my stomach growls in an instant. I pad to the kitchen and stop at the doorway, unsure about where I'm welcome.

I see a spread of Chinese take-out on the island, but no one is around, so I walk down a wide hallway, looking in rooms. I find a dining room, a formal living room, and then a family room toward the back of the home, where Greyson is sitting on the couch, watching sports.

He's holding chopsticks over one of the take-out boxes and has changed into shorts and a t-shirt. His blond hair looks shiny and soft, and as soon as I eat, I need him to take me to Camilla's hotel so I can get far away from him.

"Hi," I say meekly. Looking my way, he sits up straight.

"Hi. Feel better?"

"Yeah, I do."

"Are you hungry? I ordered plenty of food."

"I'm starving, actually."

His brow furrows for a second, but then he smiles.

"I set a plate out for you, so help yourself."

"Thank you." I stroll back to the kitchen, and once I've made my plate, I sit at the dinette set next to some windows. I stare out at Ellis's neatly kept property that seemingly goes on forever.

"I did shower, so it was safe to sit by me," Greyson says. I look at him, and he's giving me a charming smile as he stands by the island.

"Sorry. I worried I'd make a mess sitting in there." I can't tell him it's because I'm nervous to be around him since he's so smokin' hot. "Where's Ellis?"

"Upstairs. He's probably in his office or showering."

"Could you give me a ride to Camilla's hotel? I'm going to stay with her until I can get out on my own."

He's silent as he refills his plate. He strolls over and sits across from me. Ugh, I don't want to eat in front of him.

"About that ... I have a proposition for you."

What?

"Um, OK..."

"I was thinking you could come stay at my house temporarily. I'm the only one living there, and although it's not as spacious as this pad, I have a couple extra bedrooms. I have a housekeeper, too, so the place is tidy." That dashing smile returns, and my heart begins to pound in my chest.

"Why would I do that? I mean, why would you offer?"

"I know it seems weird when you don't know me, but I think I might've convinced Ellis to talk to Camilla. She's coming back tomorrow, and I believe they need time alone to work on their relationship."

"So, what you're saying is I'm a burden they don't need." Laying my fork down, I look at my plate.

"I'm sure neither of them sees you as a burden. It's just that Ellis gets overwhelmed when a lot of people are around, which in turn makes him grumpy. Also, since Irene is here through the week, Christopher and the nanny, too, I figured you'd like my quiet place better."

I rub my sweaty hands on my jeans. "I can't let you do that. I should talk to Camilla and see what she suggests."

"If you don't want to go back to California, then inpatient treatment locally would be the next best thing."

"I can't afford that, and I won't let you or Ellis pay for it."

"I figured you'd say that, so live with me, and go to NA meetings. It's the perfect setup. You'll have space while Ellis and Camilla work out their shit. I have an extra car you can drive. I wouldn't offer if it was an inconvenience."

"Camilla says I'm a terrible roommate. If she and Ellis stay together, then you and I will be around each other the rest of our lives. It's a bridge I don't want to burn."

"If you're living a sober life, then I doubt it'll be terrible to have you as a guest. Look, I'll sweeten the deal. Stay with me, and I'll give you a job, too. Do you feel you're above filing paperwork?" He rolls his eyes. "My paralegal sure thinks she is."

"You can give me a job just like that?"

"I have my own law office and real estate company, so yeah, I can hire you if I please."

Having lost my appetite from the knot in my stomach, I start to get up, but he stretches over and grabs my wrist. "Please sit. Don't dismiss this because you think it's too generous or because of the self-loathing shit that's going through that pretty head of yours."

Pretty?

"Look, I got messed up with drugs in college, and my family helped me get clean. We all need support from time to time, so take this opportunity. You can pay it forward once you get your life together."

"Wow, you have a lot of faith in me."

Giving a half shrug, he looks out the window.

"Camilla seems great, so I figure you can't be all that bad." He braves a look at me, and if the sight of dimples could kill, I'd be struck dead by his and that smile that accompanies them.

I'm going to regret this, but I'm beginning to think he'll never let me out of this room without a yes. I twirl the ends of my long hair and stare at the table.

"You're coming around. I feel it. The Burke men always get their way."

I smile. Dammit, why am I smiling?

"OK, I'll stay with you." I shake my head. "This is crazy, but I guess my sister deserves a longer break from me, and I don't want Ellis angry before he even gets a chance to know me."

"Awesome, and thank you. I get more help at the office, and you get a place to crash. It's a win-win."

"No, thank you, and I'll do my best not to let you down."

CHAPTER FIFTEEN

Ellis

While I'm examining the large painting Christopher was so hell-bent on winning, Greyson pokes his head inside my office.

"Got a minute?"

"Sure. I'm trying to figure out why Christopher was determined to take home this painting. He was up to something, and it's the reason I had you bid against him."

Turning the artwork over, I lay it across my desk and survey the mounting board on the back. "This frame is deep. Do you think there could be something hidden inside?"

"I guess it's possible. Let's open it. You can always have it repaired."

"Maybe I'm reading more into this."

"I'm sure he has a nest egg from working for both you and Tony, but I doubt he'd blow it on a painting for only the sentimental value."

Greyson helps me remove the mounting board with minimal damage, and the second I see inside, I swallow.

"Holy shit, how much money is that?" he asks. Picking up one of the many bundles of one hundred dollar bills attached to the back of the mat, I fan them with my fingers.

"There are a hundred bills to a band, so there's ten grand in each one."

Greyson adds them up. "Two rows of ten... There are twenty bundles here. No wonder he wanted the damn painting. He thought he was going to profit almost two hundred thousand, especially if I hadn't pushed the bidding up."

"He said Tony wanted him to have the painting, but I wouldn't give it to him. I felt like a dick at the time, but Tony didn't leave it to him in the trust, and I figured those benefiting from my mother's literacy program deserved it more."

"What's this?" Greyson peels off a white envelope that's below the bills and tears it open. Inside is a slip of paper, along with a key he hands me. "There's only an address on here. It's in Isla Mujeres."

"I think that's an island in the Caribbean. I wonder if he owns it."

"He never listed the asset in his trust."

Sitting at my desk, I open Google Earth on my laptop and type in the address, bringing up a virtual view of the property.

"Damn, it's a home, and from the looks of it, it's an expensive one. Do you think he left it to Christopher?"

"I don't know, but I believe the fucker knew all this was here. Maybe Tony did tell him he could have it, but like you said; there's no proof of that."

"I don't trust him, Greyson. I've been keeping him around to see if he comes up with any information about Tony's death, but his so-called friendship with Camilla is pissing me off. I can't stand seeing them together, especially knowing he's in love with her."

"Does this mean you're forgiving Camilla?"

I start removing the bundles of cash taped to the back of the mounting board.

"I don't know. I need time to think about it."

"At least that's not a no. Uh, I came up to tell you something. Sasha's going to come live with me temporarily so you can work on things with Camilla without having another distraction in the house."

"She agreed to this?"

"It took some persuading, but she finally caved. I'll make sure she works and goes to NA meetings."

I stare at him and consider his motives.

"Whitney's going to lose her shit when she finds out. Is that the angle you're working here? Are you hoping she'll dump you over it?"

"Give me some credit. I have no ulterior motives here."

"Maybe not consciously."

"I'm helping her out–helping you out, man."

"I don't know how Camilla will feel about it."

"Sasha's an adult. She can make her own decisions."

"True, and I'd like to see that happen. She's relied on Camilla way too much over the years." I give him a look of warning. "All right, but don't think about touching her."

"I'm only being a friend. Sasha and I couldn't possibly have a thing in common."

"When has that ever stopped you from sleeping with someone?"

He flashes a sly grin. "Point taken, but she's different. She's Camilla's sister, and I know she's fragile right now. I won't mess with her head."

I hand Greyson six of the bundles of money. "Here ... for the painting."

"Hey, now, I bought that painting. I think I'm entitled to it *and* all the money stashed inside."

Smiling, I pick up the rest. "Fine, here."

"Cuz, I was joking." He shoves them back toward me, so I set all of them down but one.

"Here, put this in an account for Sasha. She has nothing. She's even borrowing Camilla's clothing."

He laughs. "I think she's wearing her own shirt today. It has a bright fucking unicorn and rainbow on it."

"That means you checked out her tits." I smile since I'm only messing with him.

"I couldn't help it. Her shirt was glowing with all these neon colors." His sly grin returns. "OK, and she has an amazing rack for her petite body. I might've noticed."

I point at him. "Don't touch her."

"I know, I know." He holds up the extra ten grand. "She'll probably refuse this."

"Then I guess you'll have to use your persuasion skills yet again. Oh, and thank you for helping me out earlier."

"Same here for last night." He strolls out of my office with ten grand for Sasha and sixty for the painting. What's a few extra thousand? It was all worth it to confirm what a slimy worm Christopher is.

It's time I find out everything about him. I figured if Tony trusted him enough to call him a close friend, then I could, too, but that's not the case.

After finding out he lied to Camilla for years, ignored my demands to stay away from her and now tried to undermine me with the painting, I'm doing a thorough check on him. I'll call my FBI friend and set up a meeting for tomorrow.

Camilla

Liam and I are playing with his action figures on the hotel bed when I hear knocking. I leave Liam in the bedroom and head to the door, expecting it to be Sasha.

"Hello, who's there?"

"It's room service, ma'am."

"But I didn't order anything." I look through the peephole, and there's a man in a hotel uniform.

"Someone called in an order for you." Hmm ... Ellis maybe? I inch the door open and spot the cart of food with him.

"Sorry, I was only being cautious."

The young man smiles. "I understand." I step aside for him to enter, and the amount of food delivered confirms that it's from Ellis.

I'm comforted by the gesture, even if he only did it for Liam. Hurrying to my purse, I find some cash and tip him before I wheel the cart to the living room.

"Guess what, sweetie," I yell, craning my neck to see Liam. "Ellis surprised us with dinner. Are you hungry?"

"Yessss," he says excitedly before he jumps off the bed, almost falling on his face.

"Oh, be careful."

"Boss is nice."

"Yes, he sure is." Of course, he booked us in a suite that's close to the size of my previous apartment. An apartment I'm wondering if I should've kept. Who am I kidding? There's no way Ellis would allow Liam to live there again. Where will we end up now?

After I get Liam set up to eat at a desk in the living room, I fix myself a plate and sit on the couch. Holding my phone in front of me, I debate on texting Ellis. This is an excuse for me to reach out to him, so I'm taking advantage of it, even if it hurts me in the end.

Me: *Hi, thank you for dinner. Liam's thrilled. He also loved the pool.*

Ellis: *You're welcome.*

I wait and wait, but he doesn't text again. It's time to open up to him, and maybe then he'll do the same.

Me: *I need to tell you something. Besides Liam and my father, you're the only male to ever breathe to me the three beautiful words I love you. Only you.*

I thought they'd be the most special words I'd ever hear from your lips, but I was wrong. There are two words that would mean more to me than any in our language. "Come home." Please say them, Ellis. Please…

Clenching my eyes shut, I breathe through the heartache so I don't shed tears in front of Liam. Unable to eat, I look at my phone in my hands. I stare at the screen and stare some more. I wait and wait until my fingers hurt from gripping it so hard.

He isn't going to message me back.

Me: *I'm sorry. I'll respect your wish for space, but don't think for a second that I'm giving up on us.*

Tossing my phone across the cushions, I look at the plate in my lap. I glance at the room service cart, and the guilt creeps in over the food that will go to waste.

I've felt true hunger before. When I first rescued Sasha from our parents, I went several days without food on more than one occasion as I moved us around, searching for jobs.

I would eat ketchup on cheap, stale bread, or I'd survive on Ramen noodles for days straight. Sasha was always fed first. I didn't rescue her from a horrific home life to let her starve to death, so if I had to skip lunch and dinner to ensure she had a meal, I did it.

My phone rings, and I lunge across the couch to grab it. Sasha.

"You must've sensed me thinking about you."

"Hi. I called to tell you I'm not coming over."

"Why is that?"

"I'm going to live with Greyson for a while. He's giving me a job, too, and I'm gonna go to NA."

"Wait, how did all this happen?"

"He offered, and at first I refused, but he kept pushing until I accepted. He thinks you and Ellis could use the time alone to work on your relationship, and I agree. I've been a burden long enough."

"You're never a burden."

"Right. I want life to be easier for you, and I think this will help, so I'm going."

"Listen ... Greyson isn't exactly single."

"He said he lives alone and that it was no inconvenience. He has to know better than to let a chick move in with him if another woman's in the picture, even if our relationship is platonic."

"You'd think, but don't spend too much time with him. I don't want you to get hurt."

"I'm not stupid. I'm aware he's out of my league, and besides, you know the sober Sasha won't get close to him."

"No man is out of your league."

"I have to go. Greyson's ready for us to leave."

"Did Ellis speak to you?"

"No, he's been hiding out in his office. I'm sorry."

"That's OK. Call me tomorrow so I can hear all about your job."

"I doubt I'll know much by then. I imagine he won't have me start right away."

"I love you, Sasha, and never forget that I'm here for you."

"I love you, too. I'm gonna make you proud, sis. This time I will."

We end the call, and I sigh. Her news didn't ease my tension whatsoever. She'll be back in my care in no time since the Whitney I met last night would never go for another woman living with Greyson.

CHAPTER SIXTEEN

Camilla

The knock on the door startles me. I sit up in bed and pull on the pajama pants I had laying at the end of it. The clock reads 12:30 a.m.

Not wanting to wake Liam, I forego turning on the light and instead walk carefully to the living room of the suite, feeling my way as I go.

I flip on a lamp by the couch and hurry to the door about the time the person knocks again. Looking in the peephole, I see him. It's Ellis, and I can't open the door fast enough.

The light in the hotel hallway reveals his handsome face. His blue eyes are weary, and his hair's disheveled, but he's still sexy in loose jeans and a black hoodie. A Denver Broncos graphic is across the front of his broad chest. He stares into my eyes without a word.

"Ellis, hi. Is everything OK?"

"Come home."

My body begins to tremble as his words sink in and we gaze at each other. Is he truly in front of me, saying what I long to hear, or is this a dream? He said the words, but his eyes expose his anguish.

I should wait to be sure that he means it, but I can't wait, so I throw my arms around his neck. He only hesitates a few seconds and then brings me in close, hugging me snugly. I feel his nose in my hair and his heavy breath on my neck.

"Thank you," I say. "Thank you for giving me another chance."

He stiffens but doesn't let me go. After a few seconds, I pull back to get a better read on him. Not wanting him to disappear, I keep hold of his waist. He doesn't look down at me. No ... please no. "You're not here for me, are you?"

His head falls back, and he blows out a breath.

"Let me inside." I walk back into the suite so he can come in and shut the door. While my body shakes, I cross my arms and grip my biceps. My mind races with a hundred scenarios of what he'll say and do.

He strolls over, so I lower my arms, wanting him in my personal space more than ever. He slides his fingers through my hair and grips it, and I can't help but lean my cheek against his warm hand.

"I'm here for you, too, and I'm not leaving town, but I need space and time to think about everything. I want to believe we can get past this, but I can't make any promises.

"What Tony did, the years I missed with Liam, and not feeling like I can trust you spurred an anger that's clawing at my insides."

"Ellis, there aren't words to express how sorry I am for my part in this. My heart breaks for the time you lost, as well. But I refuse to be angry at Tony any longer.

"What he did led me to you, and we created that special boy in the other room. I would never wish to change the past. I can't regret it."

He exhales what I pray is a fraction of his anger.

"I want to stay mad at you, and I hate how you make it so damn hard."

"I don't believe that. You wouldn't be here if you weren't hoping we could work things out." With his fingers deep in my hair, he massages my scalp and wraps his other arm around my waist.

His eyes tell his urge to resist, but I won't let him go. I shove my body forward, determined to show him how perfectly we mold together ... how magical it is when we touch.

He eyes my lips and dips his head to kiss them, and as soon as our mouths collide, relief washes over me. He slips his tongue inside, but it doesn't become the fervent kiss I expect from him, where his hands are everywhere and I'm breathless in seconds.

He's not fisting my hair or bruising my lips with his carnal touch. Instead, it's a languid kiss, one expressing apprehension or maybe appreciation, relief of his own. I can't tell, and it's increasing my anxiety.

Regardless, there's that slow burn in my belly that spreads to between my legs. My body doesn't care what's garbled in my mind.

It only yearns for more of his touch. It needs to be possessed by his mouth and hands, his warmth and strength. I pull away and grab the back of his hair.

"Take me right here. Make me submit. Punish me if it will bring you back to me."

He pulls my arms down, and the same hurt swims in his eyes.

"Not yet. I told you I need time." Dragging my teeth over my bottom lip, I nod swiftly. I'll obey his wishes and find patience so I don't scare him off. "I want to see him and take him home," he adds.

"He's sleeping." Ellis strolls toward the bedroom, and once he reaches it, he stares at the bed where Liam is curled into a ball on his side facing us.

Light from the living room casts on him, and it's enough to see our child's parted lips and little hands resting near his face. Striding to him, Ellis drops to his knees next to the bed. He places a hand around Liam's back and the other on his head and strokes his hair.

Then I hear it; Ellis's soft cries give sound to the silent space. His body shakes as he gazes at our child. Emotions overwhelm him, and his head falls forward to rest on Liam's waist.

"Liam..." His cries grow louder, more gut-wrenching. He continues to stroke his hair as he nudges him closer.

"You're my son. I have a son."

I lean against the doorframe and slide down against it until I'm a puddle on the floor, weeping, too. I'm trapped in a cage of emotions: guilt, despair, joy, and love.

Regret I said I wouldn't feel for what Tony did is in the cage with me, trying to take hold to strangle my resolve, but I won't allow it. I can't.

No, instead I'll cling to the hope that through Tony's actions and death, Ellis, Liam and I will be given a beautiful life ... a magnificent future.

But it will only happen if we believe in the possibility. I do believe, and I'll hang on to that faith for Ellis, too, until he trusts in us again. I'll fight for our family. I'll make us whole.

Ellis

For minutes, I let out the grief I've held in from losing Tony. I release the pain from the years I lost with Liam, but mostly I cry for the overwhelming amount of love I have for my son.

I felt a strong fondness for him when I believed he was my nephew, but it doesn't compare to how I feel knowing he's my flesh and blood. My purpose for living expanded exponentially by hearing that single truth.

Wiping my eyes, I ponder how I'll tell him I'm his father. How will he respond? Will it scare him away or bring us closer? Neither of our lives will ever be the same.

Camilla sniffles, so I look over my shoulder at her. She's sitting on the floor, taking a front row seat to my most vulnerable state.

She gets up and walks over to us. Sitting on the side of the bed next to me, she places her hand on his legs. Her long hair shrouds her swollen eyes, and her skin is blotchy and pink.

I realize she's the stark contrast to how she was the night she got inside my car and listened to my terms. She was defiant and angry, tough and strong, and the precise challenge I was looking for.

Unlike the women who repeatedly threw themselves at me, she was going to fight, and I looked forward to breaking her to prove I was powerful and in control of my life and those around me.

Dominating her would rid me of the inadequacy I'd felt all my life. She was going to symbolize the room full of people I ran away from in a fit of panic. She was going to pay for hiding Liam from his family.

So, I moved her in under duress, and lied to her, too, making her believe I knew what it meant for her to submit to me. The truth was, I didn't have a clue what respect a submissive deserved, but I did accomplish one of my goals; I broke her.

Now, she sits before me, plagued with the guilt and pain I initially wanted her to endure, but instead of it giving me satisfaction, it makes me feel like scum.

And the reason is because I now understand what she was fighting for and feared she'd lose. She would've done anything I asked to keep Liam.

"I hate to wake him. Why don't you sleep in the bed, and I'll take the couch? We'll go home in the morning," she whispers.

Considering her statement, I could be suspicious that she's still living with that fear, being compliant only to please me so I don't take Liam away from her.

But her eyes always tell a different story. They gaze at me like I can do no wrong, and her body responds to my touch as if it could never get enough of it. The words she breathes seem straight from her heart.

She claims she loves me and wants to be my submissive in its authentic form. What do I do with that? ... Nothing. I do nothing and keep my distance from Camilla unless I can forgive her for hiding Liam all these years and for the role she played in Tony's deceit.

I can't be anything to her if I don't trust that her actions are genuine. I want more than anything to believe this is more than her surviving … more than a way for her to keep her son. It has to be more than another form of running.

"Or, we can sleep in the bed together with him between us," she adds. Probably because I've not replied to her previous suggestion.

"No, I'll take the sofa. If he wakes up and I'm in bed with him, he'll be confused."

Scrunching her forehead, she nods. "OK."

I eye my child one last time before I walk to the entrance of the living room. I turn back to Camilla.

"Two things… Tomorrow I'm telling Liam I'm his father. He might not understand now, but he will in time."

"I think that's wonderful. What's the other thing?"

"If I'm to trust you, then you need to tell me about your past. I want to know why you took Sasha from your parents. Why have you been in hiding? I can't trust someone I don't know, so you have to let me in, too."

She swallows and tucks hair behind her ear.

"I can do that. As hard as it will be to talk about it after all these years, I want someone else to know. I want you to know."

Nodding, I leave her alone in the room and head for the sofa. I remove my shoes and strip off my hoodie before I lie down.

Why did my life take this turn? If my brother were here, I'd cuss at him, lay him out cold, and then I'd help him up so I could hug him. I'd thank him for creating this domino effect, which gave me that amazing kid.

Yes, I could've had a child already if I'd wanted to, but he wouldn't have been Camilla's. She's the reason he's so damn remarkable.

CHAPTER SEVENTEEN

Sasha

"Shit, why are you so loud?" Without opening my eyes, I slam my hand down on the alarm clock next to me, but it doesn't help, so the annoying thing keeps blasting in my ear.

Dammit. I sit up and lean on one elbow while I figure out how to shut it off. I finally find the right button. "Thank you, Jesus, for reminding me I have sight and hearing."

Falling back on the bed, I cover my head with the blanket and yawn. Drugs. They're my next thought, so that means I need more sleep to make me forget.

***

"Wake up." My blanket is yanked back, so I open my eyes wide.

"Greyson! What are you doing in here?" I grab the blanket and cover myself back up. "What if I had been naked?"

"Hmm ... I hadn't thought of that." He shrugs. "You're not. Now, get ready. We're leaving in twenty minutes." I sit up in bed, in my white tank top and shorts, embarrassed that he saw me braless.

He looks handsome in khakis and a navy dress shirt he hasn't tucked in yet. I turn my head away with the hope that I won't get another whiff of his enticing scent.

It's soap, cologne or aftershave. Whatever the concoction, it made him smell delicious. Like lickably so. Yes, I made that word up.

"Did you set the alarm after I fell asleep?" I ask.

"Yep, and I thought the volume would do the trick, but no such luck."

"I'm grateful for getting to stay here, but you should respect my boundaries. If this is my room, then don't come in here without knocking first."

He scratches the back of his head, which I've noticed he does when he's nervous or thinking. Or, maybe he does it with the hope that when his shirt lifts from doing so, I'll see his washboard stomach and forget how he misbehaved. Strategic on his part since it's working.

"You're right. I wouldn't want someone barging in my room without permission. Get ready. We're leaving in fifteen minutes now, instead of twenty."

"Where in the world are we going?"

"To work. Where else would we go on a Monday morning?"

"You want me to start today? I thought I'd have time to rest after that awful bus trip."

"Hmph. I guess we need to go over the terms of this arrangement. One, you don't get to lie around here and do nothing like some sloth. Two, you will work, starting today."

He's holding his hand out in front of him, counting off his fingers like some disgruntled teacher I've pissed off in the classroom. I'm surprised I remember what that feels like seeing how I didn't go to school past the eighth grade.

"Are you even listening to me?"

"Sorry, yes."

"Three, you will not bring drugs into my home, *nor* will you do them while living here. Four, you will not have strangers over without my prior knowledge, especially no dudes.

"Five, you don't treat my housekeeper, Theresa, like she's your servant. She's fucking awesome, and I'll be pissed if she quits, and lastly, my home gym is off limits from five to six every weekday morning. That's my time to work out."

I roll my eyes. "No worries there, Mr. Probation Officer. I have no plans to be up at five, *nor* do I have the desire to exercise."

He wrinkles his forehead. "I caught that. The snide nor reference. I hope you're quick at getting ready because you now have ten minutes."

"But I don't have any dress clothes."

"You can wear jeans until you get some." He strolls out, and I'm stunned by the change in his demeanor. Where did yesterday's sweet Greyson go?

Greyson

Yeah, I was a little hard on her, but I had to treat her like a child so I didn't *get hard* from thinking of her as a woman.

I could see her tits through her tank top. Although brief, it was long enough to turn me on. They're the ideal roundness, heavy I'm sure. Fuck, I can imagine the weight of them in my hands.

Whitney's are too small. I'm such a douchebag. Wait, no, I have a right to my opinion about tits, and my personal preference is big ones. I'm sure Whit prefers my long dick over Sebastian's three inches. She thinks I don't know she's screwing him, but I do.

Anyway, I knew I was wrong to invade Sasha's personal space, so I admonished her instead of myself. I'll blame it on the lack of caffeine and her fine assets.

Once I've put on my shoes and watch, I walk to the kitchen and start my Keurig. It's moments like this when I wish Theresa worked every day, but she's only here on Tuesdays and Fridays, cleaning and preparing my meals for the week.

The ten minutes I gave Sasha have long passed, and I debate on harassing her to hurry up. I can get to work whenever the hell I want unless I have an early appointment, so I decide to cut her some slack today. I only pushed her this morning to see how cooperative she'd be.

I hear her barrel into the kitchen behind me. I look back at her, and the poor girl's hair is wet, and she's out of breath. I smile, happy with her commitment to this.

"Do you drink coffee?"

"Yes."

"Go dry your hair. I'll make you a to-go mug while I wait."

"Are you sure you won't be late?"

"Yep. Go before I change my mind." She disappears, and her footsteps thump loudly on my hardwood floors as she runs down the hallway to one of my three bedrooms.

Once I've fixed our drinks, I stroll to the living room and admire the mountains in the far-off distance. My penthouse condo is in the Cherry Creek neighborhood, which is in the center of the city.

"I'm ready now." I turn around, and Sasha is even more out of breath. She's smiling this time, her eyes brighter than yesterday, and I imagine that'll continue if she stays clean.

A somberness settles over me when I recall the first time I saw her in her apartment. I think about how easy it would be for her to go right back to that state of despair.

"What's wrong?"

"Uh, nothing. Your coffee's on the counter, and you can grab anything you want from the refrigerator or pantry to eat on the way."

"OK, thank you." She leaves, and I gaze out the picture window again, warning myself not to get attached to her. I've felt the disappointment before when a friend I helped didn't stay clean. There's a fine line between supporting someone's sobriety and becoming emotionally involved with them.

"You have so much food," she says excitedly. I turn, and her eyes are round as saucers, her grin surrounded by caramel-brown hair that's naturally highlighted throughout. She's too pretty, smiling like that as she holds a muffin, banana and her mug.

I push out my lip. "You think?"

"Yes, your pantry is stocked full. When the zombie apocalypse begins, I'm hiding out here."

"Zombies?" I ask with a chuckle.

"I'm just joking. Well, sort of. Do you not watch *The Walking Dead*?"

"I can't say I have. Isn't it cheesy with all those zombies?"

"Oh, no. The acting is incredible, and the special effects make it so real. You *have* to watch it. We can start from the beginning and binge watch every season if you'd like."

I smile, enjoying how happy-go-lucky she is. Don't get attached, Greyson. She can't stick around. You'll soon be living in a custom-built home with whiny Whit, listening to her go on and on about how gifted she is and how lucky I am to be graced by her angelic presence.

"I don't have much time to watch television, but you're welcome to hang out in here and watch TV whenever you want."

"Right. I'm sorry I asked. I get excited about shows and movies. I guess they're an escape for me. I fantasize about lives I'll never get a chance to live."

It takes effort to hold my smile. I'm frustrated that I want to stay right here and learn more about her. She's different from any woman I've known.

Maybe it's her youthful maturity level. I think she's twenty-five, but she acts more like a twenty-year-old. I don't want to call her immature because if I had to guess, there's a dark explanation for her childlike nirvana. An explanation that was out of her control.

"We should go."

Ellis

Feeling a poke on my shoulder, I wake up to find Liam smiling down at me. I've often noticed how similar his blue eyes are to mine, but now I *really* see it.

"Boss, whatcha doin' here?"

"I came to see you, but you were sleeping. I thought I would, too." I start to sit up, so he moves to allow me room. I grin at how his hair is sticking up in the back like it often does.

His *Batman* pajamas are funny, too, and I try to recall if I ever wore clothes with action figures on them. I don't believe so. My parents dressed us in stuffy attire, so I'm sure mine were some atrocious plaid.

"Did you come to swim? They have a pool, and it's so, so big aaaaand deep." He spreads his arms apart.

"No, I don't have my swim trunks. I do have a surprise for you at the house. Would you like to go see it?"

"At your house?"

"It's your house, too."

"My house?" Pointing to his chest, he grins broader.

"Yes, and you can live there for as long as you'd like."

"I want to wive there forever. I love my room and Iwene and Em."

I chuckle from his excitement and over how damn happy he makes me. Camilla strolls in, yawning with her steps.

"Good morning," she says.

"Morning."

"Momma, Boss says I can wive with him forever."

Her eyes flit to mine and hang on tightly. They study me, looking for evidence that I've had a change of heart. I don't want to hurt her, but nothing about us changed overnight.

"Would you mind if we checked out soon and head home? I have a meeting somewhere at eleven and need time to shower. I took a taxi here, so we can ride back together," I say.

Sighing heavily, she turns her back on me and starts walking to the bedroom.

"I'll go pack our things and dress."

"Liam, you should get dressed, too," I say, "and once we're home, I'll have Irene make you pancakes. Then, after my meeting, I'll show you your surprise."

"Yes!" He jumps up and down, hopping like a rabbit all the way to the bedroom. I wish I had his energy this morning. I also wish I could forget about the past, but the second I saw Camilla, it resurfaced, along with the pain. I want to find a way to bury it with my brother.

CHAPTER EIGHTEEN

Sasha

Greyson holds the glass door open for me to enter his business, G. Burke Enterprise. I walk in and smile at a young brunette behind a curved desk.

Right away, I notice her lavender silk blouse and worry about being underdressed. I cross my arms and glance around the space.

A window spans the entire front of the brick building, and like Greyson's home, his office's décor is rustic and not what I expected. Maybe it's because of his wealth, but I pictured him with a modern style.

The lobby reminds me of ski resorts I've seen on television. Wooden crown molding and beams are overhead, and there's a colossal grey stone fireplace with a sizable cream rug lying before it. A brown leather sofa rests on top, across from two comfy chairs, making the space welcoming and cozy.

"Kaylie, this is Sasha. She's going to be assisting Rhonda. Sasha, this is Kaylie, our receptionist." She stands to shake my hand.

"Nice to meet you, Sasha. Mr. Burke's a cool boss. I think you'll like it here."

"Kaylie's the cool one. You should hear her mess with the telemarketers." He gives her a nod. "Send my calls to voice mail for the next thirty minutes."

"Yes, sir," she replies before taking her seat.

I follow Greyson through another glass door. There are offices on both sides of me as we stride down the long hallway. He stops at one on the left and taps on the open door.

"Good morning." Greyson motions for me to step up to the doorway.

"Morning," the guy replies.

"I want to introduce you to Sasha. She's going to be assisting Rhonda."

He arches an eyebrow and comes around the desk. Smiling, he shakes my hand.

"I didn't know she was getting an assistant. It's a pleasure to meet you, Sasha. I'm Terrence, the appraisal manager and Greyson's right-hand man."

"He is when he's not braggin' about it," Greyson says. I take a glimpse of him, and his smirk exposes a hint of his dimples.

"Welcome, Sasha. If you need anything at all, you come see me, and FYI, this one's grumpy before his morning cup of Joe."

"Yes, I found that out earlier this morning."

Scrunching his forehead, he shoots Greyson a look.

"Oh, I'm sorry. That wasn't an appropriate comment," I say.

"Uh, come on. I'll introduce you to Rhonda." Greyson practically shoves me through the doorway, and once we're out of earshot, he takes hold of my arm to stop me.

"Listen, I'd rather you not tell anyone that you're staying with me. Terrence and I are friends, so I'll fill him in later, but otherwise, I'd like to keep it under wraps. I don't need my staff gossiping or thinking I'm giving you preferential treatment because we're friends."

"I'm sorry. I'm not used to having to censor my thoughts in a work environment."

"I should've discussed that with you before we arrived."

"You think of us as friends?"

"Yes, don't you?" His crooked smile is heart-stirring, so I feel the heat creep up my neck.

Biting the corner of my lower lip, I reply, "Yes."

"Let's go. I need to introduce you to Rhonda." Greyson taps on a door on the right, and an older woman at a desk lifts her dark brown eyes to look at me.

"Good morning," Greyson says. "I have some news. This is Sasha, and she's going to be assisting you to alleviate some of your workload. Sasha, this is my senior paralegal, Rhonda."

Clearing her throat, she sets her lips in a flat line.

"It's nice to meet you, Sasha. Mr. Burke, may I have a word with you in your office please?"

"Sure. Sasha, have a seat. We'll be back shortly." They both leave the room, so I sit down. My hands are sweating, and my heart is racing.

Every person I've met is dressed up. Terrence is wearing a tie, and Rhonda's in a business skirt. I stare at the picture frame hanging across from me, and it's her college diploma. I don't belong here. I'm not smart enough or experienced.

I fidget with my hands ... cross and uncross my legs. I need out of here. I'll thank Greyson for the opportunity and tell him I want to find my own job.

"Sasha, come with me," he says as he steps in front of the doorway. Rhonda waltzes in behind him, feigning a smile.

"As soon as Greyson is finished meeting with you, I'll get you started with something to do." Although I'm glad there's been a slight change in her demeanor, I'm feeling more trapped by the second.

Greyson leads me to a door at the end of the hallway. I follow him inside another office, and wow … this must be his. Could his desk be any more massive? I walk right over to it and run my fingers along the intricately carved edging. The swirly walnut finish has character.

"This desk is amazing."

"My grandfather had it custom-made for me. I think it was a peace offering."

"For what?"

Slipping his hands in his pockets, he shrugs.

"He wanted me to go into the oil business. My brother did– I didn't. He shut me out for a few months, and I wondered if he'd ever speak to me again.

"I don't know what changed, but this was delivered the same day he invited me over for a drink. He said he would support me, but he added that one day I'd come to my senses and join my father and Lawrence to run the family business. I was glad we made amends, though, because he died soon after."

"I'm sorry. Do you think that day will come?"

"Never. I only planned to dabble in real estate and stick with law, but once I got a taste of buying up property, I couldn't stop.

"It's challenging to juggle both careers, but my father's side of the family has always dealt in real estate. I figured Lawrence could carry on our mother's side, and I'd carry on our father's."

I glide my fingers over the wave-like carving again.

"That's admirable. I wish I had parents who were worthy enough for me to follow in their footsteps. Look, I appreciate this opportunity, but I think I should find my own job.

"I don't fit in here, and Rhonda didn't look happy with the arrangement. Then, there's the whole ... what is it called? Conflict of interest?"

He shakes his head. "Rhonda's happy now. She just needed to hear my intentions. Also, I don't hire mean people, so once you get to know them, you'll feel at home.

"And as far as it being a conflict of interest, it's my damn company. I get to make the rules. I only told you to be quiet about it because I don't want to hear any whining from my other employees."

He nods toward the door. "Let me show you the break room, and then Rhonda can start training you."

"What if I can't learn?"

"Well, I have faith that you can. If there's a problem, we'll deal with it then."

Can I be the whining employee? All I want to do is go home and hide under the covers. Then, I'd fix a bowl of chicken Ramen noodles and watch reality television that would make my dysfunctional existence not seem so bad.

Instead, I say, "OK. I'll give it a try."

Ellis

"Pull over right here, Fletcher," I say once I spot my contact from the FBI. "I shouldn't be long."

"Yes, sir."

I scope out the area of the Washington Park Boathouse as I approach Lawson, who's resting his elbows on the railing that overlooks Smith Lake.

"Hi, thanks for meeting me."

"It's no problem, but I'm wondering why we couldn't handle this over the phone."

"It's not government business."

"Shit, what now?" He rakes his hand over his black hair, which considering his career, he keeps longer than he should. I shoot him a sideways glance.

"I'm not the only one who asks for favors."

He grins cockily. "Here lately, it's *only* you, but what do you need?"

"If you'd prefer, I can nullify our agreement and dig for the information myself."

"No, you stay the hell out of our network. I don't want to risk the agency cutting you off."

"I need you to check out this guy." I pull the envelope from my blazer pocket and hand it to him. "Everything I know is in there. It should get you started."

"Is there something specific you're searching for?"

"Mainly older shit. I guess I'm looking for something from his past to confirm my suspicion that he's a conniving dirt bag.

He works for me, and I should've checked him out before I hired him."

Shoving the envelope in his suit pocket, he pulls out a pack of cigarettes and proceeds to light up. We're overdressed for a visit to the park, and I know the real person behind that suit of his. Lawson's a badass motherfucker, who I could envision wearing a biker's cut more than a tailored suit.

"That's not too difficult of a task," he replies.

"I need something else..."

He chuckles. "Of course you do."

"That woman I had you check out a few months ago, Camilla Rose ... I need you to investigate her parents for me."

"I see why you didn't want to have this conversation over the phone." He takes a drag off his cigarette. "I should've turned her ass in when I discovered her true identity, but I let it slide because of you."

"It has to stay that way, too. Actually, I want you to wipe out every piece of information that shows she's wanted by the authorities."

His head whips in my direction. "Fuck, no. You're getting greedy."

"There's a critical reason I need this from you."

"Then you better be sharing that critical reason, but my answer's still no. I'm not losing my whole damn career over you and some chick who broke the law."

"She's the mother of my child."

He squints at me before taking another puff off his cigarette.

"Damn. Why didn't you mention that before?"

"I just found out the kid's mine."

"So, you don't want to chance her going to prison."

"Exactly. She's a good mother, Lawson. Better than good. My son's extremely attached to her, and Camilla and I can't worry every day that she could be taken away from him."

"And taken away from you?" he hints.

"Can you help me or not? I'm willing to do whatever is necessary to make this happen."

"Not all the records are electronic."

"No, but most of them are. It would minimize the risk. Also, I want her identification officially changed to Camilla Rose. Somehow, she managed to get fake IDs, but I want real documents: a birth certificate, social security card, driver's license and a passport... I want it all for her *and* her sister. Their information's in that envelope."

"Seriously?"

"I know I'm asking for a lot, but I promise to make it worth your while."

"You know I can't take a bribe."

"No, but I can give my *friend* a gift once he retires, which could be at a fairly young age."

"You're straying a little far from the red road, *friend*."

"I'll do anything to protect Camilla and my child. Please, think about it." Pulling out my phone, I scroll through my photos to find one of Liam. "Here, this is my son, Liam."

Tilting his head back, he eyes the photo.

"You're such a manipulative fuck."

"I like to think of myself as resourceful."

"Fine, but you're still a fuck."

Smiling, I slip my phone back inside my pocket.

"Do it for my kid. He needs both his parents."

"I'll see what I can do."

Camilla

Liam and I are eating lunch in the dining room, and Christopher is joining us. Irene put me on the spot, offering to feed him, too. I'm stressing out since Ellis doesn't need another reason to be angry with me.

"You're picking at your food. That means you're upset about something. What did he do this time?" Chris asks.

"Ellis didn't do anything. It was me, but I can't talk about it."

"He probably convinced you of that. He never takes responsibility for anything."

"Please stop speaking negatively of him in front of Liam."

"I still believe you'll come to your senses and realize I'm the one who would never let you down."

"Stop. I love him, and you bad-mouthing him won't change that."

"Then I'll let him screw that up on his own. We need to discuss Saturday night," he adds, refusing to let me eat in peace.

"Which part? The one where you bid over fifty thousand dollars for a painting?"

"Tony left me that painting."

"Then he should've said so in his will or trust, whatever it's called."

"I guess he was *trusting* that Ellis would believe me instead of being a greedy bastard."

"Bastard," Liam says.

I glower at Christopher. "I told you to watch your language around him."

"Sorry."

Wiping Liam's mouth with my napkin, I give him a stern look.

"You're not allowed to say that word until you're a grownup. Do you hear Momma?"

"I can't say bastard?"

Chris chuckles, so I swat at him from across the table.

"Stop encouraging him. I need to use the restroom. Can you stay here with him?"

"Of course."

I walk to the bathroom, and once I'm finished, I grip the vanity and stare in the mirror. How did my life get so complicated? I thought not having two pennies to rub together was the biggest stressor in life, but I'm beginning to think otherwise.

Once I'm back at the table, I eye Liam. He's looking down at his lap and playing with a cheese cube. I always wonder when he does this if he's thinking about the food in his hand or something else.

"Sweetie, are you OK?" Nodding, he puts the cheese cube in his mouth.

"Why did Ellis tell his family that Liam is...?" Chris asks.

"I can't talk about it."

"You say that a lot." I don't reply, hoping he'll take the hint. "It was ridiculous, Cammy. Are you going to tell Liam a lie his whole life?"

"Stop talking about him. He's right here and staring at you. Make this right," I say through gritted teeth.

"All right. Liam, I saw the jungle gym's finished out back. Would you like me to take you outside to swing?"

"Chris, stop," I say.

"There's a swing?" Liam asks.

Lord, things keep getting worse. "Christopher, that was a surprise from Ellis. He's going to lose his mind." With my elbows on the table, I rub my forehead with my hands.

"Shit, I didn't know."

"Chris said another bad word, Momma. Boss!" I hear him shout. I jerk my head up, and Ellis is standing at the far end of the table, leveling Christopher with a dirty look, which is nothing new.

"Boss, Chris is taking me outside to swing."

"He thinks so, huh?"

"Ellis, I didn't know it was a secret."

"Right. I only told you that a few times last week."

"Christopher," I admonish. He tosses his napkin on the table and stands.

"I forgot, OK, and it's not like it's the end of the world. You can still show it to him yourself. I'm going back to work."

"That's wise of you. I left a file on your desk. I need you to see if there's a backdoor on that website."

"Sure," he replies sarcastically. "I want to speak with you later."

"After I take Liam out."

Christopher marches off, and the tension between the two of them couldn't be stronger.

"I had nothing to do with him eating with us. Irene invited him."

Ellis takes his seat at the end of the table next to me, and Irene steps up with his plate. Her eyes dart to mine, and I realize she overheard me.

"It's fine, Camilla." He gives his housekeeper a reassuring smile. "Irene has always been kind and fed my employees, too. Speaking of employees, where's Emma?"

Returning a smile to Ellis, Irene leaves the room.

"I called her yesterday and gave her the day off since we were at the hotel," I say.

"Oh, right. I'm sorry I messed with her schedule. I'll pay her regardless." Ellis takes a bite of his roasted chicken.

"I wike Em and her shoes."

I snicker. "He likes her pair of Converse because they have superheroes on them."

"I'll get you a pair, Liam."

"Ellis, you can't buy him every single thing he wants."

"Don't tell me what I can't do, especially in front of him. It's a pair of shoes." Wiping his mouth, he stands up. "I've lost my appetite. Liam, are you ready to see your surprise? Well, your jungle gym?"

"Yes!" His arms shoot in the air before he hops off his chair.

"I want to take him by myself," Ellis says.

"Are you going to tell him now?"

"Yes, and I'd rather do it alone. You can talk to him about it afterward."

"Oh, OK. I'm behind on my assignments, so I'll be in my office if you need me." I give Liam a hug. "Have fun and be careful."

My stomach sinks as I leave the room. In two sentences Ellis managed to make me feel unneeded. Before Saturday night, I thought we'd be telling Liam this news together, sealing our fate as a family.

Instead, he's defensive, obviously bitter that he missed out on time with his son. I can't fault him for that, but I don't think I'm the one who should be on the receiving end of his anger.

For those first few years of Liam's life, I didn't know Ellis Burke was a good man, and I sure didn't know he was my child's father.

I guess he views the situation differently. I want to believe the time he asked for will heal his heart, but I can't help but wonder if it's too late.

CHAPTER NINETEEN

Ellis

Liam skips ahead of me to go out the back door. He runs across the patio and into the yard. His feet dig into the grass as he forces himself to stop a good forty feet from the wooden jungle gym.

"Wow, it's so tall." Looking over his shoulder at me, he grins. "This is all mine?"

"Yes, I had it built just for you." He runs over and surveys it, jogging around each side to get a good look. His smile is radiant, his silky hair shining from the sunlight. He's in a yellow t-shirt, too, that only adds to his brightness.

I experience a pang of guilt for not inviting Camilla out with us. Her smile would be radiant, as well, from seeing Liam excited. I'm angry with her one minute, not the next. This whole situation is fucked up, and I need it resolved.

"Thank you, Boss. Can I swing?"

"Of course. I'll push you." Liam skips over, meeting me at one of the three swings. He gets in the seat with no trouble, and I begin to push him.

"There's no kids here," he says.

"No. This isn't like the park. You have your very own playset." He's quiet as I push him. "Do you wish there were kids here?"

"I like playin' with kids, but I wike that I have my vewy own swing and slide."

"When you go to preschool in a few months, you'll have other kids to play with. You'll make friends then. Would you like for a kid to come over here and play with you?"

"Yes. That'd be fun."

"Liam, do you know what a father is?" Besides the swooshing sound after my push of the swing, it's quiet. "How about a dad?"

"Kids at the park come with their daddies. Miles on my show has a daddy, too." Grabbing hold of his swing, I bring it to a stop and step around to face him. Here goes... I crouch in front of him and suck in a breath.

"I want to tell you something."

"K. Then, can I slide?" Just like his mother, he bites his lip.

"Sure. Uh, you know how kids have mothers and fathers?" I avoid an eye roll. "I mean mommies and daddies?"

"Yes."

"Well, Camilla is your mommy, and I'm your daddy." Putting his finger inside his mouth, he looks to the ground. "I didn't know I was your daddy before, but now I do, and it's important for you to know that I'll always be here for you.

"Anytime you need something, you come see Boss. Anything at all. OK?" He nods but doesn't make eye contact. "We're going to spend a lot of time together and do fun things."

"Will Momma be there?"

"Liam, your momma will always take care of you, but now you have two parents."

He glances up at me and smiles. "OK. Can I slide now?"

I chuckle. "Yeah, sure, but can I have one hug first?" He hops off the swing, and I bring him in close to me. That was easier than I expected, and I wish life could always be this simple for him.

Greyson

Returning from a late business lunch, I stop at Rhonda's office to check on Sasha. My paralegal looks up at me from her desk.

"How's it going?"

"If you're referring to Sasha, she's doing fine. Her enthusiasm over her ability to file papers correctly is odd, but otherwise, she seems to catch on quickly."

"Where is she?"

"Lunch."

Oh, shit. "She didn't bring lunch, and she doesn't have a car."

Her eyebrows lift, and I realize I'm busted for knowing too much.

"I have to get to my office." I disappear before she can reply and walk down a side hallway to the break room. Sasha isn't inside, so I leave, and as I pass the conference room, I catch a glimpse of her through the cracked door.

I step back and look inside. She's sitting on the table, gazing out the picture window at the mountains. There's empty saltine cracker wrappers on the table and an empty white cone cup from the water machine. Shit.

"Sasha, hi," I say as I push the door open. Scooting off the table, she turns around.

"Hi."

"I completely forgot you didn't have a car to go grab lunch. Would you like me to run out and get you something?"

"No, I've only got a few minutes left, and the crackers were enough." She picks up the wrappers and dusts the crumbs off the table. "I never eat three meals a day, anyway."

"You should."

Letting a laugh slip, she says something under her breath.

"What?" I ask.

"Nothing. I should get back to work."

"All right. Come find me if you need anything."

"Thanks." Leaving her alone, I walk to my office. I no sooner sit down when my HR manager, Deedra, charges in.

"When were you going to tell me you hired someone? And why would you do that without informing me first?"

"Don't raise your voice at me, and shut the door please."

She does as I ask and marches to my desk with crossed arms. Her face is as red as her short hair, and although I understand why she's angry, she's also getting a little too comfortable barking at me.

"I'm sorry, but I'd appreciate a heads-up when you're going to have a new employee start."

"It was unexpected, and if I hadn't been on the phone all morning and had a lunch meeting, I would've told you already. She's a friend, but that stays between us. I'm helping her out until she gets on her feet."

"Once I *stumbled* upon Sasha, I had her come to my office to fill out paperwork, and I'm fairly certain her driver's license is bogus."

"Why do you think that?"

"I've been doing HR for fifteen years now. I know a fake ID when I see one."

I sigh. "I'll find out, and keep this between us."

"Of course."

She leaves, and I rub my eyes before I pick up the phone to call Ellis.

"Hey, cuz. Are you busy?"

"I just put Liam down for a nap. What's up?"

"Damn, your life has changed."

"No, shit."

"Does Sasha know how to drive?"

"I believe so because Camilla mentioned giving her sister her old car. Why?"

"HR thinks her ID is fake."

"Uh, I'm working on remedying that."

"What? It is fake?"

"Yes."

"Are you going to explain, or do I need to get the pliers out like every other time you're keeping something from me."

"It's Camilla and Sasha's personal business. It's not my place to tell, and it can't get out."

"You know, I thought you trusted me, but I'm not sure anymore. Fine, I'll ask Sasha myself."

"Greyson, stop. I do trust you, but I need to ask Camilla if she minds if I discuss it with you since it's so personal."

"Whatever, man. I have a lot of work to do, so I'm gettin' off here."

"Look, it's about their past, and I'm trying to straighten it out for them. As soon as I do, she'll have a valid driver's license. Can you cover for her in the meantime? It's extremely important."

"Yeah, sure."

"Thanks. I'll talk to you later."

Tossing my phone on the desk, I lean back in my chair and lace my fingers behind my head. I figured Sasha had a few little secrets buried, but I'm getting the feeling they're not buried or small.

Maybe I jumped the gun on offering her so much help. It's not normal for me to get this involved, but ever since I carried her in my arms out of that shithole apartment, I've felt a need to protect her.

Deedra isn't going to be the last person to bitch me out over Sasha. Whitney's wrath will be unleashed once she discovers that another chick is living with me. Fuck, I just made my life a hell of a lot more difficult.

Ellis

Christopher sits down in a wingback chair in my office.

"What did you want to discuss?" I ask.

"I need Greyson's phone number?"

"Why?"

He purses his lips. "It's about the painting. I came up with more cash, and I want to buy it from him." I'm not surprised by his response. Who wouldn't want to fight for a free house and all that money?

"It's not for sale."

He looks heavenward, and I guarantee that's not where he's headed after this lifetime.

"Tony said if anything ever happened to him, he wanted me to have it."

"It's a painting. You've never breathed a word about the expensive paintings displayed throughout my home, so I find it hard to believe you have an interest in art. You need to let it go."

With his leg resting on his other knee, he messes with the hem of his pants.

"Why are you keeping me around? It's obvious you don't like me."

"If you want the truth, Camilla is the main reason you're still here. She says you two are friends." Stretching back in my chair, I tent my fingers and touch my lips as I stare him down. "You know what I think?"

He gives half an eye roll. "No, but I'm sure you're going to enlighten me."

"I believe she feels indebted to you for being by her side the last few years, but we both know the only reason you did that; you wanted her and still do."

"And how is that any different than the reason you're supporting her?"

"The difference is that she wants me in return. Once and for all, you need to stop trying to get with her. She's not going to suddenly leave here to be with you, and she wouldn't remove Liam from this house or his father."

Christopher laughs. "I think you're the one obsessed with Camilla, and you're obviously delusional, thinking Liam's yours. I couldn't believe you told your family that lie."

This is the moment I've been waiting for. I lean over and rest my elbows on my desk.

"He is mine. Camilla and I slept together at one of my brother's parties. We took a paternity test. He's mine, not Tony's."

His jaw drops, and I think he's lost the ability to breathe. He struggles to swallow, too.

"Camilla wouldn't keep a secret like that from me."

"He's mine. I can make you a copy of the test if you'd like."

Standing, he shoves his chair back. "I'll pass, and I'll also find another job as soon as possible."

"I think that's wise." With his fists clenched, he stomps to my door. "Oh, Chris, one more thing... If you get time, I'd like you to research Isla Mujeres. It appears my brother had a home there."

Christopher's head falls back. "Fuck," he breathes.

"What was that?"

"You're a dick," he says with his back to me.

"And you were an idiot for thinking your plan would work. It's my job to uncover what's hidden. You weren't going to get this past me."

He tears out of my office, and I have no remorse for how I treated him. He tried to pull the wool over my eyes, and my gut tells me he's still hiding something.

I'll figure it out, and then he's never stepping foot near my son or Camilla again. I'll prove to her he's not worthy of her friendship.

Sasha

"College and hard work are paying off for you," I blurt out as Greyson and I ride in the elevator up to his penthouse.

"Yes, they are. Have you ever thought about going to college?"

"I doubt I could get in, and I definitely couldn't afford it."

His head cocks to the side. "Why do you think you're not smart?"

"I didn't say that, and I don't wish to talk about it." The elevator dings, and we step into the hall.

"Then let's discuss why you have a fake driver's license."

I come to a stop at his door and cross my arms.

"How do you know about that?" I begin to pace. "Oh, god, that means Deedra knows. This is so humiliating." Panic pummels me, so I reach out and clench Greyson's arms.

"Please don't turn me in. Will she tell on me?"

Pulling my hands off of him, he holds them between his.

"Calm down. No one is turning you in."

"I should go. I knew this was a bad idea." Jerking free, I start down the hallway to pack my things, but he clutches my arm and turns me around.

"Tell me what's going on."

"I can't, and you need to let me leave."

"Sasha, I'm not the enemy here. Your secrets are safe with me."

"They're not safe with anyone, and Camilla would kill me if I told you."

He blows out a lengthy breath. "Look, I'll let it go if you stay. I think I still have a frozen lasagna Theresa made Friday, so let's eat dinner, and you can unwind in front of the television." He smiles. "You did say you like that."

I study his face, looking for a reason not to trust him since he does and says everything right.

"If you promise we won't talk about my past, I'll stay."

"I promise, but if you're going to remain clean, you have to get your shit straightened out. It's part of the process."

"Then that's going to be a problem seeing how my shit can never be straightened out."

He scratches the back of his head. "You can't talk in code, Sasha. I hear enough of that from Ellis."

"Then, let's not talk. I'm hungry."

He smiles. "That's one problem I can fix."

CHAPTER TWENTY

Camilla

I open Liam's door after being awakened from his cries.

"Sweetie, what's wrong."

"I peed," he replies with a whine. Wonderful. I turn on the light and go to him. He's sitting up, and I see that his pajama pants are soaked.

"It's been a long time since you've wet the bed. Let's go give you a quick bath."

The door swings open, so I glance over my shoulder.

"What's wrong?" Ellis asks.

"I heard him crying from the monitor. He had an accident. Liam, go in the bathroom and undress." Still whining, he leaves Ellis and I alone.

"Why did he wet the bed?"

"I don't know. It happens sometimes."

"It hasn't happened here."

"Ellis, it's not a huge deal. He still has a small bladder. He drank a lot today, too, from playing outside."

"What if this is because of what I told him?"

"I'm sure it's not."

"What can I do?"

"You can either help him take a bath, or you can change his bedding."

"I don't know where Irene keeps his extra sheets."

"OK, then you go run his bath water, and I'll find the bedding."

Ellis passes by me in only his sweats, so I look away and begin stripping the bed. In a breath, Liam begins to cry. I hear Ellis's voice next and then Liam sobbing. I'm too tired for this. Can we rewind to Saturday when I was Cinderella and it hadn't struck midnight yet?

Ellis bursts back in the room. "He started crying the second he saw me, and he won't tell me why. He's just standing there naked, rubbing his eyes, and I can't understand him. I don't know what the hell I'm doing. You go in there."

"Welcome to parenthood, Ellis, where you never know what the hell you're doing, or if your decisions are right or wrong, so you do the best you can and pray it doesn't screw up your child for the rest of his life. Check the closet for the bedding."

***

"I was useless in there," Ellis says before he takes a bite of the French silk pie I made after dinner. We're sitting at the dinette set in the kitchen with the pie pan between us.

"Have you ever made a bed before?"

He fires a look my way. "Yes, Camilla, I've made a bed. I had to while I was at college." I lower my head to hide my snicker. "I was talking about how useless I was at helping Liam."

"Don't be hard on yourself. It's two in the morning, so we were all tired in there. You have to expect that it might take him a while to adjust to the news you gave him."

"He did ask me outside if you were still going to be here."

"See, he doesn't understand. I'm sure as he realizes things aren't going to change, he'll be back to his old self." I think about the possibility of having to move out and lower my head again. I lay down my fork, too.

"What's wrong?"

"I only hope he doesn't end up with two homes."

"I don't want that, either."

I look up. "You don't?"

"No. He needs both of his parents under one roof, and obviously I need your help."

"I don't want to be kept around for only those reasons." His gaze averts to the wall, and the silence fills the room fast and heavy. "I'm going back to bed," I say as I stand with my glass of milk. "I have a live lecture I can't miss in the morning. Good night."

Reaching across the table, he clasps my wrist. I glance down at his hand and relish in how good it feels and how my body responds to him in one beat of my heart.

"Come here."

I lift my gaze to meet his. Come home ... come here ... they're two-word sentences I don't believe I could live without. I set down my glass and pad around the table.

Taking hold of my hips, he brings me right onto his lap. He grabs my face and stares into my eyes as if an unyielding force is driving him.

"I want you right now."

"When the sun rises, will you feel the same?"

"I'll always want you, but it doesn't mean the darkness from the night won't still linger."

"We can outshine it, Ellis. Through Tony's death, we were brought to life, and I refuse to let our love die, too." Climbing off his lap, I urgently strip my clothes and drop to my knees.

"You promised you were going to pleasure me and inflict pain on me until I was splintered down to my soul. You said I'd be stripped bare and kneeling at your feet, begging for you not to stop … to never let me go." I clench his knees.

"This is that moment, Ellis. I'm begging you. Please, don't let me go." His fingers delve deep in my hair, and my scalp prickles from the feel of the tips of them. I pray he never stops touching me.

"You're everything I've ever wanted but also feared. No matter how much I fought it, you always came back in my dreams. It's impossible to let you go." Breathing out the rest of the fight he's been holding in, he whispers, "I love you."

Yanking down his sweats, he grasps my arms and brings me up onto his lap again. His lips crash to mine, and he fists my hair. His groans are penetrating, his kiss desperate and aggressive. He lashes my tongue and moves his hands to my breasts, where he squeezes them and tugs on my nipples.

I'm losing myself in the pleasure, falling into the abyss of Ellis Burke, where his soul resides and I could live for all of eternity.

Coming up for air, he scoops out a handful of the fluffy chocolate pie filling from the pan and spreads it across my throat and breasts. He laps at it and kisses me all over while grinding his cock against my pelvis.

The sensations are jarring, heightening my senses. His sizzling mouth on my skin mixed with the cold chocolate filling makes my pussy throb. He grabs a handful of my hair again and clutches my hip as he sucks the cream off my stiff nipples.

"Fuck, how I've missed this. Ride me, and don't stop. I'm coming inside you."

"Yes, Sir." I raise up and sink onto his cock. He jerks his head back and presses his fingers firmly against my hips. It feels hard enough to bruise me, and I want him to leave marks. I want the evidence that he's taking back what's his.

Lifting me, he slams me down again and growls from the sensation. I moan from how deep he fills me—how complete I am with him inside me. Tugging my head back by my hair, he sucks on my throat, my breasts and my nipples. His urgency never wanes while I ride him like he ordered.

Feeling the tightening of my muscles, he shoves his head against my shoulder, and we orgasm together before he can tell me to come. I shudder from my contractions and the way his cock pulses inside me.

The pleasure is inundating, divvied out across every inch of my being until I collapse against him, forcing him back so I can press my chest to his.

We're skin to skin, sticky and sweaty, and he has come back to me. He's the Ellis I love and want to serve. I'll give him anything so long as I'm able to share my life with him.

Greyson

Grabbing Sasha by the ankles, I yank her toward the end of the bed. Her head slips under the blanket, and she's soon flailing about, trying to get out from under it. Her eyes appear, and they're round, the color gold like cognac. They're also drilling me with spite.

"Greyson! What the hell are you doing?"

"Waking your ass up so you're not late for work."

"We agreed you wouldn't barge in here."

"That was before I knew I'd have to hear your alarm go off a dozen times. If you don't want me in here, then get your damn self out of bed."

Brushing strands of her long hair away from her face, she huffs, "Well, maybe you need to have your coffee before my alarm goes off, and then it won't bother you so much."

"You need to grow up, Sasha. You're not a teenager. If you want to amount to anything and get out on your own, you have to be responsible. Did your parents spoil you or something?"

"Get out. I'll be ready in twenty minutes."

"I'm leaving in five. There's keys on the kitchen counter. You can drive the white BMW in the parking garage, and you can explain to Rhonda why you're late."

I march from her room to the kitchen. My housekeeper, Theresa, holds out a mug of coffee for me.

"I couldn't help but hear your disgruntled guest."

"That's Sasha. She'll be staying with me for a while, and I have a strong suspicion she won't be picking up after herself, so I'll increase your pay while she's here. If she's ever rude to you, you let me know." I point a finger at her. "Do you hear me?"

"Yes, sir."

"How many times do I have to tell you not to call me that?"

"Each and every time as long as I work for you, sir." She flashes me a smile, and if she wasn't so damn good to me, I'd probably bite her head off this morning, too.

I hate how Sasha's getting under my skin. I should've left her ass in bed this morning. Then, I could kick her out this evening for not appreciating the opportunity I gave her, but somehow, I already care too much.

I guess I'm waiting to hear her story from either her or Ellis, but I suspect I'm only going to care more once I do, and that can't happen.

I peel out of the parking garage, and my phone rings. The screen on the dash in my Wraith reads Whitney. Fucking great.

"What?" I ask.

"Good morning to you, too."

"What do you want, Whit?"

"I love when you call me that. I remember when you first started shortening my name. It was when you looked at me and talked to me like you gave a damn."

"You want something. What is it?"

"I'm coming over this evening."

"I'm busy tonight, tomorrow night and the night after that."

"We can't avoid this forever, Greyson."

"I know, but I have a lot going on this week. Let's discuss it next week."

"Look, I'll make this super simple for you. I picked out the engagement ring I want. All you need to do is pick it up and slide it on my damn finger. I'll say yes to your *implied* proposal and make up a convincing story about how romantic it was."

"Do you hear how jacked up that is?"

"It's only because you won't cooperate."

"Right, like that's the only reason, but like always, you would think it's my fault. I have to go." Ending the call, I slam my head back against the seat. Her surly voice is like nails on a chalkboard. How in the hell will I live with her for the rest of my life?

CHAPTER TWENTY-ONE

Sasha

"I'm sorry I'm late."

"Thirty minutes late to be exact, and don't blame it on traffic."

"I won't make excuses. I overslept, and it won't happen again."

She lifts an eyebrow. "Good answer. I won't tell HR this time."

"Thank you." I truly am thankful for her acceptance of my apology. Theresa had a packed lunch waiting for me in the kitchen this morning. She'd never met me, yet she still took time to make sure I would eat today.

Combine that kind gesture with driving Greyson's luxurious car, and it was impossible not to consider all that he said to me. He was right; I need to grow up. I have to get my shit together and prove to him that I'm grateful and can make something of myself.

Maybe one day I'll have a home of my own. It won't be a penthouse, but I don't need a lavish home to be happy. A hot meal and a bed, and I'm one content girl, but I guess I haven't shown him I'm grateful for even that.

***

"Hi, do you have a minute?" I ask Greyson before I leave work at the end of the day. He tosses a pen on his desk and motions to the chair in front of it. "I don't need to sit. This should only take a minute."

I do shut the door behind me before I proceed. "I'm sorry for this morning. I wouldn't have yelled at you, but you scared me. I can't be grabbed or touched like tha—"

"Sasha—"

"Please, let me finish. I was in the wrong for not getting out of bed this morning. You're putting a roof over my head, feeding me and giving me a car to drive. On top of that, you provided me with a great job here. I promise I'll get up every day and come to work. I won't let you down again."

Blinking slowly, he smiles. "I only push you because I want the best for you."

"I know that. I don't understand why, but I believe you. Anyway, that's all I wanted to tell you. Oh, and I won't be home this evening. Camilla and I are going to the salon and to dinner.

"She's giddy that I have a job, so she wants to treat me. I can't wait to return the favor once I earn a few paychecks. I've never been able to do anything for her."

"That's great. I'm glad you're taking this opportunity and running with it. What about your recovery?"

I look to the floor. "Uh, I probably shouldn't have told him this soon, but Terrence and I were talking at lunch, and he mentioned first that he was a recovering addict.

"He said you gave him a job here, too, so I shared about my drug problem, and he offered to take me to an NA meeting tomorrow evening."

"Sounds like everything is coming together for you."

I clutch my hands in front of me, feeling giddy myself.

"It is, thanks to you. I'll leave you to your work now." He nods and smiles, but there's a sadness in his turquoise eyes. Deciding our conversation was personal enough, I leave it alone and exit his office. He hasn't mentioned there being a woman in his life, but it's hard to believe. His heart's too big not to love someone.

***

Pulling up to the gate at Ellis's home, I smile at the guard. Recognizing me as Camilla's sister, he opens it to let me through.

Cammy's already waiting on the steps outside as I approach. She gets in the passenger seat and laughs.

"I never imagined we'd both get a chance to drive such luxurious rides."

"I know. It's crazy, and I'm so nervous I'll hurt the pretty thing." As I pull away, I rub the dash. "Where's Liam? I figured he'd tag along."

"Ellis offered to keep him while we're out. He said he has a lot of time to make up for. I can't describe the feeling I get when I see him smile at his son." She rests her head back against the seat. "I'm so fortunate he forgave me."

"Sis, that's great."

"He knows everything about me now except for the reason why you and I left South Carolina. I have to tell him, Sasha."

"I know. I don't like it, but I understand."

"He will, too. I believe that we can trust him, and it feels good to finally have someone to count on."

"Yeah, I'm beginning to understand. I've only been at Greyson's a few days, and I'm already seeing how nice it is to have a responsible man to count on instead of the losers I've dated in the past."

I feel Camilla's eyes on me, and the purr of the engine is the only other sound I hear. "It's not like that." I give her a reassuring look. "I only mean I feel safe ... and lucky."

"Maybe you should come live with us."

"No, Greyson was right when he said you and Ellis needed time together. Actually, you, Ellis and Liam need time to be a family."

"I shouldn't tell you this, but Greyson's getting engaged. It's an arranged marriage with someone in their high-society circle," she says in an irritated tone. "It's absurd to me. I mean, what century do their parents think this is?

"And what's odd is his father seems like the most laid-back man. He was sweet and funny, and I can't picture him making Greyson marry someone he's not in love with."

She touches my arm. "Please don't say anything to him, though. We're not supposed to know about it."

"I won't." I do, however, ponder the news she briefed me on. There's a tinge of jealousy that someone else gets to have a future with Greyson, especially someone he doesn't love. Is this why he hasn't mentioned her to me? If so, that's sad.

If he's really engaged and I can't talk to him about it, then what am I supposed to do about living there?

Greyson

Once I finish eating the awesome steak, scalloped potatoes and asparagus Theresa left in the oven for me, I change into athletic shorts and a t-shirt.

It's almost nine o'clock, and I'm tired, but it's too early to crash, so I sit on the couch and turn on the television to catch the latest sports news. About ten minutes in, the doorbell rings. God forbid I ever relax.

Few people have access to this floor, so I'm curious who it could be. I tread to the door and swing it open.

"Whit, what are you doing here?"

"It can't wait."

Rolling my eyes, I step back for her to enter. Her long lashes flutter up at me as she brushes against my body to step inside. I follow her to my living room, and she takes a seat on the couch in her slinky hot pink dress.

"Would you like to have a seat?" I mumble sarcastically. I also cross my arms and keep a safe ten feet between us. I'm being a dick, but she brings it out in me.

"Stop, Greyson. You act like I'm a stranger."

"You pretty much are."

She pats the spot next to her. "Sit so we can talk." Fooling with my hair, I trudge over and take a seat. "If you don't want my father showing up here or at your office, then you need to put a ring on my finger.

"I'll set the date, and our mothers and I can arrange the wedding. I swear all you have to do is show up for the parties and the wedding. That's it. Oh, and get fitted for your tux."

"That's it?" I ask with aggravation. "I think you're forgetting the most important part of this deal. It's where I agree to spend the rest of my life with you.

"We'll have to live in the same house and be there for one another not only in health but in *sickness*, too. We're also supposed to remain faithful."

Whitney tears up, and her lip quivers. Ah, shit, this never ends well.

"You act like I'm diseased or something. Greyson, I know we've both screwed around. I won't try to hide it."

"Good because I have a mental list of guys you've fucked all this time we were supposedly in a relationship. The latest being that douche, Sebastian."

"Oh, don't you point fingers. At least he wants to touch me. What about all the women you've slept with? I saw you sneak off with Penny at the gala."

"I wouldn't let her wet my dick for a million bucks."

Whitney smiles, and it reaches her glassy green eyes.

"Really? You didn't sleep with her?"

"No, but I'm not innocent, either."

Scooting closer, she wipes a stray tear from her cheek.

"Let's start over, Greyson. When we first got together, we couldn't keep our hands off each other." She slithers her fingers over my thigh. "You used to look at me like I was your whole world. What changed?"

"We did. We grew up and became two different people. I'm sorry to say it, but you don't think about anyone other than yourself. It's always about what's best for you, and I grew tired of watching the Whitney show."

"That's not true, but I'm willing to try harder to make this work. An engagement could be our fresh start. We can work on our relationship and agree not to sleep around."

"That's the thing, Whitney; we shouldn't be getting married when our relationship needs fixing. Hell, to me we don't even have a relationship."

"Together, our grandfathers built an empire in the oil industry. We're the two people they're counting on to link our families together. Look, I promise I'll be the person you need me to be. Just give us another chance."

Her hand slides over my cock, and rubs all rational thought right out of me. My dick hardens beneath her palm, and I'm fucked.

Her pouty lips press to my cheek next and kiss their way behind my ear and down my neck. I get a whiff of the familiar fruity scent from her strawberry-blond hair.

Angry that her seduction is working, I groan. She always wins, and I'm tired of it, but on the other hand, I need a release from the sexual tension I've been carrying lately.

"Take me to your room, and I'll show you I'm willing to change. Do what you want to me, Greyson," she whispers in my ear, "or I can suck your cock right here."

A blowjob sounds appealing, but I don't want her in control. She thinks she owns my balls as it is. I'm not giving her access to the real pair. No, if she's so determined to give me what I want, then I'll fuck her doggy style right on this couch.

"Shift around, and bend over the arm rest." She starts to say something but wises up. Setting her purse on the floor, she gets in position for me.

She lifts her dress, and I eye her smooth, bare skin. A slip of light pink lace runs down the crack of her ass, and it matches the lace that trims the top of sheer stockings that cover her shapely thighs.

Damn, one thing I do love about a woman with money is how they pride themselves on the sensual lingerie beneath their clothing. Opening the drawer on the side table, I fish around until I find a condom.

Yanking down my shorts, I roll the latex over my cock quickly before I lose my hard-on. I stroke myself a couple of times while I shove her thong aside. She whimpers and sinks against the two fingers I push inside her.

We haven't slept together in six months, and although I know I'm an idiot for sticking my dick in her again, I have this strong urge to hate-fuck her senseless.

Grabbing a hunk of her hair, I wrap it around my wrist and slam into her. She gasps, stunned by my aggressiveness. I've never been this rough with Whitney.

We were each other's firsts, so it was all gentle and sweet back then and set the stage for the sex to come, but I'm over doing things the way she wants, and I'm done pretending that we love each other.

Remembering that I'm fucking her, I drive into her harder. The self-loathing rises from the ashes for being weak and caving in.

I'm doing this so I can punish her while I get off, and she's doing it so she can marry a man that doesn't even want her. We're sick, and I don't see how I'll go through with the wedding.

Catching sight of a shadow, I look up in time to see Sasha. She's standing paralyzed and watching us. I should stop this instant, but I can't any more than she's able to stop watching.

It hits me like a bolt of lightning. I'm angry because it's not Sasha I'm fucking. It's not Sasha I can get to know or let in. I can't spend time with her, and in about two seconds, I'm going to be reminded why she can't live with me. Whitney's body tenses, and Sasha's eyes grow rounder.

"Who the fuck are you?" Whitney yells. Sasha turns toward the foyer but then turns back the other direction toward the hallway.

She wants to run, and I know what's going through her head. *The car's not mine, and the bedroom's not mine... Where the hell am I supposed to go?* The realization makes me sicker than before because she was supposed to feel safe here. She was counting on me.

I slip out of Whitney and pull up my shorts about the time Sasha runs to her room and slams the door. Whit's on her feet in a flash. "Who the fuck was that? And why did she head toward the bedrooms?" Her nostrils flare, and her skin is scarlet.

"It's not what you think. She's the sister to Ellis's girlfriend and needs a place to stay. She's an addict, and you know I've helped out several people during their recovery."

"No, you helped out several *males* while they recovered."

"It shouldn't matter what sex she is."

She grabs her hip. "When did you plan on telling me this?"

"I didn't think it was a big deal, and I doubt she'll be here long."

"She's not staying here *period*. Do you know what people will say if they find out you have some other girl shacked up with you? You're not humiliating me in front of our family and friends."

"What you said about changing is total bullshit. You plan on bossing me around like you always have, and it's not happenin'. She can live here as long as she wants, and there's not a damn thing you can do about it."

Swiping her purse off the floor, she huffs and straightens her hair.

"I better get a fucking ring by the end of the month, or I'm telling your father about your slutty side piece."

Grabbing my head, I let out a roar that echoes through the house, but it's not as loud as the sound of the lamp crashing to the floor after I throw it.

Sasha

Flinching from the sound of something breaking, I toss my suitcases on the bed and begin stuffing them with the few clothes I'd found a home for. I shove the dresser drawer closed and turn around to soak in the last sight of the spacious room and solid oak furniture.

Greyson told me yesterday that he'd let me decorate it however I wanted, and I was already thinking up a color scheme. After I saved some paychecks, I was going to buy my first comforter set.

It was stupid of me to think this could ever feel like home. Seeing him with her made me ill, and getting caught watching them was humiliating. How will I ever face Greyson again?

Leaning back against the dresser, I sink to the floor and pull my phone from my pocket. I'll text Camilla and see if she'll come get me, or maybe I should call an old friend instead. I'm a burden my sister doesn't need.

I jump from the pounding on the door.

"I'm coming in. We need to talk."

"No. Go away. I'll be out of your hair as soon as I get a ride."

"You're not going anywhere." He tries to come in, but the door's locked. "Open this goddamn door. There's things I can't fix in my life, but this isn't going to be one of them."

"Please, go away." I begin to sob, and I'm not sure of all the reasons why, but one that I'm certain of is I officially have a crush on a man I could never be with. It's why I have to get out of here.

"Dammit, why are you crying?"

"Go. Away. I'm leaving."

He mumbles something unintelligible and stomps away. Relieved he's leaving me alone, I wipe my eyes and get up off the floor to finish packing. Within a minute, the handle jiggles again, and in seconds, Greyson shoves the door open.

His blond hair is in disarray, and his t-shirt hugs his muscles so beautifully tight. His face reveals anger and desperation, and I don't want to hear why because I don't want to care.

"I believe in facing things head on, if you haven't noticed, so we're airing this out now."

I cross my arms. "Head on you say? It looked like from behind to me."

Tightening his lips, he brings a fist up to his mouth, locking down whatever anger he'd prefer to unleash.

"OK, I deserved that, but only because you're staying here. I have a right to fuck whoever and wherever in my own home, but since you're living here, I should've remembered that you could walk in on us. I wasn't thinking."

"You should've told me you had a girlfriend. I never would've agreed to come here, and you should know a girlfriend would never approve of me being here, either."

"I don't care what Whitney thinks, and stop calling her my girlfriend."

"What is she then? A random hookup?"

"No, she's, she's ... it's complicated."

I stick out a hand. "This early in my recovery, I can't get caught up in your drama, so I'm going to find somewhere else to stay. Thank you for all you've done for me. Now, please get out so I can pack in peace."

Greyson stalks toward me like I'm some sort of prey, so I step back until my legs hit the bed.

"Why were you crying?" He brushes tears from my cheeks, so I pull back and look away.

"My own shit's complicated, too, so let's part ways now before we make our situations more fucked up than they already are."

"I meant it when I said I wanted to help you. I slipped up, OK? I'm sorry. I'm used to being here alone, so when Whitney showed up uninvited and came on to me, I didn't think about you walking in on us.

"I swear I won't let it happen again. Actually, you saved me from a head-on collision. I was making the biggest mistake of my life letting her back in my personal space."

I look at him and smirk. "She was definitely backing into your space."

He cracks a grin, his dimples finally coming out to play along his flushed skin.

"That was another good comeback. Fucking embarrassing, but clever. See, I need this banter to keep me in check, so stay here. I promise I'll behave."

Exhaling, I examine his handsome face and a mouth that's making promises I want to believe. He might behave, but my emotions won't. I like him, and that won't change if I continue to live with him.

"I'll stay, *but* only for a short time. As soon as I save enough money, I'm moving out."

"Thank you. Now, unpack your clothes and come watch some trashy television with me."

"Uh, I have no desire to ever sit on your couch."

"Oh, right." He tilts his head to the side. "You did something to your hair. I like it."

"I got it layered and added some highlights."

"You already had those. Natural ones in about three different shades of brown."

I scrunch my nose. "You noticed that?"

"Yeah, I did." Lifting a piece of my hair, he eyes it. "I like this, too."

"Thanks. I want to be sure I get up in the morning on time, so I better go to bed."

"Yeah, I probably should, too. It was a long day. You promise you won't sneak out of here?"

"I promise."

CHAPTER TWENTY-TWO

Camilla

"I'll check on him," I say to Ellis as I hurry off the bed and throw on my robe. Liam is screaming for me, and I can hear it on the monitor next to Ellis's bed.

I run down the hallway and sling open his door. He's reaching for me, his small hands opening and closing, and I have a flashback to when he tumbled down the staircase with Ellis. That same terror is etched on his face.

"Momma, Mommyyyyy," he cries.

"Sweetie, what's wrong?" Sitting on his bed, I pull him onto my lap. As I rock forward and back to soothe him, I stroke his hair and hum a song. Sniffling, he wipes his wet face and nose on the sleeve of my robe. "Did you have a bad dream?" I ask him.

"Chris," he says before he cries again.

"Chris? Our friend Chris?"

Liam nods.

"What about him? Was he in your dream?"

"Secret," he mumbles.

"Secret? Baby, I don't understand."

"Will you sleep with me?" Turning himself around in my lap, he wraps his arms around my neck like a vise. I kiss his head as I think about Ellis's disapproval.

"Sure, I'll sleep in here with you. Just tonight, though."

***

"Camilla, wake up," Ellis says. I open my eyes, and he's touching my shoulder. Smelling his clean scent, I admire him in jeans and a thin brown sweater.

"Good morning," I say before I look down and see that Liam's still asleep next to me.

"What happened?"

"I guess he had his first night terror. He was petrified when I came in here. I'm sorry, but I couldn't leave him."

His gaze softens. "Don't be sorry. I get it now."

"I love you."

"I love you, too. Emma will be here in thirty minutes, and don't forget that Liam's first Italian lesson is at ten. The tutor's name is Lorenzo, and he's actually Italian, so maybe he's familiar with the town your grandmother lives in."

"I can't talk to him about her."

"Then, you need to talk to me soon. You have to tell me why you haven't seen her in years."

"I will, but right now I better get moving."

"I have a business meeting at ten, so I'm leaving soon, but I'll meet you downstairs for breakfast first."

"Sounds good." Waking Liam, I help him get dressed for the day. He takes his baths at night, so it normally makes for easier mornings, but not today.

He's difficult and whiny and refuses to go downstairs, so I carry him there, which flares up my back pain. We reach the dining room, and his face lights up.

"Boss-Daddyyyy."

Ellis and I both chuckle. "Hi, kid. That's an interesting combination, and I can only imagine what my parents will think of it." He brushes Liam's hair from his face before he gets up to help him into his chair.

"Speaking of my parents, they're coming for dinner at six this evening," he says. "I couldn't put them off any longer since they're eager to meet Liam."

"I want them to meet him, too. I'm excited for him to know his family." I sit down at the table, and Irene serves Liam and me breakfast. As she begins to walk away, Liam crosses his arms.

"I don't want eggs. I want French toast," he spouts.

"OK, my piccolo. I'll make you some," Irene says.

"No, Irene, please don't, but thank you," I say as I look at Liam. "We're not having French toast today. Irene was nice enough to make you breakfast, so we're going to eat it and be thankful."

I glance at Ellis, expecting him to disagree, but he gives Liam a stern look instead.

"Eat your eggs, and I'll have Irene make you French toast in the morning. If you don't eat your eggs, I'll have her fix them again tomorrow with tuna fish on top."

Liam's little brow furrows the way his father's does, but then he breaks into a smile over his dad's funny comment. I stifle a giggle, wondering how I ever missed the uncanny similarities between them.

"I hate to run, but I have to get to my meeting," Ellis says.

"OK. Be safe, and maybe this little guy will know an Italian word besides piccolo when you return."

Ellis kisses the top of my head and Liam's, too, and my heart is filled with joy this morning. My sister was happier than I've ever seen her last night, and Ellis and I are pulling off this parenting gig together.

Now, all I need to do is tell him about my past and have him take me back to the playroom. Then, I'll be content.

Ellis

"Here's what I have so far. It's on Mr. Day, and you're not going to like it," Lawson says after handing me a file folder.

"You mean I'm going to dislike it more than meeting you at this busy coffee shop?"

He takes a sip from his cup. "I think you can make an exception, considering all I'm doing for you."

As I open the file, I say, "Does this mean you're going to take care of the more sensitive matter for me, as well?"

"Yes, but I need more time. I should be able to wipe her slate clean, and I'll get you the documents you wanted, too. Oh, and I'll check out her parents."

"I can't thank you enough." I read over the first page in the file. "Wait, this can't be right." Sitting up straighter, I read the page again. "Are you sure you got the correct Christopher Day?"

"Yes, it's him."

"But this says his mother is Sandra Buchanan."

"That's correct. I'm guessing it's not the news you were expecting."

"I don't know what I was expecting, but not this. Sandra Buchanan is his mother. This is unbelievable but explains so much."

"What's the significance?"

"Christopher's mother is also my brother's birth mother. Christopher is Tony's half-brother."

"Shit, did Tony know that?"

"If he did, he never told me. Did Sandra raise him?" I flip to the second page, looking for more information.

"Yes, she had custody of him. I couldn't find where his father was ever in the picture, but his info's in there, too."

"Thank God we don't share the same parents." The anger swells inside me, and my pulse accelerates until there's a pulsing in my temple. "Christopher Day is full of secrets."

"There's another one in there, and I have a feeling you won't want him working for you after you read it. Page four." Swiftly, I look for it. "What exactly happened here?"

"At sixteen he was charged with sexual assault against a fifteen-year-old girl, but due to lack of evidence, the case was closed. Then, he had a robbery conviction at seventeen and spent some time in juvenile detention."

"This bastard's in my home every day, and he's spent more time with Camilla and my son than I have. This news makes me want to kill him."

"Settle down there, cowboy."

"As far as I know, Tony never saw his mother. He hated her for giving up custody in exchange for cash. If I had to guess, Christopher found Tony and befriended him for his personal gain. Hell, this makes me wonder a lot of things."

I slam the file closed and drop it on the table. "Shit, do you think it's possible he killed my brother?"

"I'm not on Tony's case, but I can look into it for you."

"I've tried to keep you away from the investigation since we don't want it getting out how closely we work together, but if I haven't used up all my favors, could you talk to your colleagues on the case and plant the seed of suspicion about Christopher?"

"Why not? What's one more favor among friends?" He pushes back his dark hair and grins. "While I'm doing my research, I'll envision my brand-spankin'-new lake house and boat. It's the one you and I will be fishing from while we drink bourbon and celebrate my *early* retirement."

"One day, my man." I stand. "I have to get home. That scumbag's working there this very minute, and I want him as far away from Camilla and my son as possible. Thank you, Lawson. I owe you big-time."

Camilla

"Oh, my gosh, kid, what is going on with you?" I ask, exasperated by Liam's foul behavior. He stomps his feet violently, and if his screams reach a decimal higher, Lorenzo will call Child Protective Services on me for suspected child abuse.

Needing to get back to the Italian tutor, I leave Liam in his room, along with the tantrum he's throwing. Emma is waiting outside his door with round eyes.

"What's that about?"

"I have no clue, but let him get it out of his system. Can you wait here by the door? I need to reschedule with Lorenzo and see him out. That is if he'll even come back to teach the devil's spawn."

Beginning to laugh, she falls short at a giggle.

"Sorry, but that was funny."

I head downstairs, and Lorenzo rises from the couch. Thankfully he grants me a warm smile as opposed to a look of horror.

The second he said hello to Liam in the grand hall, my child began throwing a hellacious fit I couldn't get a handle on. I finally picked him up to remove him from the scene, and he proceeded to kick his legs at me all the way up the staircase. There was no consoling the little monster.

"Lorenzo, I'm so sorry. Liam's normally well-behaved, but he had a nightmare last night and was up for a while. I believe the exhaustion and anxiety spurred his foul disposition this morning. I hope you're willing to try again."

"Absolutely. He's not the first child who was alarmed when meeting me."

"Thank you. This was especially important to Ellis."

"Would you like to try again next week?"

"That'd be perfect."

I show Lorenzo out, and I'm only midway up the staircase when I hear Liam again. Thankfully, his full-blown meltdown has run its course, and his cry is taking turns with a whine.

"Emma, you can go hang out in the family room and watch TV or play on your phone. I think I'm going to put him down for a nap. Maybe in a couple of hours, he'll eat lunch and be more tolerable afterward."

"OK, no problem." She strolls off, and I enter Liam's room. He's lying on his back in the floor, holding a few Lego blocks above his face.

"Do you feel better now?" He only grunts and whines, so I sit next to him on the floor and pick up a red and blue block. "That man, Lorenzo, only wanted to help you like Emma does.

"He was going to teach you some cool, special words. Momma doesn't even know them, but Boss does. I know you want to be like your daddy. He's smart like you."

Liam smiles, but once he realizes I can see it, he frowns. I pick up a few more blocks and begin building something. "Do you want to help me build a fort?"

Sitting up to face me, he rubs his nose on his arm. His eyes are swollen, and every inch of his face is pink.

"I can do it myself."

"OK. You can have these, too." I drop the Legos and reposition myself to sit more comfortably. "What's got you upset today?" He shrugs and snaps two blocks together. "Is it about the bad dream you had last night?"

"It's a secret. I'm not awoud to tell you."

"Who told you the secret?"

He sniffles. "Chris."

"Oh, he did, huh? Liam, you don't keep secrets like that from me. It's my job to take care of you, and if something upsets you, you can always tell me."

"I'll get in trouble."

"You won't be in trouble for telling me your secret. I promise."

He looks up at me for confirmation. "I promise, sweetie, now tell me what Chris said."

Cocking his head to the side, he sniffles again and stares at his blocks.

"He said I might take a trip wif him. I asked him if you was going, too, and he said no. I don't want to go wifhout you."

My mouth dries in a split-second. If my blood could boil, it would spill over the pot. Speaking of stoves, I'd like to stick Christopher in the oven and set it to broil.

I take Liam's hands in mine. "Listen to Momma. You're never going on a trip with Chris. Not ever, so you don't need to worry. You'll always be with me."

"And Boss-Daddy?"

I find a grin amid my anger. "Yes. Boss-Daddy and me will always keep you safe, and if you go on a trip, it will be with us. I'm proud of you for telling me the truth. That shows you're growing into a big boy."

Smiling, he hands me some Legos. "Here, let's build a fort. I want to make it super tall so my Army men can fit inside it." Holding up a green block, his face brightens. "Let's use all the gween ones so it matches the gween guys."

I'm utterly amazed by his ability to move on so quickly. It shows the trust he has in Ellis and me, but I'm feeling unworthy for not having a gut feeling that Christopher was up to something. Maybe it was a misunderstanding, but I find that hard to believe after the way Liam explained it.

I pull my phone from my pocket and text Emma to come up. I need her to distract Liam so I can confront Christopher. This can't wait.

"Hi," she says after cracking open his door.

"Change of plans. Can you build a fort with him? There's something I have to take care of."

"Sure."

"Liam, Emma's going to play with you, but I promise I'll be back in a little while. I'm only going downstairs." I kiss his forehead.

"Em, you can build with all the blue ones," he says. Relieved that he's comfortable with me leaving, I stomp down the stairs. I head straight to the library and find Christopher working at his desk. Shutting the door behind me, I march over to him.

"We need to talk."

"Yeah, we do." He backs away from his laptop and clasps his hands in his lap. I cross my arms and glare at him.

"What the hell did you say to Liam when I left you two alone the other day?"

"It wasn't a big deal."

"You think the fact that you told him you were taking him alone on a trip isn't a big deal?"

"Look, when I'm around you and Liam, Ellis becomes jealous. Taking the kid on a short trip would be a way for me to spend quality time with him. I was going to discuss it with you today."

"I don't believe you. You would've asked me first before mentioning it to him, and you sure as hell wouldn't have told him to keep it a secret."

Chris gets up from his chair and strolls around the desk.

"Speaking of which, I heard you've been keeping a secret, as well."

"What are you talking about?" I ask.

"Let's see ... that you slept with Ellis years ago. That he's really Liam's father, not Tony." Without warning, Chris backs me up against his desk, and by gripping it, he cages me in with his arms.

"What are you doing?"

"Saying my peace. I think I at least deserve that after kissing your ass for four years. If I'd known you were such a slut, I would've made a move on you a long time ago."

"Shut up. I'm not a slut."

"Really? So, you fucking one brother while you were dating the other makes you what then? Considering how they both threw money and possessions at you, I guess that makes you a whore, too."

Squeezing my hand up between us, I smack his face. He grabs my wrist and brings my body closer to his. His hot breath is on my skin but his eyes are glacial. He's not the Christopher I've been fond of for years.

"What happened to you?" I ask.

"I've grown tired, Camilla, of your games. You're buying into Ellis's bullshit that he cares for you when all he really wants is his child. I don't know how you're so damn blind."

"That's not true. I love him, and he loves me." I try to free my wrist, but he only squeezes it tighter. My lower lip quivers, and I feel the hammering of my heart. Leaning forward, he forces me to bend back over the desk even farther.

"Now that I know he's Liam's father, I have no use for you. You screwed up all my plans and are nothing but a dumb, greedy whore."

I squirm against him to get away, but he won't budge, and I feel sick over having his body pressed to mine.

"Get away from me. If you don't, I swear I'll press charges."

"For what? Making you see the truth about yourself?"

"Get away. Let me go!"

"You get your fucking hands off her!" Ellis says. His voice booms from the door before he barrels toward us. Christopher looks over his shoulder about the time Ellis gets a handful of his shirt.

Grabbing his body, too, he throws Chris on the hardwood floor, and instinctually, I bring my arms up for protection.

"Where's Liam?" Ellis asks.

"He's safe upstairs with Emma," I reply.

Grabbing Chris by the shirt collar, he lifts his upper body enough to punch him in the face.

"Ellis, stop!" I yell. "Just make him leave." He drags him up to his feet next and clutches his shirt.

"Give me your keys. Then, get out of my house, and don't ever think of coming back. I know who you really are."

Christopher turns his head to the side and spits blood on the floor. I eye his busted lip that's swelling up. "The question I have is did my brother know the truth?"

"What's going on, Ellis?" I ask.

"Tell her," he says to Christopher.

"I don't know what you're talking about."

"Bullshit. Camilla, Chris and Tony have the same mother."

"You can't even say it, can you?" Chris spews. "That I'm his brother, too."

"Did he know the truth?" Ellis asks. "Answer me!"

"Wouldn't you like to know?"

Ellis sucker punches him in the gut, and Chris falls over against him. "Let me go, asshole, so I can leave." He groans and coughs. "I was done here, anyway."

While still holding him by the collar, Ellis peers at him, contemplating what he wants to do next.

"Please let him go so you don't get in trouble." Listening to me, he shoves Chris away, who stumbles back a few feet.

"Give me your keys, and get the fuck out."

Wiping his mouth with the back of his hand, Chris pulls out his keys to the property. He walks up to Ellis and drops them on the floor next to him before storming out. Ellis follows right behind, and I hope it's only to be certain he leaves.

I blow out a long breath and brush tears from my cheeks. I don't know who that person was, but I'm thankful Ellis showed up and nothing happened to Liam. I can't believe Chris and Tony are brothers.

After a few minutes, Ellis returns. While stroking my hair, he scans my face.

"Did he hurt you?"

"No, he only scared me. He said the most awful things, Ellis. I've never seen him like that."

"He's not the person you thought he was."

"I believe that now. I was sure he was going to hurt me."

"He's gone and finally out of our lives."

CHAPTER TWENTY-THREE

Ellis

As I hold Camilla's shaking body against me, I have the overwhelming desire to hunt Christopher down and kill him. I pull back and touch her quivering lip with my thumb.

"It's OK. He's gone. Why were you in here talking to him?"

"You're going to be even angrier when I tell you." Her face turns away, so I bring her chin back to me.

"Tell me."

"Promise me you won't go after him."

I huff out a sharp breath. "Fine, as long as he doesn't come back here."

"When Lorenzo showed up, Liam threw a temper-tantrum, and it was so bad that I had to reschedule his lesson. Once he calmed down, I asked him what was upsetting him, and he said Christopher told him a secret he wasn't allowed to tell or he'd get in trouble." She shakes her head.

"Ellis, I swear I only left them alone together for a minute while I went to the bathroom. It was when we were having lunch in the dining room.

"Christopher told him they might take a trip together, just the two of them, so I came downstairs to confront him. He tried saying he was going to discuss it with me, but then he completely changed and showed me a side to him I'd never seen before."

Her eyes flood with tears. "Do you think he was considering kidnapping Liam? I'm so afraid of what he's capable of doing now."

Bile rises in my chest, and every muscle in my body is rigid, tense with fury. It's going to take all my strength not to harm him.

"He's gone, and I told security to never let him back in. I'll change the locks and the security code on the house, as well."

"That makes me feel better."

"I'll postpone dinner with my parents until tomorrow. I don't believe Liam needs the stress of meeting someone else today."

"I hate to do that, but I agree. You would've been beside yourself if you'd seen him acting out today. I know it's normal for kids to throw fits, and it wasn't his first one, but it was the worst I've witnessed from him. This incident with Chris explains the way he's been acting."

"I thought he was upset that I'm his father."

Camilla touches my cheek. "When I told him he'd never go on a trip with Chris and would always be with me, he asked if he'd be with Boss-Daddy, too." She giggles. "He was happy once I assured him you'd always keep him safe."

So that she doesn't see me emotional, I grab her and hug her.

"Thank you for being an incredible mother to him all this time. I hate to think about how you've struggled alone, and I assure you it will never happen again."

Pulling back, she glides her fingers through my hair and gives me a look of adoration.

"It wasn't your fault, and we're more than OK now. We're becoming the family I've always wanted." Her warm, soft lips press to mine, and I squeeze her waist, craving more of her.

"I need an escape from the day I've had," she adds. "Will you take me to the playroom soon?" With lashes fluttering up at me, her eyes tell me how naughty she wants to be.

"I'll call Beatrice."

Greyson

As I sit in the living room, I hear the front door open, followed by Sasha's footsteps. Each one is sluggish before she cautiously peeks around the corner of the living room.

"Greyson, hi."

"You were hesitant to walk in here."

Blushing, she smiles. "OK, a little."

"I told you it won't happen again." Glancing to her shopping bag, I frown. "It doesn't look like you bought much."

"I didn't have time since I had the NA meeting after, and the other reason is because I don't feel right using Ellis's money. I spent a hundred, and I'm giving the rest of the thousand back to him."

"He genuinely wanted you to have it and will be insulted if you try to return it."

"I didn't do anything to warrant him giving it to me."

"You're trying to better your life and are family now. Both mean something to him. Besides, it's pocket change for the guy."

"I can't comprehend that. It's so much money for someone like me." She'd shit if she knew Ellis gave her ten thousand, not one. I didn't tell her because she would've flipped out and not taken a dime of it.

"There's dinner in the kitchen if you're hungry."

"Oh, I ate with Terrence. He wanted to go shopping with me, which I thought was odd. He went to the NA meeting, too.

I hope he's not trying to get with me because I don't want to date him."

I smirk. "Trust me, he's not."

"You were quick to say that." She clutches her hip. "Is there something he wouldn't like about me?"

"Yes, the fact that you're a girl. The guy has a vagina allergy."

Her hand smacks over her mouth, but it doesn't muffle her giggles.

"A vagina allergy ... like he's gay?"

"Yes."

"You're funny, and few guys make me laugh."

"I'm glad I'm amusing to you." I slide my hand forward and back over my hair.

"It's not in a bad way." As she gazes at me intently, her smile fades. Actually, it's more like she's looking through me. Realizing she's staring, she breaks eye contact.

"Uh, I guess I'll go to my room."

"I was thinking about what you suggested the other day, about us watching that zombie show, and I'm down for it if you are."

"That's OK. I know you weren't that interested in it. I'm still adjusting to getting up early and working all day, so I think I'll hang out in my room and crash early tonight, but thanks for the offer."

"Yeah, sure. I should probably do the same." She strolls out, and I shut off the television. I'm alone, and for some reason it bothers me. I'm not accustomed to rejection from a chick.

Too restless for sleep, I consider my other options. I need to get laid to release my sexual frustration from sharing space with Sasha, but I don't have the urge to hook up with anyone else, so that's marked off the list.

I don't want to work out again, and I definitely don't want to sit here and think about my impending engagement.

Tapping my fingers on the couch, I look down at it, and a thought comes to mind. I'm an idiot, and I wonder how late a furniture store is open.

Camilla

Ellis clasps my pear-shaped ruby necklace and kisses the back of my neck. It's the only red item he requested I wear tonight. He stalks around my body, his fingers skimming down my arm in the process. Bumps rise to the surface, and I shudder beneath his lingering touch.

"Do you know why I gave you this necklace?"

"I believe it was a gift, Sir."

"It was. I wanted to imagine you as the lady in red who made me vulnerable in my dreams, and you were indeed her. In this playroom, you're the vulnerable one, anticipating the unexpected from me."

"Yes, Sir."

"I also wanted you to wear it so you'd come on command by simply touching it ... by hearing me say, '*Come, my Rose.*'"

As my heart flutters in my chest, my eyes close.

"Baby, it's going to happen soon. Touch it. I know you're itching to. I'm also aware that your pussy is spasming, yearning for me to fuck it. Look at me now."

My eyes open, and his hands slide across my collarbones and down to my breasts. He massages them gently, but the heat in his eyes, and the blue veins cording in his neck, convey that today will be more about pain.

"Hold the ruby in your hand, and don't let it go." His fingers travel downward and brush along my skin. He squats and presses his open mouth to my body, skirting it along my stomach.

Flinching, I whimper and let my head fall back. His strong hands grip my hips, his fingers pressing into them forcefully. "All mine. Every single part of this body belongs to me when I want it ... when I crave it ... when I'm hungry for a taste."

The heat from his mouth is what I feel first. He covers my pussy with his lips, and I shove my pelvis forward, needing more, but he pulls away. "Look down at me."

Already dizzy, I lower my head and stare into his smoldering eyes that are tilted up at me. He slides his hands around to my ass and brings me closer to his mouth, dragging his tongue down my slit.

I cry out from the sensations and grab hunks of his hair. Releasing my ass, he smacks it hard, and the unexpected impact causes me to yelp.

"Have you forgotten you're to do as I say in here?"

"No, Sir."

"Did I tell you to touch me?"

"No, Sir."

"It's time to restrain those eager hands of yours." Rising, he leaves me alone, and it's vital I have his touch, his mouth, and his tongue on my skin.

His dirty words and gruff voice ... I yearn for them, too, along with his muscular body pressed to mine as he claims me as his.

Walking to the middle of the room, he points to the black framework he'd shown me the first time I entered the playroom. The slotted metal is a couple of feet wide and spans the width of the ceiling and down each wall to my right and left.

"Stand in the middle." As I pad over to it, he goes to the wall at the front of the room and gathers black wrist restraints hanging from it. Once he returns, he pulls down a silver chain that's attached to the framework above me. "Hold out your wrists."

He buckles each of them in a thick leather restraint and lifts my arms above my head. "Hold them still." While I do as he instructs, he hooks the quick-release silver lock in a notch on the hanging chain.

He said he designed this room once he met me, and I believe him. It's as if it was made to fit me precisely. The framework and chain are the right height to where I'm able to stand while my arms are pulled tight above me. There's no getting out of the restraints or any give for me to touch him.

I'm vulnerable like he stated and horny as hell. Wet between my thighs, I'm already panting. He steps back to admire me, and his eyes are blue flames, his desire ignited as he picks up the flogger from the floor and drags his fingers over the leather tails.

"You said flogging was a soft limit for you, and since it's our first time, I'm going to be cautious and gentle at first. What's your safe word?"

"Marshmallow, Sir." Tilting my eyes up at him, I watch his mouth quirk into a smile.

"Marshmallow it is." He prowls around to the back of me and skims the tails of the flogger over my ass. Bumps rise to the surface of my skin again, and the first time the flogger connects with my back, I exhale a lengthy moan.

"Please, Sir, punish me."

"It's my pleasure." The flogger strikes my back, and I flinch. It's only a light sting at first, but as he continues, the endorphins flood my system, the lightheadedness building to where I can hardly hold my eyes open.

He stalks around my body to stand before me, and with a gentler motion, he connects the flogger to my breasts. His mouth parts, and there's a gleam in his eyes as he strikes them again and again.

He continues, breathing harshly between hits. The rush is overpowering him, dictating his every move, and as my skin turns a darker shade of pink, the more insatiable he becomes. He's staring at my tits, his pupils dilating as he gets sucked into the euphoric moment.

Abruptly dropping the flogger, he's on me fast, sucking one of my nipples into his mouth. He's careful with my breasts but continues to take out his urges on the pointy tips, biting down on them and tugging them outward.

I cry out from the sting, but I can't resist shoving my body forward, wishing to bring him more pleasure and excitement. I need him to punish me, as well, for all my wrongdoings in the past.

"Please, Sir, inflict more pain."

Crouching below me, he drapes one of my legs over his shoulder and buries his mouth against my pussy. The pleasure is instantaneous and enthralling as he licks me rough while the bristly growth of hair on his face rubs my inner thighs raw.

Unexpectedly, he sucks the hood of my clit inside his mouth and bites down on it, causing me to buck against him and cry out. I'm balancing on one leg, trying to squeeze his head with my thighs.

He licks me again, and I'm about to come when he lets me go and steps away. His mouth is soaked as he wipes it with the back of his hand. "Since you want to be punished so badly, you can hold on to that orgasm a little longer."

I whimper, and my body quivers from the need to come. Every part of my pussy throbs, the ache spreading up throughout my pelvis.

"Please, Sir, make me come."

"No." Unhooking the restraints from the dangling chain, he unbuckles them, freeing my wrists. "Walk over to the bed, and bend over it." His command sets my skin on fire, and the bundle of raw nerves beneath tingle.

I hurry to the side of the bed, eager to do what he wants so I can come as soon as possible. Clutching the back of my neck, he braces me and connects his palm to my ass. My face buries in the comforter, trapping my moans.

He spanks me several more times, but I lose count as I'm swept up in a violent storm. I'm swirling inside a funnel of delirium. It's a brilliant chaos in my mind, an internal scream belting from my soul.

"Fuck, your scarlet ass has me so turned on." Pinching my neck more firmly, he grips my waist and stands me up. "On your knees, my Rose. Suck my cock now. Make me come, and I'll do the same for you."

"Yes, Sir," I say as breaths burst in and out of my lungs. Willingly, I kneel in seconds, and having the green light to touch him, I clench his ass cheeks and bring him closer.

Sliding my lips over his rigid cock, I take each glorious inch in my mouth slowly ... tauntingly. He hisses and shoves his pelvis farther against me.

Gathering all my hair, he twists it around his hand and tugs so hard that I feel the pull and sting at the sides of my face. I don't let up, though, and suck his dick, dragging my lips firmly up its thickness.

Every groan from him eggs me to continue. "Earn your orgasm, Camilla. Bury me so deep in your throat that you gag. I want to hear you gagging on my cock."

Gasping from his erotic command, I do as he orders and open my mouth wide until the thin corners of it stretch and burn. I take him deep until I'm gagging, and rather than feeling humiliated, I experience only pride. His growl exposes the ecstasy he's drowning in; a euphoria I created.

Thrusting forward, he clamps down on my hair and explodes in my mouth, shooting his cum down my throat. He convulses to the point I grip his ass to keep him from stepping back.

"Fuuuck, baby," he yells. I wipe my mouth and stay kneeling as he massages my scalp, making up for the hair-pulling, which I secretly love. "Lie on your back on the bed. I'm licking you until you're screaming fuck, too."

He doesn't have to tell me twice. I'm on my back in a heartbeat, and he yanks me to the edge by my ankles. His mouth covers my swollen bundle of nerves, and he blows his searing breath on it.

I arch and strangle the bedding with my hands as my nails bite into my palms. He languidly licks and flicks his tongue, delivering delicious sensations before taking them away.

He leads me to the cusp only to pull me back again, the torment yo-yoing me between heaven and hell. It's tantalizing one second and torturous the next.

"Please, Sir, just make me come." Growling, he licks me faster and slides a finger down my slick crack until he reaches my asshole.

"Wrap your hand around your necklace." Carefully, he dips his finger inside, pushing it in, and I writhe. "Come now, my Rose." I'm done. Shattered. Crashing into the oblivion, the most vulnerable state of all.

"That's it. Ride it out. Next time, I won't need to touch you with my mouth or my hands to make you come. You'll see."

CHAPTER TWENTY-FOUR

Sasha

Today I'm working alone in what Rhonda calls the multi-purpose room. Copiers are on the left after you enter, and straight ahead are two work tables, which I've been sitting at today.

I just finished putting sticker labels on file folders so they'll be ready when the company acquires new clients. Now, it's time to file one of eight enormous stacks of papers that Rhonda let pile up on the table.

I pick up one I've already alphabetized and walk to the file cabinets behind me. There's a long row of them horizontally that create a barrier in front of the bookshelves that are beyond that. I call it the library section since there are six rows of them running vertically.

Filling the shelves are rows of books and binders that are mostly about the laws in our country. Who knew there were so many? I've flipped through one or two of the books, and the fact Greyson can make sense of them reaffirms how smart he truly is.

I have no desire to be an attorney, but I do wish my job was more challenging. I was terrified to work here, certain I'd feel stupid, but the duties are simple. They're so easy that after only a few days, I'm bored.

Since I'll be filing the next two hours, I stick in my headphones, find a pop channel on Pandora and slide my phone between my thin tan belt and short green dress.

I guess I should see about getting my own phone plan soon. It's another bill Camilla's been paying for years. She couldn't afford it, but she feared she'd never reach me if I didn't have one. I feel shitty for that. I would disappear for weeks at a time whenever I was hitting the drugs hard.

She must've worried so much, but during those times, I didn't want to talk to her. Seeing her meant having to stay clean. That equated to living with horrific memories in a sober state.

The only reason I'm able to right now is because I'm getting help and staying busy. Oh, and I have a shiny new toy to look at, Greyson. It sucks that I can look but not touch, and it's embarrassing how I'm his and Ellis's charity case.

Greyson probably thought he needed to watch television with me to make amends for when I walked in on him and Whitney. Or, maybe it's because he wants to help me stay clean.

Regardless of the reason, I don't want them to feel obligated, so that's why I stayed out with my sister the other night and Terrence all evening yesterday. I'm trying to give Greyson the space he needs and deserves.

Opening the first metal cabinet, I start the monotonous task of filing papers away in the letter A folders. I'm singing, bobbing my head, and I can't help but shake my booty a time or two while I'm at it. I need some sort of excitement while I do this boring job.

I move to the letter B and come out of my skin when someone grabs me by the shoulder. I spin around, and Greyson is laughing, so I yank out an earbud and grimace.

"You can't deny it any longer. You take pleasure in scaring the crap out of me."

"I haven't intended to, but I can't lie; it's entertaining when your eyes grow that round. You're a great dancer, by the way, but I wouldn't take up a career in singing."

"You weren't supposed to hear me." I punch his arm as heat travels all the way to my cheeks.

"That song sounded familiar and super annoying. Who's the artist?"

"It's Justin Bieber, and I happen to love him and his songs."

He rolls his eyes. "I should've known."

"Why is that?"

"It's nothing."

"No, tell me now."

Shoving his hands inside his pockets, he shrugs.

"You act younger than your age, but in a cute way. I mean, it's not a bad thing."

Wow, I can't count the times I've heard those words from my sister or counselors, or deadbeat boyfriends.

"Did you need something? If not then I should get back to work." He touches my arm, but I step back. "I told you not to touch me, yet you continue to do so."

"Sasha, I wasn't trying to insult you about the age thing. I like that you're not so serious. Being an attorney, I deal with stuffy and serious every day. It gets old."

"Did you need something?"

"Yes. Are you coming home after work?"

"Does it matter?"

"It does to me, and stop giving me attitude. I'm still your boss."

I sigh. "If you're having a girl over, or that Whitney, and need me to disappear, I can find something to do. It's no problem at all."

"Jesus, no chick is coming over." As he grows increasingly frustrated, he rubs his forehead, and I don't get why when he's the one who insulted me. "I have a surprise for you."

"Why?"

Looking to the ceiling, he clicks his tongue on the roof of his mouth.

"Can't you just smile and be excited I have a surprise for you like other women would do if I told them that?" His pouty expression should take away from his sexiness, but it doesn't.

"Aww, does your ego need stroking?"

He slides his gaze back to mine, and it's suddenly smoldering. "Don't use that word."

"What word? Ego?" Yes, I'm playing the clueless card here because if not I might hyperventilate over the instant sexual fog we've entered.

"Look, are you coming home today or not?"

237

"Yes, sir. See you then." I pop my earbud back in and expect him to leave, but his eyes linger several seconds until I'm forced to turn away from him to file again.

The moment I know he's gone, I lean my head against the cool metal of the cabinet and take deep breaths. Given the opportunity, most women would fall for him. He can't be blind to the fact, so why won't he leave me alone?

***

On the way to Greyson's, I'm nervous about the evening. He left the office before me, which hasn't happened this week, so I'm curious as to why.

I park his BMW in the lower-level garage and take the elevator up. As soon as I step into the foyer of his penthouse, I smell something delicious, and I'm like a dog on the hunt for scraps as I follow the scent right to the kitchen.

Greyson is pulling a sheet pan from the oven, so I admire his muscular thighs as his legs bend in his jeans. He changed into a black t-shirt, too, and his bicep flexes as he sets the pan on the stove. Moving here was such a bad idea.

"Hi," I say.

"Do you like hot wings?"

"Yes." I stroll over and snicker once I spot the sloppy mess of them.

"These chickens are lucky enough to swim in my homemade secret sauce."

"Don't you mean their wings? Do you love cooking?"

"Hell, no, but being a single guy, I have to fend for myself occasionally. I came up with the sauce when my buddies were coming over to watch football once."

"How can I help?"

"There's potato salad in the refrigerator that Theresa made. It should still be good."

"I'm starting to feel like I'm living in the south again."

"I heard Camilla say you're from South Carolina."

"Uh, you have so much stuff in here. I can't get over the amount of food in this place for only one person."

"Two people, and I think you're trying to change the subject."

"Yes, I'm from there, but I haven't been back in years. Where do you keep your plates?"

Greyson points, and it's quiet as I set the two-person table in his kitchen. "What would you like to drink?"

"With wings, I need beer. Wait. I'll have tea."

"It won't bother me if you want a beer."

"No, I want tea."

Striding back to the fridge, I bring out a pitcher of iced tea. I pour us both glasses at the counter, and as soon as I take a sip, I want to spit it out.

"Oh, this is terrible. There's no sugar in it."

"Yes, there is."

"You call this sweet?" His arm brushes against mine as he points next to me.

"There's a container of sugar in that cabinet that I use for coffee."

His face is so close to mine, and instead of turning my head toward the direction I should, I turn to look at him. His eyes remind me of tropical waters I've seen on TV shows, and I'd like to drown in them.

He's eyeing mine, too, and then my lips, so I quickly turn to the cabinet. I grab the small container and laugh.

"This is *not* going to be enough."

"There's a bag of it in the pantry." While he dishes out our food, I make sweet tea that reminds me of home. Once I've stirred it good, I pour fresh glasses and take them to the table.

"Here, try this. It will give you a taste of the south." Cocking an eyebrow, he takes a long drink and smacks his lips together, making the funniest surprised face. I take a drink, too.

"Damn, there's just the right amount of diabetes in here," he says. Losing it, I shoot tea from my mouth and nose. I laugh so hard that tears run down my face. This is embarrassing but couldn't be funnier. Grabbing napkins from the table, I dry my skin. My nose burns, making my eyes water further.

"Oh, that was hilarious, but my nostrils are on fire." Greyson gets a roll of paper towels off his kitchen counter, and we both get down on the floor to clean up the mess I made.

"I'm sorry," I say.

"Don't be. I'm glad someone finds my jokes funny. Someone else would've told me to grow up. Actually, she would've never put sugar in my tea."

"Whitney..."

"I shouldn't have brought her up."

"Why? She's obviously a part of your life."

"Unfortunately. Uh, you have tea on your dress." Without warning, Greyson dabs at the front of it, just above my boobs. I glance down, and his hand freezes. "You look pretty today. Green's your color."

"Thanks." Hurrying to my feet, I go to the trash can and discard the wet napkins I was holding. "I don't know how I made that big of a mess. Are you ready to eat?"

He gives me a puzzled look. "Yeah, sure."

Dinner is awkward and quiet, and I'm self-conscious over how messy the wings are.

"You won't let me in," he says.

"What do you mean?"

"You won't talk to me like friends usually do."

"We haven't been friends long, and I'm not used to sharing my personal business with people. I'm not supposed to."

"See, right there. What does that mean?"

"I have an upsetting past that I'm not comfortable talking about, and you didn't want to talk about Whitney, so what's the difference?"

Wiping sauce off his hands, he leans back in his chair.

"All right. I'll tell you about her, but then you have to answer one of my questions. Agreed?"

"OK..."

"Her grandfather owned a business with my grandfather, and now our fathers share ownership of it. Our parents decided it would be perfect if Whit and I fell in love and married so our families could have the ultimate empire. I didn't know all this back then." He laughs. "I just thought damn, she's hot, and sure I'll date her.

"We fell in love, but once we went to college, things changed between us. Honestly, I stopped liking her as a person. Then, I realized I never loved her the way you should love the person you're going to spend the rest of your life with.

"The problem is that our families feel differently. Everyone besides me still wants us together. My brother, Lawrence, got to marry who he wanted since he joined the family business, but since I chose a different career path, I'm expected to marry Whit.

"It was supposed to happen years ago, but I've put it off as long as possible, hoping she'd bail on the deal first." Greyson tosses his napkin on his plate. "No such luck, so my time at running is over. I have to get engaged very soon."

"Damn. That's deep and depressing."

"No, shit."

"I'm sorry, but you're an adult, and this is America. You don't have to agree to some arranged marriage."

"I do if I want to maintain a decent relationship with my family."

"It seems like they'd get over it."

"I thought that, and it's why I've held out as long as I have, but my father has only grown more demanding about it."

"I can't judge you since I'm not in your shoes, but there's no way in hell I'd agree to something like that."

"All right, it's time for your question. Why the fake ID?"

Laying my napkin down, I stare out the window in his kitchen. We're high off the ground, and it makes me feel physically safer, but it can't erase the haunting memories of my past.

"I can't believe I'm going to tell you this..." I shake out my sweaty hands. "OK, here goes. Rose is not my last name. It's an alias Camilla and I use to keep me safe from people who could hurt us and destroy our lives, my sister's in particular."

"That's still code. I don't understand, and what's your real last name?"

"I answered your question. I told you why I have a fake ID, and that's all I can share." I won't put my sister's freedom in jeopardy by telling him the whole truth. Liam's not losing his mother because I trusted the wrong person.

"Fair enough, but don't forget that I'm persistent."

"I've noticed."

"Are you finished eating? I want to show you something, along with your surprise." To tease him for earlier today, I clap my hands and bounce in my chair.

"Oh, I love surprises. You're the sweetest guy ever, and I can't believe you'd do something for me. How did I get so lucky?" Batting my eyelashes, I giggle.

Greyson rolls his eyes, and his cheeks redden.

"Real funny. I can think of something that needs to be stroked, but it's not my ego."

Oh, my god, did he just say that out loud?

"Uh, sorry. I guess that was out of line." To make things less strange than they've already been this evening, I swat my hand toward him.

"Hey, it's fine. We're friends, and friends should be able to crack jokes with each other, even crude ones."

"I guess that's true, but you're not one of the guys."

"It's cool if you treat me like one, though. Now, show me my surprise."

Greyson

Sasha follows me to the living room and comes to a stop once she spots the new leather sectional.

"You bought a new couch? When? How? The old one was here last night."

"There was a half hour to spare before the furniture stores closed, so I drove down there and bought one they had in stock. That's why I left work early today. I needed to be here while it was delivered."

She turns her head to me, and instead of the grin I'm expecting, she pierces me with a look of disgust.

"I can't believe you just ran down to the store and bought a sectional like it was no big deal whatsoever. This couch had to cost thousands of dollars. Look at it." She waves her arms toward it.

"Yeah, I see it, and I thought I'd get a different response from you. I did it so you wouldn't mind sitting on it. I was trying to be considerate after what happened with Whitney the other night."

"So, you went out and bought a sectional?"

"Yes, I believe we established that."

"You could've had the old one steam cleaned or something. You don't go buy a new couch." Sasha stomps to her bedroom, and this chick makes me crazy.

I get right on her heels, and about the time she goes to slam her bedroom door, I catch it. Shit, she's really going to freak in a second.

Yep, here goes... She spins around. "Is this my surprise?" She points toward the fifty-inch flat-screen television hanging on the wall.

"I thought you'd be happy since you like watching television so much. I mean, you can still hang out on the couch, but this way you can watch TV when you're in here lounging."

Sitting down on her bed, her foot taps, and she drags her teeth over her bottom lip. "Talk to me, Sasha. I'm not gettin' what's happening here." Her eyes fill with tears, and if there was ever a woman I didn't understand, it's this one.

"I felt lucky whenever Camilla would surprise me with a twelve pack of generic Dr. Pepper. This is the first bed I've slept alone in since I was a teenager. I always shared one with Camilla, and once Liam was born, I moved to the couch."

Walking over to the bed, I sit next to her.

"You've been sleeping on a couch for years?"

"Yes," she whispers, "and can you please go? This is humiliating."

I scratch the back of my head. "It's not a lot of money to me. I can't help that I was privileged growing up, and I won't apologize for having worked hard to maintain that wealth."

Falling back on her bed, she covers her face with her hands. Her dress rides up, and I can't help but admire her attractive legs. Her hands drop to the mattress, so I hurry and look up.

"I'm sorry I seemed ungrateful. Thank you for the television ... for everything you've done for me. It's an adjustment to see how wealthy people live, so I was surprised that you made this happen so fast. What you spent on that sectional could keep me in a crappy apartment for six months."

Lying on my side next to her, I prop my head up.

"You don't need a crappy apartment. You have an awesome place to stay for as long as you need."

"As much as you want me to be, I'm not a shield for your inevitable future. You're getting engaged, and we both know I can't stay here once that happens."

Like she always does, she turns her head away from me. "And the fact that news upsets me so much means I need to leave sooner rather than later." I shouldn't do it, but I grab her hand and lace our fingers together.

I'm surprised when she lets me. "Look, I'll make a deal with Whitney. I'll get engaged but only if she agrees that you stay here until we're married. That way you'll have plenty of time to save up the money to move into your own place. Hell, I'll buy a small house and give you a cheap price on it."

She shakes her head like she can't believe the words coming out of my mouth, and I can't believe my current behavior, either. Looking back at me, she yanks her hand away.

"Having to move wasn't the part that upset me so much. Now, thank you again for dinner, the television, the job, the *everything*, but will you please get out? Your mixed signals are company I can't keep."

She's right. Not only is she in recovery, I'm getting engaged. I'm flirting with her and disaster. It's my engagement she's upset about, and at least that makes two of us now.

CHAPTER TWENTY-FIVE

Ellis

"You seem nervous," Camilla says to me as she buttons Liam's khakis. He did try to do it first, but the pants are new and stiff, and his little fingers couldn't do it, so he became frustrated and is irritable now.

"Sit down so I can help you get your shoes on."

"Those hurt my feet," he whines. He's wearing a matching dark brown polo shirt, and I'm having flashbacks to my youth.

"Let him wear his play clothes and socks if he wants."

Camilla stands and studies me. "What's going on in that head of yours?"

"I've come to realize he can be brought up differently than how I was raised. He's already a happier kid than I was at his age."

"There's nothing wrong with Liam learning that there are times we dress more formally out of respect for the occasion or our company. I'm suspecting your change of heart on this matter might have more to do with your defiance against your parents."

"And I think you need a punishment for challenging my request and for knowing me so well."

"Momma, Boss-Daddy is going to get you in trouble if I can't just wear my socks. You should wisten to him 'cause he's the boss."

I throw my head back in laughter, and Liam joins in, even though he doesn't understand why. As much as Camilla doesn't want to, she finds it funny, too.

"You're going to look nice to meet your grandmother and grandfather, so I will happily accept my punishment." She flashes me a look, and the craving I can't shake for her intensifies.

"Ah, maaan," Liam says.

"You win some, you lose some, kid," I reply. "Behave tonight, and I'll take you to the bookstore tomorrow to pick out a new book."

"I like the toy store better, and they have books there, too."

"Have you ever been in a toy store?" Camilla asks.

"Not since I was a child."

"I'll show you," Liam says. "You'll have fun when you buy me toys."

This kid's a riot. "Are you listening to him?"

"Yes," Camilla replies. "I see your training is working. He's already learned his father's manipulation skills."

"And I see his momma wants extra spankings."

Hurriedly, she covers Liam's ears. "Watch it please. I don't want him to think you punish me for real."

"Oh, but I do, and after the last time in the playroom, I can hardly keep a lid on my urges." The doorbell rings. "My parents are here."

As my feet hit the marble floor in the hall, my heart thuds fast. I don't know why I'm nervous since I'm certain my parents will love Liam. I think I'm concerned over what they'll

249

think about my parenting. My *brief* experience sure hasn't made me an expert.

After I take a deep breath, I open the door.

"Mother, Father, welcome." As they walk in, my mother kisses my cheek, and my father gives my shoulder a squeeze. Camilla and Liam are standing several feet behind me.

I turn around, and he's gripping her leg. "Liam, I want you to meet my mother and father, your grandparents."

"Oh, he's so precious," Estella says. Her heels tap against the floor as she rushes over to meet him. Liam's face is scanning hers, and he smiles faintly over her enthusiasm.

"Hi," he says. My father bends over next, moving my mother out of his way.

"Hi there, young man. I'm James, but you can call me Grandpa." My eyes bug out over my father's statement. I never dreamed *pa* would leave his lips.

"I think I want to be called Nana. Liam, would you like to call me Nana?"

Say what?

"OK, let's give him a little space," I say.

"Camilla, it's lovely to see you again," Mother says. "You birthed a handsome, young man."

Lord, it's going to be a long evening.

"Oh, I think he was blessed with the fabulous Burke genes more than anything," my girl replies, being gracious as always.

"Irene's still preparing our dinner, so let's move to the living room." Taking Liam's hand, Camilla leads us down the hall.

"Look how cute he is, James."

"I see, dear."

Once we're inside, Liam runs over to the coffee table.

"I helped make you snacks," he announces, pointing to a tray.

"You did? Well, that was very kind of you," Mother replies before she picks up a cracker.

"There's cheese, too. Momma says it makes your bones stwong."

My father lets out a hearty laugh, and Mother grins.

"Well, I guess I need a piece to go on my cracker then." Sitting down on the sofa, she looks at me with glassy eyes, and I can't recall a time she appeared prouder.

This is why it was important to me to tell her Liam was my child, and I couldn't be more thankful it's the truth.

Camilla

Our dinner is delicious. Irene prepared seared scallops and shrimp in a creamy alfredo sauce over a bed of noodles. Liam's having the same, but she fixed him his own side of macaroni and cheese.

Estella informed Liam that she brought him a present and will retrieve it from the car if he eats most of his dinner. The only problem with that is he's scarfing down his meal to make that happen faster, so naturally, he'll end up with a bellyache.

"Camilla, how is school going?" Estella asks.

"Great, but I need to find a place to do an internship. Do you have any suggestions?"

"Hmm ... since you're passionate about helping the hungry, would you be interested in working at a food pantry? I'm on the board for one here in Denver."

"That sounds perfect."

"Wonderful. We'll get it set up right away. The staff consists of mainly volunteers, and you can work as many hours as you'd like."

I look at Ellis with a smile, but he meets it with a frown.

"Oh, this is exciting," Estella adds. "This will give me an excuse to put a press release in the paper to draw more attention to the pantry. I'll announce your arrival and add a photo, too, and maybe that will get us some new sponsors."

"Oh, no, I can't be in the newspaper. I mean, I'd rather you wait until I've accomplished something to earn the recognition."

She waves her hand my way. "Don't be modest."

"Mother, she doesn't wish to be in the paper." Ellis's tone and narrowing gaze challenge her, and I sense our dinner is going south.

Irene enters just in time. "Irene, would you mind serving dessert now?" he asks her.

"Yes, sir, right away."

"I really want my present," Liam says.

"Son, why don't you and I go to the car to get it," James says to Ellis with raised eyebrows.

"Can I go?" Liam asks excitedly.

Sensing that James wants a moment alone with Ellis, I say, "Sweetie, you stay here. They'll be right back. Hey, why don't we show Nana your bedroom and some of your toys while we wait for your present."

Estella covers her chest. "Aww, I already love being a grandmother. This is going to be so much fun."

A moment of discomfort flashes across Ellis's face before he follows his father out. He's brooding, and I'm curious as to why.

Ellis

"What do you wish to discuss? I know there's something," I say to James.

"Your disapproval over your mother suggesting Camilla work at the food pantry was evident. I suggest you be more supportive in both of their endeavors if you'd like to keep that fabulous woman who seems accepting of your surly disposition."

"How I am with Camilla is none of your business, and I don't understand your hang up with me disapproving of the endless hours my mother has given to her community, rather than to her family."

My father leans back against his black Cadillac. He's in a dark grey button-up shirt that draws attention to his light grey hair. He nervously brushes the front of it back with his fingers.

"Contrary to your belief, your mother and I are regretful for the hours we put toward our careers while you and Tony were growing up. His death forced us to see all that we missed.

"We're excited about having a close relationship with Liam, but we also feel it's our opportunity to make amends with you. I hope you can set your pride aside, as well, and leave behind some of this anger."

I shift my jaw, grinding my teeth in the process. He's sure not wrong about the anger I'm carrying. It's only exacerbated since I began caring for Liam. That kid's made my life so much richer, and unlike my parents were with me, I don't want to miss a minute of him growing up.

"It's time to bury the hatchet, son. Your child and Camilla deserve a happy man in the house. I do hope you're going to marry her soon."

That's the best apology I'm going to get from my father.

"I'll work on the anger issue. As far as my relationship with Camilla, it's private. Mother gossips, and I don't want everyone knowing our business."

"Fair enough. I only ask that you inform us of future life-altering events in private as opposed to say a gala with five hundred people."

I smirk. "Sure. You'll be the first to know and in private. Now, what did you buy your grandson?"

James opens the back seat of his car and removes a large square package. The paper it's wrapped in is covered with red, blue and yellow balloons, and it's topped with a bright yellow bow. He hands it to me to carry inside, and it's heavy.

"It's a train set, and you get to put it together."

"I'm sure Liam will help me, and he'll be thrilled. He loves trains."

My father clasps my shoulder as we return to the house.

"You're going to be a fine father."

Maybe Liam will do what James is hoping and bring us all closer. I'm only worried about my mother's interference. I won't stand for her sucking Camilla into her world, which will take her away from Liam and me. That's not happening.

Camilla

"You called it. He said he had a bellyache," Ellis says as he shuts the door to our bedroom. "He did fall asleep after I read him a story, but I wouldn't be surprised if he wakes up in the night."

"Then we should go to bed. I feel like we never get a solid night's sleep."

"We need to have a discussion first."

"Yes. I was wondering what was wrong with you at dinner. You seemed upset when your mother suggested I intern at the food pantry, and I thought you'd be happy for me."

"I am happy for you. That's not what I want to discuss."

"Oh, OK."

"You panicked when Estella mentioned putting your picture in the paper. It's time, Camilla. I need to know about your past in order to build our future. If there's something I can do to ensure the past *stays* in the past, I'll make it happen."

Looking to the bed, I pick at the fabric.

"There will always be the risk that the past will catch up with me. It's another reason I'm grateful Liam has you. He might *only* have you one day."

Walking over, Ellis leans down and cups my face.

"Listen to me. You're not going anywhere, but I have to know what happened to help."

"All right. Have a seat, and I'll tell you."

Once Ellis has changed into some pajama pants, he sits next to me and takes my hand in his.

"The first ten years of my life were OK. Not great, but tolerable. We didn't have much, and my parents fought a lot, but I thought my home life was like any other child's.

"Then, my father hurt his back at work and couldn't keep his job. He became addicted to the pain pills his doctor prescribed him. My mother hadn't held a job in years, but she tried to work."

I shake my head. "Dad hated it. He was extremely jealous, and I guess ashamed that he was no longer the breadwinner, so he made her quit.

"He started using other drugs and began dealing. He and my mom were hanging out with his supplier and other bad people. Of course, I didn't understand all this at that age, but I pieced it together over the next few years.

"By the time I was fifteen, both my parents were using crack. Our home life sucked. My parents seldom fed us, the house was disgusting, and they were mean. They only cared about getting their next fix.

"Sasha wasn't as strong as me, and their behavior was almost all she'd known, so she tolerated it, whereas I'd challenge my parents.

"I got in a huge fight with my dad one day, and I was done with his shit. I packed a bag and moved in with a friend. I think he let me leave out of fear that I'd turn them in if he didn't." Picking at the comforter, I think back to that upsetting day.

"The terrible treatment Sasha endured only became worse as my parents' drug use increased. I'd visit her or take her out for the day, and I witnessed her decline. She wasn't the happy girl she once was. I saw her slipping away, Ellis. She turned into this hopeless, lifeless being."

Pulling my head to him, he kisses my forehead. He's here for me without judgement. I know it and trust him, but it doesn't make this any easier.

"I got a part-time job and swore that when I turned eighteen, I'd rent Sasha and me a place to live, but over the next few years, things only got worse, and I had no idea just how awful it truly was for my sister.

"Once I turned eighteen, I tried to get her out of there, but my dad said no. He was determined to keep her there. I got her alone one day and found out why my father needed her so badly."

The overwhelming shame and pain from that day return, and the tears come with it. Swallowing, I look past him at the wall. "I found out my father had been allowing Sasha to leave with his supplier for a day or two at a time in exchange for my parents' drugs.

"Horrific things happened to her the hours she was away and by more than one man. My mother knew this and looked the other way so she could keep feeding her addiction."

The veins in Ellis's neck cord, and his lips curl.

"Camilla ..."

"Don't, or I won't be able to finish." I swipe the tears from my cheeks. "Sasha told me she couldn't take it another day and would kill herself if she had to stay there.

"I didn't know what else to do. She was fourteen, and this had been happening for two years. She was only a child, Ellis, when this began.

"I feared that if I told the authorities, they'd put Sasha in a foster home and she'd take her own life. I also worried my parents' supplier would kill us for telling, so I fled with her. I took all the money I'd saved and got us the hell out of there.

"I didn't think my parents would look for us, but I was wrong. They got their shit together enough to report Sasha missing, and it wasn't long before I was wanted for kidnapping. I couldn't believe it, so I kept moving us west, and that's how we ended up here."

"Baby, you were brave. I can't get over your strength."

"It was the scariest, hardest thing I've ever done, Ellis. I was young and naïve, thinking if I got her out of that environment she'd be fine, but it didn't work.

"Yes, the physical abuse stopped, but she's harmed herself every day since by either getting high to numb her pain or by dating losers who made her believe she was worthless. It wasn't hard since she'd been treated that way for years.

"It's why I've cut her so much slack, and maybe it was wrong of me, but it's difficult to come down on someone who's already beating themselves up. I was terrified I'd push her away and lose her for good.

"It's hard to believe Sasha's only four years younger than me. She's trapped in that teenage state, and I think it's because she thinks that's all she deserves."

I smile. "At least she was stuck, but maybe that's finally changing. I've never seen her as happy as she was the other night. Greyson's giving her an amazing opportunity, and I believe she's going to blossom from it. I couldn't thank him enough, but I do worry about her getting hurt.

"I think she already has a crush on him, so would you talk to him for me to be sure he doesn't give her the wrong impression, especially if he's getting engaged?"

"I did warn him, but I'll talk to him again. Listen to yourself. You're still only thinking about her. Have you ever thought about what you've endured?"

"I know I've been through a lot. The years on the run have been rough, but it'll never equate to what she went through or the torment she carries with her every day.

"Being hungry more times than not is why I'm passionate about helping others in need. I don't want anyone to feel that degree of hunger. I visited several food pantries myself over the years, and I'm grateful those days are over."

Ellis pulls me into a hug and kisses my head.

"Baby, you'll never want for anything again. You can have everything your heart desires, and if I need to build another pantry to stock full of food so you'll feel more secure, I will. I'll do anything for Sasha, as well."

"I love you."

"I love you, too, and you no longer need to worry about being taken away from us. I can't tell you how, but I'm handling the situation. I promise."

Sasha

Hiding out in the empty conference room on my lunch break, I pull out my phone and call Camilla. I hate to dump my shit on her again, but I can't keep staying with Greyson. Maybe she'll have an idea.

"Hello," she says.

"Sis, hi."

"Hi ... are you at work?"

I roll my eyes. "Yes, don't worry. I'm only on my lunch break."

"I'm so proud of you."

"Thank you. Other than the job being too easy, I like it here." I would tell her that I'm finding another job soon so I'm not subjected to seeing Greyson every day, but I've learned to dish out the bad news in increments. It shortens the lecture I receive from her. "So, is anything exciting happening in that mansion?"

"Ellis's parents met Liam last night, and they won him over with a train set and loads of attention, so that was a relief. I hate that we're apart, Sasha, but you and Greyson were right about Ellis and I needing some time alone with Liam. Things are finally calming down, and we can enjoy each other and our time with our son."

"Uh, that's great, sis. You deserve to be happy, and you definitely deserve to have some weight lifted off of you."

"How was your NA meeting?"

"It was difficult, but I'm attending another meeting tomorrow."

"I'll go with you if you ever want me to."

"Thank you, but I'm good right now. A friend here at work is going with me."

"Did I say I'm proud of you?"

"Yes, several times this week."

"OK, and you better get used to it. I hate to go, but I need to get back to studying."

"And I better get back to work. I love you."

"I love you, too, and let's get together next week."

"Sounds perfect." Shutting off my phone, I lay my head on the table. So much for that idea. I guess I'm stuck living with stud boy until I save up some money. At least I have a ginormous new television in my bedroom. I'll sequester myself there as much as possible.

CHAPTER TWENTY-SIX

Greyson

I'm driving home from the office, thinking about how it's been one week since Sasha and I spoke more than a greeting to each other.

I get fleeting glances of her at work, and every other evening she waltzes past me from the kitchen to the bedroom while sucking on a bright-colored popsicle. What the fuck is that about?

I missed Whitney's deadline to put a ring on her finger. I figured she was bluffing about telling anyone Sasha's living with me. She doesn't want to blow our image, but it's too late for that.

Everyone is well aware that we fuck around on each other and don't want this. OK, she wants to marry me, but it's not for the right reasons. She's fooling herself if she believes she loves me.

It's time, though. I have to buy an engagement ring, and dammit, I'm spending time with Sasha this weekend before I do it. It's selfish of me, but at the same time, she deserves to have some fun, too.

Once I'm home, I loosen my tie and stroll down the hallway. Hearing her singing, I smile. I'm instantly happier, and my heart begins to race. I pound on her door so she'll hear me with her earbuds in.

She swings it open, and I clear my throat to calm my nerves.

"Hi," I say. "Bieber again?"

Pulling one of her headphones out, she blushes.

"No, Selena Gomez. What do you need?"

I grip the doorframe up high with both hands.

"I need you to stop avoiding me. We're friends, and friends talk and hang out. Do you have plans this weekend?"

Turning around, she strolls over to her dresser, and I stare at her ass that's in black yoga pants. Other than seeing her in tight jeans, this is my first opportunity to admire how phenomenal her ass looks.

She unplugs her earbuds from her phone and sets both on the dresser, but the headphones fall to the floor. She bends over to pick them up, and I fight a hard-on from the even better view it gives me.

Her shirt lifts, and there's a tattoo on her lower back of a ladybug. I think that's what it is, but I need a closer look. It's fucking sexy. Whitney would never ink her body. She wouldn't do anything that fun or daring.

Hell, I want a tattoo. That would surely piss her off, and if I have to be married to her the rest of my life, I want her to look at it for that long. She'll bitch about it, but it'll be worth it.

Turning back to me, Sasha rests her hands on her hips.

"I'm going to a meeting tomorrow morning, but otherwise, I don't have anything planned."

"Cool, then spend time with me."

"Why?"

"How many times do we need to go over this? I want to hang out with you because we're friends, and that's what friends do. You said I could treat you like one of the guys."

Cracking a smile, she rolls her eyes.

"I did say that. What did you have in mind?"

"I'm going to bake the pizza Theresa prepared before she left, and then we're watching that zombie show you like. Tomorrow, after your meeting, I want to get a tattoo. You can get another one if you'd like. I'll pay for it."

"You want a tattoo?"

"Yes, and why do your wide eyes say you're surprised?"

"I guess I didn't expect a suit-wearing attorney to want permanent ink on his body."

"Well, I do, *Ladybug*." Her skin flushes, and she pulls her shirt down farther. "Too late, chick. I already had a peek." I wink at her. "Can you get the oven preheated while I change clothes?"

"Sure, and do you always wink at your guy friends?" She smirks, and now I'm blushing like a damn girl.

"No, especially not with my friends who have a vagina allergy. That could give them the wrong impression." Sasha laughs, and it's a pretty sight. Damn, how I love our banter.

"All right, I'll change and meet you in the living room."

Sasha

"What did you think?" I ask after we watch the first episode of *The Walking Dead*.

"I think you're one twisted chick."

Like I do so often with Greyson, I giggle.

"You're safe here if we have a zombie outbreak," I reply. "They won't be able to put in the passcode to get up to your fortress, and you have enough food stockpiled to last months."

"You've put too much thought into this. I'm wondering if I should limit your TV-viewing privileges."

"Oh, really?" He eyes the Pixy Stix I'm holding to my lips. I tilt my head back and let the sugary dust fall inside my mouth.

"I don't think we can live off sugar, and it's overrunning my pantry."

"Oh, sorry about that. Theresa pried the list of foods I like out of me and bought them. She's so sweet."

"Yeah, she is, and I see she's spoiling you, too."

"I didn't get this kind of stuff as a kid, so I'm making up for lost time, but I'm super grateful."

"You didn't have much growing up, did you?"

"No, I didn't."

"Where are your parents?"

"I guess in South Carolina. I haven't spoken to them in years, so I wouldn't know. Wanna watch another episode?"

"Is that all I'm getting out of you?"

"Yep, but feel special; it's more than I've told anyone else."

He squeezes my knee, and like when he held my hand on my

bed days ago, I don't pull away from him. He doesn't move his hand, either.

It sits there as the next episode begins, and I consider teasing him, asking if he's ever rested his hand on one of his other buddy's knees, but then he might remove it.

For the first time in as long as I can remember, I want a man to touch me while I'm sober. Greyson makes me feel alive, instead of numb, and I think I'm ready for more of that feeling.

Tired, I rest my head on his shoulder and yawn. I grow sleepier quickly, so I settle against his warm body, trusting that it's safe to be near him.

Out of nowhere, he presses his lips to my head. I stiffen, unsure of how to respond. He leans over, closer to my face and whispers, "Please don't move. If only for this weekend, pretend with me that things aren't going to change. I'm enjoying every second with you, and I don't want it to end."

"You're being selfish."

"I know, so when the zombies come, you can feed me to them."

I shouldn't encourage him, but I giggle. I also leave my head where it is and close my eyes. I can't face him. I can't see him look at me like I'm more than a rebellious act against his future bride. This is messed up, but I breathe, "OK."

Sighing with relief, he kisses my head again.

"Thank you." His body relaxes, and I scoot closer, pulling my legs up to tuck beside me on the couch. For now, I'll be selfish, too, and pretend this could last forever.

Ellis

Wiping the sweat off my neck with a towel, I take a drink from my water bottle. Dean's sitting on the floor, putting on his socks and tennis shoes after our jiujitsu training.

"I have some news," I say.

"What's that?"

"Do you remember when we were at dinner and I told you Camilla's son, Liam, was my nephew?"

He pauses with a sock over his toes. "Yes."

"He's actually my kid, and he's probably going to appear downstairs, so I wanted to give you a heads-up."

"A heads-up?"

"OK, I wanted to tell you. I know it's shocking. It was for me, too, and it's a longer story than the last one I told you. He's definitely mine, though, and I'm thrilled about it."

"All right. I don't need to know how you and your brother happened to sleep with the same woman around the same time, but as long as your good with it, I'm happy for you."

I glare at him. "It wasn't like that. Tony drugged Camilla and me, so we didn't know we'd slept together. It's complicated, and it's also why this training is so important to me.

"My brother was involved in dangerous shit and had dangerous people by his side. I have to be physically prepared to take someone down if necessary."

Standing, he grabs his duffle bag. "I think you're covered there, and I'm sorry, man. I shouldn't have said that."

"I get it, but Camilla is nothing like you're thinking. She's an incredible woman and raised my son on her own. She wasn't looking for a payout."

"I trust you. Let me meet him."

I motion toward the door. "Let's go. I'm sure he'll hear us and come running." We stroll down the stairs, and as I expected, I hear Liam's footsteps as he trots down the hallway. Spotting Dean, he comes to an abrupt stop.

Suddenly bashful, he sticks his finger in his mouth, and I have a thought. Nothing would build his confidence up more than some martial arts training, but I imagine Camilla wouldn't go for it at this age.

"Liam, I want you to meet my friend Dean."

"Hi," he says as he creeps closer.

"Hi, Liam. You should come upstairs and watch us work out next time."

"I wanna do that," he replies with a smile, and I'm sure he doesn't have a clue what Dean's talking about, but if it involves me, he's usually all for it. Camilla hurries into the hall.

"Hi, Dean. Good to see you again." She looks at me. "Do you mind watching Liam? I need to get ready to meet the volunteers for coffee."

"Sure, I need to cool down before I shower, anyway. Maybe I can show Liam some moves."

Camilla's forehead scrunches. "Oh, be careful with him."

"I'm not going to let anything happen to him. I tumbled down a flight of stairs for the kid." Liam's eyes widen as he looks at Dean and points toward the staircase.

"We fell really, really far, and Boss-Daddy caught me. We got boo-boos even." He strains his head and twists his arm to look at his own elbow.

Chuckling, Dean slaps me on the back. "I didn't think you could get any richer, but it appears you have."

My eyes dart to Camilla. "They're both pretty amazing."

Smiling at me, she then gives Dean a wave.

"I have to run. Bye, Dean." She takes off up the stairs, and I show my friend to the door. Liam skips along, and I never thought I'd say it, but I like having a shadow at every turn.

Liam and I head to the living room, and as we sit on the sofa, he jabbers about the cartoon that's playing on the television. He looks like me, but he acts like Camilla.

His eyes exude excitement with the same intensity, and he has many of her mannerisms, like the way he bites his lip or how he scrunches his nose when he doesn't like something.

"I do hope you're going to marry her soon."

My father's words resonate with me, and I ponder the future. There's no doubt I want Camilla in my life forever, but we haven't been together long. Would she say yes to a proposal this soon?

Patting my arm, Liam frowns. "Daddy, are you wistening to me?"

"Uh, yes, but let's go upstairs. I need a shower. I'll use the one in your bathroom so you can play with your toys in your room while I'm in there."

He giggles. "Are you gonna use my coconut shampoo?"

"So that's what turned you into a nut." I muss up his hair, and overexaggerating his laugh, he points at me.

"I'm not a nut. You're the nut."

"No, you're the nutty one, eating up all my peanut butter and getting nutty crumbs all over the floors." Pulling him onto my lap, I tickle him, and he cackles and squirms.

I glance up, and Camilla is standing in the doorway with her hand over her heart. Her eyes are watery, too. Has she always been this emotional?

Since finding out Liam's mine, she cries often, but the more I watch her now, I realize this is not her upset look. Those are happy tears. Why did I have any doubt? She'll marry me if I ask; I'm sure of it.

Camilla

Liam and Ellis sharing a fun, loving moment is a magnificent sight to see. To witness them remove their protective shields is a gift I won't take for granted.

"Hop up, Liam," Ellis says. "Let me talk to your mother for a minute before she leaves." He strolls over, and I smell his sweat and sense his frisky mood in seconds. Clenching my waist, he nuzzles his nose in the crook of my neck.

"Don't go. Stay here with us."

"Ellis, this is important to me."

He leans back. "Why? You only met them this week."

"Exactly, and they were kind enough to invite me to their weekly coffee outing. They go every Saturday after the pantry closes."

His eyes bulge. "You're going every Saturday?"

"No, not every weekend, but I don't want to decline their first invite. Most of the volunteers have been there for years, so I can learn from them, which will help me in my career."

"Camilla, you don't need a job anymore."

"This isn't about me having a job for money. It's about me having a fulfilling career where I give back to the community."

"I'll make a considerable donation and pay for other people to work there if it means you can be home with your family."

I tilt my head to the side. "I love that you want me here with you, but I need this." Remembering the promise I made to him, I look at my feet.

"I told you I was submitting to you completely, and agreeing to be your submissive meant handing over my trust to you. I believe you respect me and don't want me locked in a castle like in *Beauty and the Beast*."

"I don't want that." Taking his hands in mine, I tilt my eyes up at him.

"If you tell me again not to go, I'll believe you have an important reason in doing so, and I won't leave."

Ellis's head falls back. "Fuck," he utters under his breath. "If doing this makes you happy, then I want you to go. I only hope you won't leave us alone too often." Lowering his head, he looks at me like a wounded child.

I cup his cheek. "I wouldn't do that."

"I wonder if my mother thought the same when she first became passionate about helping others."

"I'm not going to lose sight of what's most important." Tiptoeing, I kiss his cheek. "I promise, and I love you."

"I love you, too."

"Liam, run over here, and give Momma a kiss. I'll be back before you know it, and you behave for Daddy."

"Yes, Mother. Bye, Mother."

Laughing, Ellis winks at me.

"Maybe you two don't need more time alone. He'll only discover new ways to tease me," I say.

"I don't like that Mitch is off today, but the younger guard, Todd, is going to ride with you. I told him to wait in the car while you're in the coffee shop."

"OK, and thank you for supporting me."

"I might be working the wrong angle here. Maybe I should punish you for behaving since you do way more of that. I'd have endless opportunities."

"You get to make the rules, *Sir*."

Yanking me to him, he growls in my ear.

"And don't forget it."

CHAPTER TWENTY-SEVEN

Greyson

Sasha's been quiet since we left the NA meeting. As I drive, I reach over and squeeze her knee. Rejecting my attention, she turns her legs inward toward the passenger door. Her arms are crossed, and she's staring out the window.

"During one of your stays in rehab, did you ever confide in a counselor about your past?" I ask.

"I told you I wasn't allowed."

"Your odds of staying clean are slim if you don't talk to someone about why you started using in the first place."

She snaps her head in my direction. "Why did you start using?" Her voice is bitter, and I know damn well what she's doing.

Her wall is boarded back up as her mind searches for an excuse to get high. She's looking for the fight, the fallout ... anything that will allow her to feel sorry for herself enough to excuse it again.

I open and close my hand that's gripping the steering wheel.

"My friends introduced me to drugs in college, but I take full responsibility for using them. I could've said no, but school was fucking hard, and the drugs got me through it.

"I was able to stay up all night and study, and then I'd take something to make me crash when I finally had a moment to sleep.

"The other reason I used was because I felt trapped over my future. It's one thing to feel shackled in the present. It's another to see your life sentence. I was expected to join my family's oil business and marry Whitney, and I wanted to do neither."

Glancing from the road to Sasha, I look for a sign that she's loosening up. Her arms have uncrossed, so I'm making progress.

"The drug use finally caught up with me, and I was going to lose my shot at law school if I didn't get my act together. Ellis knew it, and he helped me get clean more than anyone.

"I eventually got the career I wanted, but as you're aware, the bride's a different story. Do you know why I can sit here and tell you this?"

"No, why?"

"Because in rehab, I talked shit out, regardless of how uncomfortable it was. It's why I can share with you about personal, deep shit unlike most guys could."

"The meetings already make me think too much. The last thing I want to do is talk about it."

"Maybe once you talk about it, you'll think about it less."

"I want to use right now."

"I know. I feel it a little bit, too, especially with the looming wedding. It's sick but I even fantasized about us using together. Damn, I miss that high sometimes."

Sasha surprises me when she bursts into laughter, slinging her head back against the seat.

"Please don't try to be anyone's sponsor—like ever. You'd totally suck at it."

I grin at her. "Hey, I'm just being honest. I do other daring shit now to get that rush. Even closing a deal on a property can give me an endorphin dump. I'm banking on that rush when I get this tattoo. Are you going to get one, too?"

"No, I'm saving my money for a place to live."

"I told you I'm paying."

"I'm running up a large enough tab. Maybe next time."

I snort. "There won't be a next time."

"Ha. You'll see; one tattoo leads to another."

"Do you have more than one?"

"Yep."

"I want to see it."

"You can't. It's in a private place."

I grin at her again. "You at least have to tell me where and what it is."

She succumbs to the crack I made in her boarded-up wall and smiles shyly.

"I'll think about it."

A call comes in, and I see it's Ellis.

"Cuz, hi."

"Hey, what are you doing?"

"You're on speaker. Sasha and I just left a meeting. What's up?"

"Liam and I are hanging out here alone at the house. You're welcome to stop by."

"Actually, my weekend is booked. Could we grab dinner Monday evening?" Silence fills the air ... fills it ... and from Ellis, I know what that means. Shit. "Any evening next week will work," I add. "You can let me know later."

"I'll check Camilla's schedule and get back with you. Sasha, hi."

"Hi, Ellis."

"I'm sure Camilla would like to have you over. We're not leaving the house this evening or tomorrow, so you're welcome anytime."

He sure can be a dick when he wants to be.

"Uh, thank you, Ellis, but I have plans, too. Tell Cammy I'll call her Monday. Oh, and thank you for the gift, but I'm giving eight hundred of the thousand back. It was too generous of you."

"A thousand...?"

"We have to go, Ellis," I say.

"Call me, *Greyson*." I hang up since he's pissed and will blurt out something he shouldn't over the speaker phone.

"Wow, he spoke to me," Sasha says, "and he invited me over, too."

I rub the back of my neck. "Looks like you made the cut. Earning his trust is a hard one."

"I won't let him down. He's giving Liam and Camilla a life most girls only dream about."

I'm quiet until we reach the tattoo shop. Ellis doesn't need to tell me that I shouldn't spend time alone with Sasha. I know it, but I'm a selfish prick, and my conscience will tolerate the guilt while I enjoy my time with her.

Sasha

"Your pain face is too funny," I say to Greyson over the sound of the tattoo gun.

"Stop. I already have to accept I'm a candy-ass. I don't need you teasing me for it."

I giggle, and the male tattoo artist laughs, but then my eyes stray from Greyson's face to his body, and I'm distracted in an instant.

His shirt is off, and I'm appreciating his 5:00 a.m. workouts. Maybe I should consider exercising myself, but I'm thinking in the evening would be a better fit for me. His body ... I could lick Pixy Stix sugar right off those rock-hard muscles.

I can't believe I've found a man I want to touch while I'm not high, but maybe the fact I can't touch him is why I fantasize about it. I know it's not going to happen, so I feel a bit safer.

"What are you thinking about, Ladybug?" My eyes flit to his, and he's exposing his sexy dimples. Damn, I'm busted. OK, I'll play.

"I was thinking how I'd like a juicy popsicle to suck on right now. I really like them."

Swallowing, his smile recedes. "Girl, that's not funny. I'm on to you."

The young artist smirks but never looks up.

"What?" I ask innocently. His fixed gaze transforms to hungry and determined. I'm chained to it as he transmits his desire to ravish me. Through the turquoise of his eyes, I see the fantasies and feel his urges. The words from his lips aren't necessary.

Oh, no.

"I need to use the restroom." Darting to the lobby, I search for the bathroom.

I slam the door closed behind me and squeeze the handle with my sweaty hands. I want to believe it'll protect me from him, but I know the truth. I'll go back for more since the punishment is worth the high.

After I wet my face with a damp paper towel, I leave the room. Greyson is paying the artist at the counter in the lobby, and I see him hand the man a wad of cash.

"You missed the end result," he says to me.

"Sorry, you can show me later." We stroll to the Rolls-Royce, and since the tattoo is on his right shoulder blade, he winces as he leans back against his seat.

"Why did you choose a mountain and eagle?"

"They represent freedom." Starting the car, he looks over at me. I'm staring straight ahead, but after a few seconds of having his eyes on me, I steal a glimpse of him. "I want to show you something," he says. "It's something no other soul knows about."

"You want to share it with me?"

"Yeah, I do. I have a feeling you'll appreciate it and understand it more than anyone else."

Intrigued, I quirk an eyebrow. "If you're sure, then I'm down for it."

"We'll have to take a drive, and we'll stop for food on the way."

"You have me curious." Sinking down in the seat, my mind dwells on all the possibilities of where we could be going, but I come up with nothing. All I know is I feel more vulnerable than ever if he's sharing something this private with me.

***

"We're almost there," Greyson says. "You've been quiet since we stopped at the store. Actually, you've been different since you ran off to the restroom at the tattoo parlor. Don't think I didn't notice."

"Why do you have to say such honest shit?"

"It's who I am, so tell me why."

I sigh. "OK. Why do you look at me like I'm more than a blip on your radar? I'm Podunk, whereas you're like a tropical island or Times Square in New York. Hell, you probably own an island."

He laughs. "I don't own an island, but that'd be cool. Seriously, Sasha, I don't know what you're talking about. I mean, I do but it's not accurate."

"You're handsome, wealthy, educated, and it sounds like women throw themselves at you, so the fact you want to spend time with me makes me wonder who's kidding who here."

"Don't do this." He glowers. "Don't act like you don't matter. Rhonda told me you're overqualified for your position. That means you're capable of doing a more challenging job or getting a college degree if you want it.

"You're funny, kind and beautiful, too, and once you believe it, more people will. Then, more opportunities will come your way."

I break our gaze, wishing I believed what he said, but it's contradictory to how I was treated in the past. Only Camilla held on to hope that I'd amount to something, and I've disappointed her more times than I could count.

Greyson turns onto a long gravel driveway, and I see a cabin in the distance. "Pity parties are my least favorite to attend, so liven up, Ladybug. I'm about to show you my favorite place." He parks in front of a small log cabin.

"This is yours?"

"Yep."

"And I'm the only soul you've told about it?"

"Correct."

"That's weird."

"You're weird."

Finding my smile, I poke him in the shoulder.

"No, your weird."

"I've concluded we're both a little weird. Now, come on so I can show you around."

Grabbing the grocery bags, we head inside the cabin. I'm surprised over how small the kitchen and living room are, and I have a strong suspicion there's only one bedroom, too. Setting my bags on the counter, I wipe my sweaty palms on my jeans.

"It's quaint and reminds me of cabins in the Carolinas."

"I know it's small, but that's how I wanted it. It's my refuge, and I plan to keep it that way."

I stroll over to the picture window and gasp from the view of the mountains. There's a door to a deck, and I can't resist walking out onto it to suck in the crisp air. Earth is what I smell, and a cool breeze is what I savor on my skin.

"Breathtaking ... I love it here," I whisper.

"So do I," Greyson says as he comes up behind me. I jump from his presence, and I can't look back at him. All I can focus on is the view before me. Low-hanging clouds shroud some of the rocky slopes, but the peaks stand tall above them.

"What do you think of the view?"

"It's as if the trees are kneeling before their king ... the way they line the basin."

From right behind me, Greyson grips my biceps. I flinch again but don't pull away as he leans his head over against mine.

"Sasha ... I knew you'd see it the way I do." I open my dry mouth to speak, but words won't come out. Slowly, he turns me to face him. His hands cup my cheeks, his thumb skims across my lips, and I tremble uncontrollably in the process. "I want to kiss you."

"I—I don't think that's possible."

"That I want to or that I can?"

"I won't be able to handle you kissing me." Looking to the door, I picture myself running.

"Now, I'm more confused. Handle it as in you'd like it too much or would be repulsed by it?"

Glancing back at him, I roll my eyes.

"I don't believe kissing you could be repulsive."

"Explain, weirdo."

Stifling a giggle, I slap his chest. "Don't make me laugh because then you'll think it's OK for you to kiss me, which will result in me ruining your perfect place. I don't want to create a bad memory for you at your special hideaway."

"So, what you're saying is I'll be repulsed by kissing you."

"Why do you have to be so charming?"

"Why arc you putting up a fight?"

Humor vanishes from my existence, and my iron wall goes up.

"Because fighting a man off is all I've known." I stomp back in the house and head straight to the front door. I don't know where I'm going, but it'll be far away from here. Greyson grabs my arm about the time I reach the door.

"Stop running from me, and tell me why you're fighting this."

"You want to know why? I'll tell you two reasons. One, because unless I'm high, fighting a man off me is all I know to do when he touches me. Second ..." I grab my hips and shake my head. "Wait, I shouldn't have to tell you the second. You're getting married, Greyson. *Married.*"

"Maybe I won't."

"I never dreamed my entire future balanced on the cliff of a maybe."

"That means you see me as a possible future."

"No, I see you as an *impossible* future. An unattainable future. A broken heart is what I see when I think of you and my future."

"I hear Whitney's spending her time with another man. His name's Sebastian, and he's who she wants." Pulling me to him, Greyson grips my chin. "I want you, and I believe you want me, too."

"That doesn't change the other issue I have."

"No, but you trust me, or you wouldn't be living in my house, so that means I can fix the other issue."

"I'll stay, but I need time to consider the kiss."

"That's not a no."

"Let's cook dinner; I'm hungry."

"Of course you are." He winks, and my insides turn all gooey. It's going to be impossible to resist Greyson's sexiness. I want him to kiss me. I do more than ever, but I don't know how I'll feel once he begins. Maybe I'll brave a chance to find out.

Greyson

Sasha and I are sitting on the deck after dinner. While we cooked cheeseburgers, I wooed her with my charm, and after we ate, a food fight ensued with the toppings.

Best time ever.

"I could sit out here all night, but we need music," she says.

"I can make that happen. I have vinyl."

"Really? My parents had a record player." She hops to her feet, ready to see my stash of albums. "I loved setting the needle down and waiting through the pause for that first sound."

I start to shake my head but stop myself. She gets me without even trying. We go inside, and remembering the player and albums are in my bedroom, I decide it's best to bring them out to the living room.

"You didn't have to move them."

I shrug. "We'll hear the music better on the deck."

"Oh, right." She flips through the albums. "You have oldies here."

"There's no other way to do vinyl."

She hands me an album. "I know this band. Camilla said my parents would play it before their drinking turned to drug use and their drug use ruined our lives."

"Bob Seger and the Silver Bullet Band's *Stranger in Town*. Uh, are you sure you're OK with listening to it?"

"Yep." She heads back outside, and although her parents suck, I'm pleased she shared with me about her past. She then bailed, not wanting me to pry, but that's OK. She'll tell me when she's ready, and if that means a little at a time, I can live with that.

Sitting next to each other in my lounge chairs, we stare at the view and talk. The sun is setting, and the sky has morphed from blue to saffron.

"I wonder what it's like to see a band perform live," she says.

"What? You've been to a concert, right?"

"No, Camilla and I didn't have money to spend on things like that."

"Unbelievable... You *have* to attend a concert. I lost count of the artists I've seen."

Her eyes light up. "I really want to see Justin Bieber or Bruno Mars since they can dance."

"I'm taking you to a concert, girl. I'm going to pop your concert cherry, but Bieber can't be the third in this threesome." She giggles, and I love seeing her smile. She's gorgeous.

Her hair is healthier, and her skin and the gold in her honey-brown eyes glow. Her body has filled out from consuming more calories, and her curves are in all the right places. Needing to be closer to her, I stand and hold out my hand. "Dance with me."

"No, I can't."

"Bullshit, I catch you dancing all the time."

"But I was doing it solo."

"Please, dance with me." "We've Got Tonight" begins to play, and there couldn't be a better song for us. She stands, and her hand is trembling as I take it into mine.

I pull her close, but she stiffens, so I gradually move one of her arms up around my neck while I gaze at her. "You can trust me. I won't do anything you don't want me to do."

She places her other arm around my neck, and I feel victorious yet again for gaining her trust. We sway to the song, and as I listen to the lyrics, I panic over the future.

The song reminds me that we may only have tonight together. This might be the closest I ever get to her, right here in this moment.

"I like dancing with you," she says as she looks up at me. Something's different now. Her eyes are alluring, her long lashes batting as she looks at me seductively. "I think I want you to kiss me."

Hell. Yes.

I have this feeling I'm getting one shot at this, so I can't fuck it up. Stopping our movement, I stare down at her.

"Close your eyes, and stand still. I'm turning your *I think* into a *yes*." Her breath hitches as she prepares for me to kiss her. She fails to stay still as I press my lips to the corner of her mouth.

"I won't hurt you, Sasha." I press them to the tip of her nose next and the other corner of her mouth. "Do you want me to kiss you, Ladybug?"

"Yes," she whispers. Cautiously and gently, I kiss her. I repeat it, alternating between the corners of her mouth and her quivering lips.

They're soft and plump, and I'm dying for more. I inch her closer, and I'm surprised when she opens her mouth to let my tongue inside.

Cradling the back of her head, I deepen our kiss and groan as our tongues tangle for the first time. She whimpers in response, the heat from her hum filling my mouth, and it takes all my strength to go slow.

I imagine carrying her to my bed and burying myself deep inside her. Fuck, I don't want to give her up. Tonight's not enough.

She pulls back and sucks in air before she gifts me a wide–fucking–grin that's more breathtaking than the mountains ever could be.

"Thank you," she says.

"You're welcome. I've never been thanked for a kiss." Leaving one arm around my neck, she clutches my shirt and stares at it.

"Since I was fourteen, I haven't kissed a guy without being high or drunk. You're the first."

"See, I'd make a great sponsor." Her head falls over, and her body bounces against mine as laughter thaws my frigid heart.

I'm curious what the age of fourteen has to do with her confession, but at the same time, I believe the truth could be ugly, and nothing ugly is going to mess up this moment.

Ending her laughter, she rests her head on my chest.

"I can't sleep with you, Greyson."

"I know. I've been selfish long enough." I stroke her hair, which is cool to the touch from the evening breeze.

"I want to, and you have no idea what that says about you, but my sobriety wouldn't survive it afterward if you ended up with someone else."

As the heavy darkness of reality returns, I kiss her head.

"Let's go home."

CHAPTER TWENTY-EIGHT

Ellis

Answering the front door, I let Greyson and Sasha inside. He looks irritated, whereas she's grinning like she won the lottery.

"Hi," I say. Camilla and Liam join us in the hall to greet them.

"Sasha!" Liam runs to her, and she swoops him up into her arms to hug him.

"I've missed you, *Mikey*, and I swear you keep growin' and growin'."

"I know. I'm getting so, so big. I'm going to be tall like Boss-Daddy."

Greyson and Sasha both quirk an eyebrow.

"Boss-Daddy?" he asks. "I have no words."

"Sasha, would you take Liam to the backyard? He wants to show you his jungle gym. I'll be out in a minute," Camilla says.

"Sure. You have a jungle gym?" Sasha asks excitedly while grinning at Liam.

"Yes, and you can play on it, too."

"OK, you lead the way."

They wander off, and I know what's about to happen. I've had to hear it from Camilla for the last two hours, and seeing her pissed doesn't sit well with me. Greyson better listen good today.

She fists her hips. "Greyson, I like and respect you. I really do, and I couldn't be more grateful for all you've done for

Sasha, but you're crossing a line with her. She's fragile, and Ellis told you when she was moving in not to touch her."

"We're only friends."

"So, friends make out?"

"How do you know about that?"

"She called me this morning. She said you two were spending the weekend together and that you kissed her. She likes you and is sick over you marrying Whitney."

Greyson grabs the back of his neck. "I only planned to be a friend to her, but since she's living and working with me, I've gotten to know her, and I can't help but like her."

"OK, but she can't be your mistress. If you're going to marry Whitney, then don't spend unnecessary time with my sister." Camilla tears up. "She can't end up with someone like Rusty again, doing drugs in some crack house. She could end up dead next time."

Greyson points at his chest. "I only want what's best for her, Camilla. She's not some secret side piece."

"If that's true, then back the hell off before she falls in love with you and gets her heart shattered." Camilla storms away, and Greyson drags his hands down his face.

"Is this why you wouldn't wait for us to have dinner tomorrow?"

"I've had to listen to that for the last two hours, so it was only fair that you heard it, too. Let's go to the family room, and I'll fix you a drink."

Greyson takes a seat on my sofa, and I pour him a scotch.

"You didn't listen to me," I say as I hand it to him.

"I swear I didn't mean for it to happen."

"First, I want to know why you didn't give her the entire ten grand."

"I thought I'd ration it so she wouldn't freak out and give it back to you, but that's only the partial truth. If I'm honest, it's because I worried she'd use it to rent her own place.

"I like her, Ellis. She's fun and doesn't have some agenda of how to get ahead. She's—she's herself. She doesn't pretend like everyone else."

"Fun? How long will fun last? You're nothing alike."

"You and Camilla came from different worlds, and you're making it work."

"She's not Sasha. Camilla's more mature, responsible and older."

"I'm younger than you, so I can date a younger woman than Camilla, and I'm not as serious and uptight as you. Sasha and I fit together."

I hold my hands up. "Fine, you like her, but that doesn't change the fact you're marrying Whitney Peterson."

"You're like everyone else in this family, thinking I belong with someone like her."

"That's bullshit. I've been telling you for years to stand up to your father, but you haven't listened, so what am I supposed to think? Unless you're ending things with her, you need to leave Sasha alone. She's been through hell already."

"You know about her past." Downing his drink, Greyson slams his glass on the coffee table. "Tell me what happened to her."

"I can't."

"I tell you everything, Ellis. I won't say anything to her about it. I need to know."

I walk over to the window of the family room and watch Sasha push Liam on the swing.

"Fine, I'll tell you, but only so you understand why you can't mess with her head. Her parents were junkies. They traded Sasha for drugs whenever they needed them. Their dealer would take her for days at a time. I guess he and his friends would drug her up and have their way with her."

I turn around to face him. "She was a pincushion, Greyson. She was only twelve when it started. Camilla rescued her when Sasha was fourteen, and they've been on the run ever since."

As he looks to the floor, his hands ball into fists.

"I'm trying to wipe away any record of Camilla's kidnapping charges as we speak, but it hasn't happened yet. That's why I needed you to be quiet about Sasha's driver's license."

Getting up, Greyson begins to pace. He holds his head as his skin turns crimson. His breathing is labored, too.

"Calm down. She's obviously doing better."

The veins bulge in his neck while he pulls at his hair, and before I can stop him, his fist connects to a wall in my family room. I'm not sure which is louder, the punch or his ferocious yell. For fuck's sake.

"Greyson, get it together."

"She deserves better than how I've treated her. I won't touch her again."

"You have the power to end this nonsense with Whitney, but I'm beginning to think you like the safety net."

"Fuck you. I have to get out of here, so tell Sasha something came up with work and give her a ride home."

Camilla

"What a day," I say as I take off my earrings and lay them in a tray on Ellis's dresser. "Greyson must've been angry with me if he'd leave Sasha here like that." I turn around to face Ellis while he reads in bed.

"It wasn't you. I told him what happened to Sasha when she was younger to be certain he wouldn't string her along. He promised he wouldn't say anything to her, but the news upset him."

"I understand why you told."

He removes his reading glasses. "I was surprised over how angry he became. We now have a hole in the wall of the family room, so that's why I kept you and Liam out of there today. I'm sure our inquisitive child would've asked about it."

"He punched the wall?"

"I think he honestly cares for Sasha. I've never seen him that enraged."

"It doesn't matter how he feels about her if he's still going to marry Whitney. Oh, shoot, I forgot to take my pill." I walk into the bathroom and open the drawer to where I keep my birth control.

I moved them to Ellis's bathroom since I'm sleeping in his room now. I rummage through the drawer, but they're nowhere to be found, so I hurry back into the bedroom.

"My pills aren't in the drawer. Do you think Liam found them?"

"He's never in here alone. You probably moved them. Did you check the other bathroom?" He puts his glasses back on and stares at his book.

"I'm sure they were in that drawer." Starting to doubt myself, I go back to the bathroom and search the entire vanity.

"Maybe I should wake Liam to be certain he didn't take them. I mean, what if he thought they were candy?" I rub my forehead.

"Camilla, calm down. I'm sure they'll turn up."

"It's not like an aspirin for a headache, Ellis. I have to take them every day or they're pointless. I'm going to search his room. I'll be right back."

Only turning on the bathroom light, I quietly check the drawers of Liam's vanity and then various spots throughout his bedroom. Thankfully, I don't find them, but not knowing their whereabouts is driving me crazy. It doesn't make sense. No one else would touch them.

Or would they? No, surely not. We swore there'd be no more secrets between us. No deceit of any kind. After turning off Liam's light and tucking him in better, I head back to our bedroom. I close the door behind me and lean back against it.

"Ellis, please look at me." His eyes tilt up from his book. "Did you move my birth control pills?" Blowing out a breath, he removes his readers and tosses them on the bed.

"Why would I do that?"

"Answer me. Did you take my pills?" Slamming his book shut, he gets out of bed and stalks over to me. Shit, he's mad I accused him. His hands press to the door at each side of my head, and I peer up at him as he towers above me.

"Yes. I took them."

"Why?"

"You know why. I want you to have my babies." Hearing him say babies is heart-melting, but the fact he hid my birth control or disposed of it is whacked.

"I want to have your children, but not until we're married, which we haven't even discussed. We promised there would be no more secrets between us."

"I know, but I was hoping you would say heck with it after all the trouble you've had getting birth control, and then I wouldn't have to tell you what I did."

"All the trouble I've had... Oh, my god, you're the reason my appointments were cancelled." I attempt to push him away, but he grips my waist with his strong hand while his other continues to cage me in.

His bare torso is right in front of me, all powerful and sexy, and I'm mad that I'm noticing.

"Yes, that was my doing, but you were keeping secrets then, too."

"I think you're learning from Liam instead of the other way around. Look at you, trying to talk yourself out of trouble."

He flashes a devilish smile. "Is it working?"

"This is a serious matter." I cross my arms. "I think you're trying to get me pregnant so I won't have a career."

He scowls. "Please ... having kids didn't stop my mother from working."

"I don't know how many times I need to tell you that I'm not going to abandon you or our children. I would never put a job or dream before my family since having a family was my most desired dream of them all."

Kissing my forehead, he clasps my chin. "I told you I didn't want any barriers between us."

"That's not a barrier."

"If it's preventing what would naturally occur, then it's a barrier."

"OK, but we're not even married."

"We're not married *yet*. Once you and Liam filled this house with laughter and a joy I'd never experienced before, I knew I wanted a big family, and I want it with you."

"You're sweet and irresistible, and it's frustrating at times."

"I'm sorry I was dishonest, but after Tony died young, I realized how short life could be. I'm getting closer to forty every day. If we're having a bunch of babies, we need to get on it."

"A bunch? You're incorrigible, like a spoiled child who always wants his way."

He slides his hand in my hair and grips it.

"Are you looking for a punishment, my Rose?"

"I think you need the punishment." Ducking his head, he licks my ear. "OK, my punishment is that I have to eat your pussy."

"You enjoy it, so it's hardly a punishment." I'm instantly aroused by his dirty talk, so I trail my fingers down his chest. "Besides, we can't make babies if you're not inside me, too."

Leaning back, Ellis peers down at me with a pleased gleam in his eyes.

"I knew you wanted to make more little geniuses with me."

"I do, but only as a married woman."

He kisses my lips. "That makes two of us." Strolling over to his dresser, he digs around in the top drawer. He returns with a ring box, and I gasp, inwardly wanting to squeal.

"I was going to do something special and share this moment with Liam, too, but you need to know right now how serious I am about spending my life with you."

He opens the box and lowers to one knee. "My Rose, will you marry me, grow old with me, and make more phenomenal babies with me?"

"Yes, yes, yes!" I jump on top of him, knocking his feet out from under him. Once he falls to his back, I straddle him and pepper his face with kisses. "I love you, and I can't wait to marry you."

He radiates happiness as he grabs my hand.

"Then let me put the damn ring on your finger."

"Oh, yes, please do." He gets the gorgeous band out of the box and slides it on my wiggling finger. A magnificent round diamond is encircled by smaller ones.

Rose gold prongs are set between them, giving it a floral design. The band is rose gold, as well, and the details of the ring show the sincere thought Ellis put into selecting it.

Once I've admired its beauty, he pulls me snug against him and hugs me. I'm sure my hair's covering his face, but he doesn't care. He holds me tight, kissing me everywhere he can reach.

"I love you, baby. Thank you for saying yes."

Still straddling him, I sit up and grin. "Oh, like your spoiled butt would give me a choice." His eyes widen before he grabs my waist. He tickles me hard, and I squeal loudly.

"You're getting a punishment now for sure." I squeal again, and his laughter warms my heart. Other than the day Liam was born, I've never been happier.

CHAPTER TWENTY-NINE

Sasha

I knock on Greyson's bedroom door and gnaw on my lip while I wait for him to answer. This is the sixth time I've approached his room and the first time I've gotten the nerve to knock.

I hear him come to the door, but it remains closed.

"Greyson, I need to talk to you."

Opening his door, he tilts his head to each shoulder, popping his neck. His blond hair is sticking out in different directions, like he's ran his hands through it, and I have the urge to touch it. He's avoiding eye contact with me, and I don't understand what changed between us.

"What do you need?"

"That's what you have to say? We haven't spoken for three days, so can you at least tell me what I did wrong?"

"You haven't done anything wrong, Sasha. I'm trying to sort some shit out."

"Maybe I could help. Will you come talk to me in the living room?" I coax him with a smile.

"All right." He follows me, and we both sit on the couch. Facing him, I rest my bended leg on the cushion. As he tents his fingers at his stomach, he lets his head fall back.

"Did my happiness over our time at the cabin scare you off?"

"That's not it." He stares above him, so I use the moment to admire him in the grey athletic shorts and white t-shirt he changed into after he came home from work.

"Was our kiss bad? I mean, did it make you realize I'm just one of the guys?" I poke his arm, needing to lighten the mood.

Leaving his head on the cushion, he turns it and looks at me. Reaching his hand out, he hooks a piece of my hair around his finger.

"If you're a dude, then I've developed a vagina allergy, too, because that kiss was fucking amazing."

I snicker. "I knew you were still in there. Where have you been the last few days?"

"Trying to stay away from you." Sighing, he lets go of my hair and drops his hand to the couch.

"My sister told you to leave me alone, didn't she?"

"Yes, but she had a right to."

"I'm an adult. She needs to butt out of my business."

"She cares, Sasha, and there's nothing wrong with that."

Grabbing his hand, I thread our fingers. "I've never felt more alive as I did when you kissed me, and all I've thought about since is how I want you to do it again."

"I can't be selfish any longer."

"I give you my permission." Climbing across the couch, I force myself onto his lap. I straddle him and place his hands on my hips. He squeezes them, and a heady sound rumbles from his chest. "I'm asking you to kiss me. That is if you want to."

"Fuck, you have no idea how bad I want to." Grabbing the back of my head, he pulls me to him and kisses me passionately. Our tongues collide, and the exhilarating sensations I've craved for days roll over my body.

He gets hard beneath me, and I start to freeze up, but I manage to stop the knee-jerk reaction. No, I want Greyson. I want to feel his touch and taste his mouth.

Coming up for air, he nips at my bottom lip and groans. I move his hand over the top of my shirt, but he doesn't respond. He's staring at my breasts, growing even harder beneath me.

He glances up. "Are you sure?"

"I trust you, and I want you to touch me." Without further hesitation, he squeezes my breast and buries his face against my neck. Sucking and nipping, he trails kisses around to the front of my throat. My head falls back, giving him room to explore.

Grabbing the bottom of my top, he pulls it over my head and unhooks my bra in only a second. He tosses it aside and palms both my breasts, causing me to whimper.

"Your tits are sensational." He holds them as if he's feeling the weight of them. His tongue swirls around my nipple before he sucks on it, and experiencing a new depth of pleasure, I rub against his erection, the act uncontrollable and spine-tingling.

His pelvis lifts to meet mine, too, and I believe I may come from the friction alone.

"I need more," I mutter. In a swift move, he loops an arm around my waist and lays me over on my back. He grips the arm of the couch as he sucks on my nipple and grazes his fingers down my stomach.

I flinch, so he tilts his eyes up at me. "Are you OK?"

"Yes."

Out of breath, he looks down at my body, and the corner of his mouth lifts.

"I still don't see your other tattoo. Does that mean it's farther south?" Biting my lip, I lower one side of my leggings to show him the outlined tiny heart on my pelvis. "I like it, but I expected something more colorful from you."

"Once I've ... you know, reached that point of trust again, I'll finish it. It will mean I'm healing. My hope is that I can add one man's name inside it and feel confident that he's the only man who will ever see it."

He traces the heart as he faintly kisses my lips, and I'm ready to take another step with him. I'm desperate to feel his fingers inside me.

"Please, touch me." Dipping his hand into my leggings and panties, he sinks his fingers inside me. His eyes snap shut as he exhales a hiss.

"So fucking perfect." My first reaction is to resist, so my muscles squeeze, and as if he senses my tension, he presses gentle kisses to my chest. My breathing is strangled as I attempt to calm myself. You trust him, Sasha. You can handle this.

As his fingers move in and out of me gingerly, the tingling sensations dance along my nerve endings, the feeling more intense than I've ever experienced. I abandon all fear and allow the pleasure to take hold.

"You're dripping wet. I can't take it, Ladybug. Come on my fingers."

The pumping of his hand and his naughty words push me over the cusp, and I dive head first into a pool of pleasure. My nails dig into his bicep and waist as my body spasms beneath his. The colors behind my eyes are a psychedelic trip, an unparalleled high.

Dropping onto me, he buries his face at my neck, and I jerk my head back to find room for more breaths. His hand skims along my curves and back up again.

"Make love to me," I whisper.

"Now that you're sober, that's sacred, Sasha. Save it for someone special."

Grabbing his shoulders, I push him upward to lift his head and chest.

"You're special to me."

"Don't forget weird." Climbing off me, he sits on the couch.

"I'm being serious. I couldn't give my body to anyone else, and I don't want to leave you sexually frustrated," I add.

"It won't be the first or last time."

Self-conscious that I'm partly naked, I cross my arms and sit up to grab my shirt.

"That was amazing. The colors I saw were like a bag of Skittles."

He shakes his head and drags his gaze away from my breasts before I pull my shirt over my head.

"I'm surprised you have teeth left after all the sugar you consume."

"Speaking of sugar, do you want some tea? I made more today. We could junk out and watch our show. That always makes me feel better."

"Sure."

I brush the side of his hair with my fingers.

"If you're upset about Camilla, please don't be. She forgets I'm an adult. I'm often naïve, but not about what's happening between us. Remember, I'm Podunk and you're Fiji. We're not of the same caliber, and I can accept that."

Grabbing my hands, he squeezes them between his.

"That's bullshit."

"Are you saying your family would accept me?" His eyes avert to the floor. "That's what I thought." Pulling my hands free, I use my fingers to lift his mouth into a smile. "Now, stop frowning and help me get the snacks."

"You're a class act, Sasha. Far better than the bitches I've been subjected to all my life."

Ellis

"Ellis, what a pleasant surprise," Uncle Rich says in his Texas accent after opening the door of his home. His ranch in Evergreen sits on a sprawling 450 acres.

He met my aunt Mary Ann while in Texas on business, and once they married, he began working for her father's oil company. He could never call Texas home, though, and it's why he has the ranch here, where Lawrence and Greyson were raised.

"Hi, Uncle Rich. Do you have time to discuss something with me?"

"I do, but for you, I'd make time regardless. It's a nice day out. What do you say we sit on the patio?"

"Sounds good." I follow him through the house and out the back door. For as far as you can see, it's pasture and fencing. The day's a little warm for jeans and a button-up shirt, so I roll up my sleeves after I take a seat at the table.

"You never drop in on a weekday like this. Is something wrong?"

"Maybe. It's about Greyson."

As Rich sit's up straighter, I eye his wide silver belt buckle. His forehead wrinkles, and he rubs his thumb and finger together nervously.

"Please tell me he's not back on drugs."

"No, he's not."

"Oh, what a relief. He's not been himself lately."

"I agree, and I believe it's because of his relationship with Whitney Peterson, or lack thereof."

"What do you mean?"

"Uncle Rich, you must know he has no desire to marry her."

Looking out over the fields, he taps his fingers on the arm of his chair.

"I'm aware, but sometimes we have to do things that benefit our family. This union is about something much greater than any of us individually."

"From the research I've done, Gant-Peterson is doing fine without Greyson's help. You already have Lawrence on board."

"I need Greyson because his grandfather said so before his death. It was his dying wish that Greyson marry the Peterson girl."

"I mean no disrespect, Uncle Rich, but I believe your son's happiness should come before Mr. Gant's wishes."

"Ellis, there's more to it than that."

"Then explain it to me. I've been watching Greyson change for some time now. He's headed backward, and the last thing anyone wants is for him to turn to drugs again."

Pulling a lighter and cigar from his shirt pocket, he cuts off the end and lights it. The smoke from it floats up to the umbrella that's shading us from the hot sun.

"I'll tell you, but it stays between us. Maybe you can help me get my son hitched." Inhaling the cigar, he blows out the smoke again.

"Greyson believes all his grandfather's wealth was passed on to his mother and me, but there are two trusts from his estate that were not contained in the will. Greyson doesn't know about them. One is for him, and the other is for me, and they are each worth seventy-five million."

"Each?" I ask.

"Yep, and the only way we get them is if he's married to Whitney at the age of thirty-five. At that time, the money will be disbursed to us."

"So, you don't get your share, either, if he doesn't marry her?"

"Bingo."

"Damn. Why would Mr. Gant do that?"

"He was old-fashioned, and he lived and breathed oil. I'm not his flesh and blood, but the boys are. He wanted to ensure they carry on the business after we're both gone."

"I don't understand why you've kept this from Greyson."

"Lawrence received his trust with no stipulations at the time of Orson's death since he was already working with us. We've been keeping that information from Greyson.

"I mean, how would you feel if you found out your grandfather left you and Tony money, but the only way you received yours was if you married the woman he chose? Not too fair if you ask me, but that was Orson Gant."

While processing the unbelievable news, I stare out at the pasture again and the specks of color from the cattle in the distance.

"With that much money at stake for the both of you, I'm surprised you haven't told Greyson."

"Mary Ann won't let me. She's all about *feelings*, so she thinks it would devastate Greyson to know Lawrence got an inheritance free and clear. I think Orson did it to get back at Greyson for not coming to work for us like his brother did."

"He might think his freedom is worth seventy-five million."

"That's what I'm afraid of. Whitney's been pressing him hard, but it's not working."

"She knows about the money?"

"Her father told her. We knew the dollar signs would pressure her to seal the deal. Our hope has always been that if they marry, Greyson may decide to join the company, too."

"That's definitely not going to happen. He's built a successful business on his own."

"Are you seeing the pickle I'm in?"

"Yeah, and I'm seeing the one I'm in now. You have to tell him. I can't keep a secret like this from him."

"Whitney said he's putting a ring on her finger this week. We'll rush the wedding along, and then when he's thirty-five, he'll get the trust. We'll make him think Lawrence got his inheritance then, too, and the secret will be dead and buried."

"No, you have to tell him or I will."

"I thought you'd understand, considering the amount of money on the table. I was hoping you would nudge him to hurry this wedding up."

Standing from my chair, I shove it under the table.

"Then I guess you don't know me as well as you thought you did, and I see you're not the man I thought you were, either. Goodbye, *Ron*."

CHAPTER THIRTY

Greyson

"I can't believe you wanted to do this in a damn grocery store parking lot," Whitney snaps as she sits down in my vehicle.

In one second of hearing her annoying, pissy voice, my ears feel hot, and my vision clouds. I also imagine myself doing forty to life behind bars.

Shifting to face me better, she tosses her hair back. I notice she's keeping it longer and blonder these days. I hold out the small bag from the jewelry store.

"Here's my *leash*. I'll marry you under three conditions." Rolling her eyes, she swipes the bag from me and looks inside for the ring box.

"Let's hear them," she says rudely.

"One, I'm not proposing. You can put that ring on your own damn finger. Two, you better never have a man in my bed. Do that shit elsewhere. Three, we're not having children."

"Greyson, you know I've always wanted babies."

"Not happenin'. I'm not raising kids in a loveless, dysfunctional marriage."

Pressing her palms to her face, Whitney bursts into tears. Fucking hell.

"Do you think I want to be in a loveless marriage any more than you do?" she asks, jerking her hands down to scowl at me.

"Uh, yeah, seeing how you snatched that bag from me."

"I have the same pressure from my family as you do from yours. Probably more so since my father didn't have a son. He's counting on me marrying you so that Gant-Peterson Oil stays half Peterson once he's gone. That requires us having children, Greyson."

"How did we get to this place?"

"We got here from you not accepting the inevitable like I did."

Leaning my head back against the seat, I turn it toward her.

"You love him, don't you?"

"Who?"

"Sebastian. I hear the rumors."

Shaking her head, she digs for a tissue in her purse.

"It doesn't matter how I feel about him."

"It should. We could take a stand together. We'll sit down our parents and tell them we're not getting married. End of story. Leave us the hell alone."

"Daddy has given me everything. I'm not breaking my promise to him." Wiping the last of her tears, she sits up straight. "OK, so to speed this along, we're going to have an engagement party at your parents' ranch in one month. There's no way I could get a venue that fast.

"However, I did get us a cancellation for the wedding venue. It's in October, and I'll keep you up to date with emails." Pulling the ring box out, she opens it. "This isn't my fairytale engagement, but I'm sure the wedding will be spectacular."

"Get out of my car, and please get some professional help before the ceremony."

"You're such an asshole. I can't believe I have to put up with you for the next fifty years."

"Oh, please. I'm sure you'll smother me in my sleep long before then. I can dream, anyway!" I yell as she slams my door. "My fucking life!" I scream before I pound my fist on the steering wheel.

Sasha

After Greyson touched me on the couch, we spent several days enjoying each other's company, but then he began to withdraw again.

He's been distant for over a week now. A conversation every couple of days is all we share. There have been no laughs and absolutely no touching.

I do catch him watching me from the living room or at work. His eyes give away his feelings, but it doesn't matter if he isn't acting on them. I guess he wised up and saw the truth, too; we're from two different planets.

I'm heating up some dinner when the doorbell startles me. Who could that be? I wipe my hands on a towel and stroll to it. Through the peephole, I see her. Shit, it's Whitney. I debate on not answering since Greyson's not home, but the curiosity over what she's doing here gets the best of me.

"Hi," I say once I open the door.

"Hi, I'm Whitney."

"Yes, I remember. How did you get up here?" I peek around her.

She hugs her hip. "Do you honestly think I wouldn't have the passcode to my fiancé's place?"

My eyes flit to the hand on her curvy hip. The largest, shiniest rock my eyes have ever seen is on her finger. It's even bigger than the one Ellis gave Camilla.

"That's right. We're engaged, so you need to get the fuck out of his house since it's pretty much mine, too."

Tears come, so I blink several times to hide them.

"Aww, were you really so naïve to think Greyson would settle for someone like you?"

Lifting my gaze from the rock on her hand, I glare at her.

"No, I didn't think that, but I see he did indeed settle. I'm at peace with Greyson's decision since unlike you, I want to marry a man who can't see himself with anyone else.

"A man who will love me from the moment we say I do until we take our last breaths. I'm holding out for that kind of love. It doesn't have a price tag on it like that rock on your finger. I hope you love being surrounded by material things since you're going to be alone in every other way."

The elevator doors open, and Greyson charges toward us.

"Leave now," he yells at Whitney. "I told you not to come here." He looks at me with pleading eyes. "Sasha, I'm sorry. I should've told you about the engagement. I tried to beat her here when she told me what she was doing."

"It's fine. We had an enlightening discussion. I'll be in my room packing." I slam the door in their faces and run to my room. I will not cry–I will not cry. I knew this was the likelier outcome, but I guess I believed he'd have the decency to tell me himself.

I'm a little surprised when he doesn't come to my room, but then again, we both know it's time for me to move on. I stuff my suitcases, but having purchased more clothing, I can't fit them all inside. Maybe Camilla will get the rest for me.

I was so happy for her when she showed me her engagement ring, and I couldn't help but imagine being that in love one day myself.

Ellis cherishes her and Liam, but I'm not her. She's special, and like always, I'm the girl who can be used and then tossed aside. It's nothing new.

Once I'm packed up, I call an Uber driver for a ride. I drag my suitcases out to the foyer, and Greyson appears.

"Can we talk?"

"There's nothing to say."

"There's so much to say."

"The dazzling diamond on your fiancée's hand pretty much summed it up. I'm giving my two-week notice effective immediately. I would appreciate it if you didn't speak to me at work."

"You have a good job. Don't quit."

"I have a boring job, so I'll find another. All my belongings wouldn't fit in my suitcases, so I'll have Camilla get them later. The keys to the BMW are on the nightstand."

"Take the car."

"It's not mine." He sticks an envelope out in front of me. Spotting the cash in it, I push it away. "That's not mine, either."

"Yes, it is. Ellis gave it to you with the other money. I, uh, I didn't tell you about it." His fingers bend and fold the envelope as he stares at it.

"Why?"

"Because I worried you'd use it to rent your own place, and I didn't want you to go. I still don't want you to go." He lifts his eyes, and from the tears washing over them, they truly look like the glistening ocean.

"Says the man who proposed to another woman."

"I didn't ask her."

"This is ridiculous. I can't stay here." I start toward the door, but Greyson grabs my arm. "Stop!" I snap. "We both know what you're wishing for ... what you hope will gradually happen, but I refuse to let it.

"If you believe all the affirmations you've given me about how special I am and how I'm worthy of greatness, then you'll tell me to go instead of hoping I'll stay to become your dirty little secret."

Clearing his throat, he lowers his chin to his chest.

"I'd never ask that of you, and I'm sorry ... for everything."

"I'm not. I'm grateful for having met you, for the help you've given me, and for all that you've taught me about myself." I blink fast to see through my tears. "I only wish you saw your worth, too. I love you, Greyson. Your name will forever be inscribed on my heart."

CHAPTER THIRTY-ONE

Ellis

"This better be good. I don't do nightclubs," I say to Lawson as I sit next to him at a noisy bar.

"Humor me. I'm keeping an eye on someone here."

"I also don't like explaining to my fiancée why I need to go out at eleven o'clock at night."

"Well, congratulations on the engagement," he says as he slides a glass tumbler across the table. "Drinks are on me."

I eye the amber liquid, tempted to numb myself amid a room full of gyrating asshats, but I don't plan on sticking around.

Reaching in the inside pocket of his tan blazer, he removes a flash drive and hands it to me.

"There's some interesting information on there about your girl's family."

"All right. What about the other stuff we discussed?"

"Mr. Day is going to be brought in for more questioning over Tony's death. If you think of a possible motive, let me know."

"He wanted this painting my brother owned. Suspicious as to why, I opened the frame, and it was loaded with cash and a key to a beach house in the Caribbean."

"Intriguing. Send me the details. As far as the documents you wanted, they're arriving at your home tomorrow by courier." He grins. "I didn't want to bend the pretties. Nice looking ladies you got in your life now."

"Please tell me you cleared Camilla's name."

"Actually, I took it a step further. I hope Clarissa and Sasha Rosenthal don't mind being dead on paper. No one is ever going to look for them again, and there will be no charges on record if somehow Clarissa is found."

I bring my fist to my mouth as the mountainous weight lifts from me.

"I could fucking kiss you right now."

He holds a hand up. "Please don't. It'd be nice to kill two birds with one stone and pick up a chick while I'm here."

"I can't thank you enough, and if there's anything you need, you let me know."

Camilla

"Good morning," I say to Ellis as he trudges into the dining room. He's still in pajama pants and a t-shirt, and I was beginning to wonder if he was joining us, but I know he was out late dealing with something he claimed was top-secret.

"Good morning."

"Hi, Daddy." Liam waves, and I giggle once I notice the jelly all over his face.

"Hi, kiddo. I think it's time you use your napkin." Ellis kisses my temple before he takes his seat at the head of the table. "Good morning, Sasha," he adds.

"Morning," she says. At least she spoke. That's progress from yesterday. Irene brings Ellis his coffee and breakfast.

"Mr. Burke, a package arrived for you this morning. I placed it on the desk in the library."

"Thank you, Irene." The doorbell rings, and I wonder who it could be.

"Stay seated. I'll get it," she says before she hurries from the room.

"Is that Dean?" I ask Ellis.

"No, I cancelled today," he replies without looking up from his plate. I wrap my hand around his wrist.

"Is everything OK?"

"We'll talk about it after breakfast." Emma strolls inside the room, and Liam goes into a frenzy trying to get out of his chair.

"Em!"

"Hi, buddy, what's up?"

"Emma, why are you here today?" Her eyes dart to Ellis's.

"I asked her to spend a few hours with Liam. I want to talk to you and Sasha about something."

I look to my sister, and she gives a lazy shrug, knowing no more than I do on the subject. Since showing up here a couple of days ago, she's been despondent and sad.

She swears she can get through this, but when something has upset her in the past, she turned to drugs. I'm scared I'll look the other way, and she'll disappear on me.

"Liam, do you want to go outside and play, or would you like to go upstairs to your room?"

"Outside. Outside. Outside!" He marches to the doorway like a band conductor, and I wish I had half his energy. Sensing that Ellis would like to eat his breakfast in peace, I turn to Sasha.

"Sis, let's hang out in the family room." As I stand, I squeeze Ellis's hand. "We'll be in there when you're ready to talk." Nodding, he picks up the folded newspaper Irene left for him.

The drapes in the family room are pulled back, allowing in the sunlight. I walk over and peek around the thin sheer curtains hanging between them. Liam is climbing the monkey bars, and I remember that I need to make his eye appointment.

"Cammy, what does Ellis want to talk about?"

"I don't have a clue."

"He's kicking me out, isn't he?" I walk to the couch and sit next to her.

"He wouldn't do that, especially without talking to me first." I run my fingers through her tangled hair. "You can stay here as long as you need."

"I want to go to college."

"Really?"

"Yeah. Do you think I can pass the classes?"

"Sasha, you earned your diploma without even attending high school. I know you can do it, especially with our support. What do you think you want to do at college?"

Gathering her hair, she holds it back like a ponytail.

"I want to get into marketing. I gave Greyson's rep some input on a project, and he said I had great ideas."

I wrap my arm around her back and squeeze her to me.

"That's amazing."

"What's amazing?" Ellis asks.

"Sasha wants to go to college for marketing."

Ellis smiles. "That sounds like a solid plan, and we'll help any way we can."

"Thank you, Ellis. That means a lot."

"Honey, what did you want to talk about?" I ask him as he sits in a chair across from us with a large yellow envelope in his hand.

"I have some news, and I'm unsure of how the two of you will take it."

"What's wrong?" Gliding a hand through his hair, he messes with the back of it and exhales.

"It's about your parents."

"Did they find us?" Sasha asks before she clutches my knee.

"No, that's not it. Actually ... they died."

Silence.

More silence.

His eyes play ping-pong between us as he waits for a response, but I don't know what to say because I don't know how I feel, and if I had to guess, Sasha is waiting for a cue from me to know how the hell she should feel.

"Are you sure?" I ask.

"Yes, and what I'm about to tell you cannot leave this room." He points. "Do you both understand?" Sasha and I nod, but it's as if she's on autopilot. "I have a connection with the FBI. We work together often, helping each other out.

"He's been investigating your parents, and they died two years ago from overdoses. It seems they bought a deadly batch of heroin, and they died within a day of each other at the hospital."

"I don't know what to say or how I feel."

"Same here," Sasha utters.

"I know it's a lot to process, but I have more news. As far as records are concerned, Clarissa and Sasha Rosenthal are no longer alive, either, and regardless of whether you're found by someone from your past, the charges that were brought against you no longer exist. Baby, you never have to worry about being taken away."

Shifting to face me, Sasha clings to my body. She weeps against my chest, and it's not because our parents are dead. It's because she believes we're finally safe. I'm finally free.

After a couple of minutes, she releases me and wipes her eyes, so I go to Ellis and make him stand to hug me. Holding me close, he strokes my hair.

"Thank you," I say.

"You're welcome, but I did it for me, too. I could never let you go without killing someone, and Liam needs his parents."

It's not a giggling moment, but I can't help it since I can envision him physically fighting to keep me here if necessary. He really wouldn't let me go.

He steps back and opens the yellow envelope. Sorting through its contents, he hands me some documents and takes some to Sasha.

"You two are officially Sasha and Camilla Rose."

"I have a passport?" Sasha asks enthusiastically.

"Yep. You need to cut up that old driver's license of yours. You now have all the *legal* documents you need for identification."

Sasha jumps to her feet and hugs Ellis next. Noticeably uneasy at first, he finally relaxes his tense muscles and hugs her back.

"I can't thank you enough for everything you've done for my family, so I'm going to show you by being the best sister-in-law ever." Letting Ellis go, she examines the documents further.

"I'm going upstairs to shower. Cammy, can I use your laptop after? I want to research college programs in the area."

"Sure."

It's sad that she's happier on the day she finds out her parents are deceased than on the one when she moved out of Greyson's home. I hope he gets his head out of his ass and calls off this absurd wedding.

Camilla

Ellis: *You're late.*

Me: *I'm sorry. On my way now.* Shit, he's going to be furious with me, but he needs to understand that sometimes emergencies arise when you're working.

Ellis: *Thanks to your bad behavior, Beatrice had to change out of her pajamas and back into her hideous orthopedic shoes to come stay for the night.*

OK, so he's not furious. Grateful is more like it. I gave him an excuse to take me to the playroom. Not that he needs one; I go when he says to.

"Fletcher, thank you for the ride."

"You're welcome, Ms. Rose." I'm getting out of the car when my phone buzzes again.

Ellis: *Go straight to the playroom, and change into a red negligee. No panties. Put the necklace on yourself, and take the silk blindfold with you to the bed. Once you've put it on, lay flat on your back. Then ... think about what I might do to you or how hard you'll be coming tonight.*

Standing in the driveway, I stare down at my phone. Anticipation unfurls in my belly and travels to between my legs. My thighs clench, and I salivate over what's to come.

It's perfect timing since Sasha is on a trip this weekend that Ellis arranged. It's a retreat for addicts in recovery, and his thoughtfulness still amazes me. We're trying to keep her mind off of Greyson and focused on staying clean. His engagement party is next weekend, and I dread it.

329

Ellis: *Baby, what the hell are you waiting for? Do as your told, or I'm adding spankings to the list of evening activities.*

Sucking in a breath, I look around for a camera on the house, certain he's watching me, but I can't find one, so I walk to the door and let myself in.

I drop my purse on the entryway table and head straight to the door at the back of the house, which will lead me to our hideaway.

The anxiety builds with each step, and I lose my breath momentarily as I reach the playroom and eye the blindfold and necklace that are laid out on the dresser. Even the bedding is pulled back, leaving only the fitted sheet and pillows waiting for me.

Envisioning him in this room, preparing for my arrival and fantasizing about what's to come, leaves me more eager, so I hurry and change my clothes. In the bathroom, I freshen up a bit, wishing I had time for a shower first.

Once I've put on the necklace, I take the blindfold and do as he instructed. I tie it tight and stretch out on the bed. Now, I wait. Is he watching me here, too? How will he know when to come in?

The suspense makes me wetter, and I feel the silky negligee grazing against my hard nipples. What's he going to do with me today?

The door ... I think I hear it open and close. My heart beats like a race horse on speed as he steps inside the playroom.

God, the blindfold is more than I can handle. I want to see his eyes and the way he's dressed. Is he only wearing sweats?

Is he in a button-up and khakis? Either way, he's my Dom, authoritative and electric, handsome and chiseled.

"I see you're capable of following *some* instructions."

"Sir, may I explain why I was late?"

"You may."

"This woman showed up five minutes before we were going to close the pantry, and she was holding her little girl's hand, and my heart hurt for them. I had to stay after and help her. I even considered bringing them home."

"Lord, your compassion is going to be the death of me. I'm running out of bedrooms."

"But you love me, Sir."

His warm lips press to mine, and my desire forces me to exhale a long, throaty sound.

"I do love you, and I lust you, as well. Let's play." I'm strangled by his smooth, collected voice and his breath on my skin. I feel his hair next on my chin as his mouth dips into the hollow of my throat and skims down it.

He moves away, and I hear him open a dresser drawer. There's the sound of a zipper next, followed by the thud of his shoes hitting the floor.

"You're coming first tonight since you're such a compassionate woman." The bed sinks as he joins me on it, and my body shudders with exhilaration. Something faint touches my shoulder, causing me to flinch.

The item brushes my cheek next, and I can't resist scratching my face. "There's a reason I don't want to tie up your hands, so do your best to remain still."

"Yes, Sir."

"Do you know what I'm touching you with?"

"No, Sir."

"It's a long black feather. It's the only thing I'll be touching you with before you come. You're struggling to breathe, baby."

"I'm excited and nervous, Sir." The feather skirts down one arm … then the other. Trembling, I clench my thighs together. "I bet you're dripping already. Touch yourself. Sink your fingers inside your pussy, and tell me how wet you are."

My head falls back as his words wrap around my lungs and squeeze. I open my legs, and stick my fingers inside. They slide right in, and I sigh from the sensation. "Now, let me see them."

Clearing my throat, I pull them out and hold them up. "They're glistening wet. Since I'm only touching you with the feather, you'll have to taste them for me."

My breath hitches, and at once I'm relieved I'm wearing the blindfold. "Put them in your mouth, and suck your juices off. Do it now." His commanding, dirty words are enough foreplay for me. I wish he'd fuck me already.

I slide my fingers in and taste my arousal. Wanting to please him, I gradually drag my lips from the bottom up, and the guttural sound he makes encourages me to prolong the show.

"Fuck, what you do to me can't be explained." I feel the feather again as it roams over my breasts. It teases my nipples, and they throb against the satin of my negligee. The agony of waiting to come is more than I can bear. God, how I need to come.

"Slide your hands over the fabric, and play with your nipples, too." He brushes the feather along my legs as I savor the feel of the silk on my skin and the way my fingertips pinch my nipples.

As I grope my tits, I feel his gaze on me and picture his hard cock. I imagine his eyes smoldering while I flick at my stiff nipples and fist the nighty at my waist.

Parted lips.

Heaving breaths.

Toes curling against the mattress.

"Fuck, there's nothing more beautiful than you like this." Groaning, he taunts the inside of my lower legs, my inner thighs, and my pelvis as I choke the satin with my hand and flick my nipples.

My moans escape, but the weight of the pleasure brings them back like the tide. I exhale them again, each one longer and more audible than the last, the yearning a surge from deep within me.

"Yes ... more...." I whisper. The feather tickles the bottoms of my feet and along my shins. My hands move under my nighty, caressing and squeezing my breasts as the feather skims over my upper arms and top of my chest. "I'm so wet. I'm so–so ..."

"Ready to come. Wrap your fingers around your necklace, Camilla."

Leaving one hand to play with my nipple, I grab hold of the necklace. I'm begging for a release like I'm begging for air.

"Come, my Rose. Come now."

An orgasm ricochets through me, shattering me like bullets on glass. I'm fisting the necklace–clenching my breast and digging my heels in the bed, much like the ecstasy's digging its claws in me, its strength unrelenting.

Ellis jerks off my blindfold, so I snap my eyelids shut. He shoves between my legs and plunges inside of me. Grabbing the headboard behind me, he lifts one of my legs, straightening it between us. It allows him more room to pound into me, to go deeper, to claim the last of my energy.

He's merciless in his thrusts, and my head beats against the bed. He's stretching my leg, pinning me between him and the headboard like a pretzel.

So turned on, it doesn't take him long to erupt inside me. He sinks deeper, the pulsing powerful as his hand clamps around my ankle and his forehead presses against it.

The heat radiates off our skin, and air whips from our lungs. Every time I think our souls couldn't be more tightly woven, I'm mistaken. Lowering my leg, he falls beside me and grips the front of his hair.

"I want to believe I'm controlling you, but it's all a façade." Rolling to his side, he kisses my shoulder. "There's an invisible collar around my neck that's tethered to you, Camilla. I'm irrevocably yours."

CHAPTER THIRTY-TWO

Sasha

I'm in the family room, trying not to listen to Ellis and Camilla talk about me down the hall. Irritated that he has to attend Greyson's engagement party alone, he's still trying to convince her to go.

I told her I'm fine alone, but she won't budge, which means I was likely moved off the Ellis nice list, considering how severe his social anxiety is.

My phone buzzes in my lap, startling me. Holy shit– Greyson. I flip my phone over on my thigh to hide the screen. I don't know if I can handle a text from him. Why the hell is he texting me an hour before his party? Maybe ... just maybe. I turn over my phone.

Greyson: *Tell me what a mistake I'm making.*

Figures. I'm not begging. He already knows it's a mistake, but he's a coward and doesn't want to step outside the only world he's known. The only relationship he's known.

I had to live with parents who pimped me out for drugs. All he has to do is tell his parents he wants to marry someone for love. I guess things are only as bad as what you've known.

Me: *No, and you're an asshole for texting me tonight.*

Greyson: *Then please, tell this asshole something funny.*

I envision my phone flying through the picture window in front of me. My anger spills over in the form of tears, but it's anger over how I *can't* be angry at him. He was my friend first, and no matter how big of a penis he's being, I'll always owe him my life.

Me: *Considering the lavish party I imagine you're attending, I suggest eating the fish eggs on crackers. I hear it's a party in your mouth.*

Greyson: *You lie, woman. I've already had caviar, and it tastes like cat food and ass.*

I bust out laughing but sigh once I picture his dimples that wain and leave only his sorrowful eyes.

Me: *OK, then if there's red velvet cake, have a bite for me. It's even better than a party of fish eggs. It's truly Christmas in your mouth.*

Greyson: *Sasha ... I miss you.*

Covering my mouth, I squeeze my eyelids shut, but my stupid eyes leak, anyway. I muffle my sob with my hand and find my strength to reply.

Me: *Someone once told me to be the daring eagle who spreads his wings and soars above the clouds. Maybe you should take his advice. Be daring, Greyson. I hear there are rainbows and unicorns up there ... maybe Skittles, too.*

Shutting off my phone, I say a prayer that he never contacts me again.

Greyson

I pace in my old bedroom at my parents' home. It's like a college dorm room in here, and at this moment, I'm spiraling out of control like I was back in those days. What I wouldn't give for a drug-induced escape.

Sasha ... fuck, I miss her. While texting her, I could picture her smiling face and those golden-brown eyes. I could also imagine the pain I was causing her, and I hate myself for it, but I don't only want her like before; now, I need her.

So, I was a selfish prick yet again and stole another perfect moment with her. I never dreamed when I met her that she'd end up teaching me how to live ... or how to love.

I hear voices in the hall. I'm sure Whitney's grating tone will be next as she hunts me down. I should've picked a better hiding place.

Deciding I need a longer reprieve, I sneak out and head toward my father's study. As I start to open the door off the hallway, I hear him inside talking to Ellis.

"You tell him about the money right now, or I'm doing it."

"Fine, but it's not going to change a damn thing other than piss him off. He's not gonna give up seventy-five million dollars, especially when he learns I have to do the same."

"It's his decision to make."

I swing open the door. "What decision is mine to make? And what's this about seventy-five mill."

"Close the door," Dad says before he tugs on his black cowboy hat.

"Tell me what's going on."

"I came to see Uncle Rich recently to convince him that you shouldn't be expected to marry Whitney, and he told me something he's been hiding."

"Now, son, I had good reason."

"I'll be the judge of that. What is it?"

"Your grandfather Orson left a trust for you that wasn't connected to the will. You'll receive seventy-five million dollars when you're thirty-five, but *only* if you're married to Whitney."

"Damn, that's a lot of money. A ton of money." I narrow my eyes on him. "Why didn't you tell me?"

"Your mother thought it'd be too upsetting for you to know Orson pulled a stunt like this, especially once you found out Lawrence got his inheritance when your grandfather died."

I begin to pace the floor. "Let me guess. He put conditions on mine because I didn't join Gant-Peterson, and you've been pressuring me to marry Whitney so I'll inherit the money."

"Yes, but also so *I'll* inherit money. As added insurance that you'd go through with the wedding, he set up a trust for me in the same amount, but I don't get my share, either, unless you marry Whitney."

"Seventy-five million dollars. Fuck, that's so much money."

"But you have millions of dollars, and you can make more. You're great at what you do," Ellis says.

I look at my father with disgust. "If this decision wasn't fucking hard enough, you just made it seventy-five million times harder."

Unable to breathe, I rip off my tie.

"Son, I'll make a deal with you. Marry the Peterson girl. If after you get the money, you're still not in love with her, then I'll accept you getting a divorce. Just don't tell the Petersons I said that because I'll deny every word."

"Do you hear yourself?" I ask. "Do you even care if I'm happy like you and Mom?"

"You can divorce her in about five years. I don't think that's too long of a marriage for this kind of payout. Find some pussy on the side until then. After the divorce, you can marry for love."

Ellis rubs his forehead. "I can't believe the respect I've held for you all these years."

"Oh, don't give me that horseshit. If you hadn't fallen in love with Camilla, you'd be telling him to take the money, too."

"You're probably right. I can admit that, but now I see what's important, and that's partly because I have a son. I'd never expect him to make this choice, and you shouldn't expect it from Greyson, either. You're a billionaire, for christ's sake. How greedy is this family?"

Ellis clutches his hips. "I can't stay here and pretend this engagement's OK when I have Camilla at home holding Sasha together. You love her, so do the right thing here.

"If you don't, next you'll be working at Gant-Peterson and having kids with a woman you don't love while you're both whoring your way through Denver. I'll be at home, and so will Sasha." Ellis marches past me, and I look to the ceiling.

"He's not saying you love that junkie you had living with you, is he? Whitney told me all about her." I charge across the room, forcing my father to step back until he's against his desk.

I point in his face. "She's *not* a junkie. You don't know shit about her."

"Exactly. I don't know anything about her or her family. She's nobody, son. Whitney's gorgeous, educated and a Peterson. Don't you want to be a part of the Gant-Peterson empire?"

I shake my head. "No, Dad, I don't. I love the business I've built, and if Orson were here, I'd tell him to shove his money up his ass.

"If you're going to stay angry with me for not adding millions to your existing billions, then tell me now so I know to never walk through that door again, but right now, I'm going to get my girl."

I leave my father alone, and as I reach the end of the hallway, Whitney rounds the corner.

"There you are. I've been looking all over for you. The wedding planner wants to announce us and welcome everyone."

"We need to talk." Grabbing her arm, I drag her into my mother's sewing room. "I can't marry—"

"Oh, no, no, no." Her arms come up. "You don't get to do this now."

"Listen to me." I take her hands in mine, but she yanks them away. Her eyes are round, her mouth agape.

"Greyson, please don't."

"Did you know about the trust Orson left me?"

"You know?"

"Why didn't you tell me?"

"Our parents made me promise not to, but I swear I don't only want the money."

"It doesn't matter. All I care about right now is calling off this phony engagement." Grabbing her hands again, I hold them tight as tears pool in her eyes.

"I know it's going to be humiliating, but screw all those people out there. Don't worry about what they think. Only focus on what you want, and I know I'm not it."

"But Daddy will think I failed him."

"He won't. He loves you more than anything. I'll take the blame and tell the wedding planner I called it off. Go be with Sebastian. I know he's who you want."

Before she can object again, I kiss her forehead and leave her alone, for good this time.

Camilla

"I want to put the sprinkles on the cookies," Liam announces as he reaches up for a jar of them on the island. Handing them to him, I snicker over how cute he is in his little brown glasses.

He hated them and kept removing them on the way home, but once Ellis told him they were his super powers and would make him see better than anyone else on the planet, he was sold.

That earned Ellis not only brownie points but the real brownies I'm making for him right now. I'm sure he'll be a bear when he gets home from the engagement party this evening, so I'm hoping sweets will help turn his mood around.

Liam jogs over to the dinette set we've covered in a few different kinds of cookies. If my kid gets his way, there'll be bright sprinkles on each one of them.

In her tiny denim shorts, Sasha's sitting in a chair with her foot propped up on the seat. I can hear her music from her earbuds as she stares out the kitchen window. She's twirling a piece of her hair that's fallen from her messy bun.

I tap her shoulder. "Sis, are you OK?"

She turns to face me. "Like the last ten times you asked, I'm good. I need to stay busy, is all." Removing one earbud, she finds a smile for Liam. "Do you want help putting on the sprinkles?"

The doorbell rings.

"I wanna answer it," he yells before he hands her the jar. "Here, you do it, but don't put them on the chocolate chip ones. Those are Boss-Daddy's, and he told me no sprinkles." He gives her a look of warning I've seen too often from his father.

"Liam, wait for me," I call out as he runs from the kitchen. Maybe it's one of the security men needing something. With both hands on the knob, Liam pulls the door back, and Emma steps right in.

There's a look of horror on her face, and then I see them— the gun and Christopher. He shoves her forward and snatches Liam right up in his arms.

"Liam!" Emma screams as I charge toward them. Chris jerks the gun up to Liam's temple, so I freeze.

"Don't even think about it. Both of you, get back now." Emma cries, and I fight not to do the same.

"Chris, what are you doing? I know you don't want to harm him."

"Momma." Whimpering, Liam strains his head back to look at Christopher.

"You're right. I don't want to hurt him, but I will if I have to, so you're going to do exactly as I say if you want him back."

"Camilla, I'm so sorry," Emma says through her tears. "He came to my apartment and forced me to drive here so he could get through the gate."

"Why don't you let Emma take Liam upstairs, and you and I can talk this out."

He sneers, "Do you think I'm that stupid?"

"I only want to help. Something's wrong with you, Chris, and we'll get you the mental help that you need."

"There's not a damn thing wrong with me. I'm here to get what's rightfully mine."

"What's that? Is it money? I'll call Ellis—"

"Don't reach for your phone!" he yells, pointing the gun in my direction.

I hold my hands up. "OK, what if I go to the bank with you? I have a lot of money in my account."

He laughs. "You don't have the kind of money I'm looking for. Now, listen to me. I'm taking Liam, and then I'm going to call Ellis with instructions on how to get me the money. If he does what I say, I'll leave Liam somewhere safe and sound."

Covering my mouth, I envision the worst.

"No, Christopher. Please, I'll do anything you ask. Ellis will pay a ransom for me, too. I know it, so take me instead."

"Mommy!" Liam stretches his arms out for me, but Chris only brings him in closer as he takes steps backward.

"No, Ellis deserves to feel the pain of missing his child, wondering if he'll get him back. You screwed up everything by going to that funeral home.

"If you'd listened to me, we'd be on a fucking island right now with a mountain of cash. Oh, wait, no, you screwed up that plan long before when you got pregnant by Ellis instead of Tony."

As if he's calming the fury within him, he closes his eyes for a second and shakes his head. The pistol is bouncing by Liam's head again, and I'm dying inside.

"You know, I killed Tony so you'd collect the inheritance for Liam, but you fucked up everything by being a slut. You didn't want me. No, you had your eyes set on the money, too.

"I wasted years orchestrating that plan. My brother had it so fucking good compared to me, and I deserved my share."

"I can get you your share."

"Shut up! He was supposed to leave it all to Liam, and he even lied to me about that, giving Ellis everything instead. He never accepted me as a brother."

My son cries from Chris's thundering voice. Emma's sobbing next to me, and I'm trying to stay upright to process Christopher's confession and a way out of this nightmare.

Sasha.

Maybe she called the police. Liam begins kicking his legs, trying to free himself, so Chris backs up even closer to the door.

"You're not leaving with him!" I shout.

"I don't need you to make this happen. With you out of the picture, Ellis will be even more determined to get his son back."

My hands ball into fists, and I squint. "With me out of the picture, he'll find you and kill you."

Pulling the gun away from Liam's temple, he points it straight at me.

"Bye, bitch."

Sasha. I see her hair as she steps in front of me.

A gunshot.

Sasha falls.

Someone's grabbing Christopher.

It's all happening so fast.

The gun slides across the marble, and Liam falls from Christopher's arms. Screaming in terror, he gets back on his feet and runs at me.

Ellis is behind Chris, squeezing his neck in a choke hold until he drops to the floor with Ellis's arm still around him.

Scooping Liam up, I press him against me. My hand's on the back of his head as I hug him.

So much noise...

So much noise...

Slow, slow motion. Sasha... Why is Sasha on the floor? Why is there blood? There's so much blood.

"Sasha!" Handing Liam off to Emma, I fall to my knees. I roll my sister from her side to her back, and she's bleeding from a wound above her chest. "Sasha. Ellis, Ellis, help me!"

With Christopher out cold, Ellis rushes over.

"Emma, call 911, take Liam to another room, and make sure he's OK," he shouts.

Ripping off his dress shirt, he wads it up and presses it to Sasha's wound. Her eyes slightly open but roll back in her head.

"Sasha, can you hear me?" Spotting blood seeping out from beneath her back, I scream.

"Camilla, Camilla." Ellis grabs my shoulders and shakes me. "You need to stay calm and check her pulse and breathing. Keep pressure on her wound, too. I'm going to check on Liam and get security up here before Christopher comes to."

Nodding, I get it together and keep pressure on Sasha's wound. Her eyelids open halfway, and she tries to speak, but a gurgling sound is all she can manage.

"Sweetie, don't talk. Help's on the way." I stroke her hair as blood soaks through Ellis's shirt and coats my hand. She's lying in a pool of red now, and I don't know what else to do.

Her body begins to shake, so I struggle to hold her still. "You're going to make it, Sasha. Please, keep fighting."

CHAPTER THIRTY-THREE

Greyson

The gate to Ellis's home is wide open, and as soon as I start down the long drive, I see the red and blue flashing lights ahead. Gunning it, I speed toward the house. Two ambulances and three police cars are in the circle drive. Paramedics are moving a stretcher inside, so I race up behind them.

A young cop holds his hand out at the door.

"This is a crime scene. You can't come in here."

"I'm family and gettin' in that house." I shove right past him, and once I'm in the hall, I come up on Ellis and a few police officers who are detaining Christopher as he lies on the floor.

"What happened?"

"Christopher tried to kidnap Liam. I came home and heard him yelling from the other side of the door. I was able to sneak in behind him." I look over at the paramedics who are crowding around someone.

"Who else is hurt?"

Ellis grips the back of his head. "It's Sasha. She was shot." Sprinting across the room, I get to her as she's being loaded onto a stretcher. In tears, Camilla's holding her hand.

"Greyson, she was shot."

"What can I do?"

"Can you ride with her in the ambulance? I need to go with Liam."

"Of course."

Sasha's loaded up in the ambulance, and I demand to ride in the back with her. Her skin is pale, her clothes soaked in blood. No, she can't die. I take her hand in mine.

"Ladybug, can you hear me? I was supposed to be the daring one today, not you."

Sasha opens her eyes, but they close right away. She tries again.

"You're here."

"Yes, and I'm not leaving your side."

***

"How's Sasha?" I ask Ellis and Camilla after they walk into the waiting room.

"She's still in surgery," Camilla replies. "The bullet went in right below her collarbone, so they think she'll pull through."

"And Liam?"

She kisses the top of his head. "He's OK. They don't believe he'll have any permanent hearing loss from the gun firing. As far as emotionally, it's too early to tell.

"I'm worried about Emma, too. I need to call her soon." She nods toward the chairs across the room. "I'll sit over there so you two can talk. Liam needs to sleep."

Bringing his fist up, Ellis eyes the wall. "I should've killed Christopher while I had the chance, but I kept thinking about Liam watching. I was so close, and if I'd done it, we'd never have to worry about the sick fuck again. He admitted to killing Tony."

"Damn. Then he'll be in prison for years if not life."

"True."

"I have to see Sasha. What if I don't get the chance?"

Sitting down next to me, Ellis stretches his legs out in front of him.

"I saw it happen."

"You saw her get shot?"

"She stepped right in front of Camilla to protect her. I was coming in, but I wasn't fast enough."

"What if you hadn't left the party?"

"But I did, and you left, too."

"I wised up and finally grew a pair."

"I'm proud of you."

"You were right about Sasha. I love her. It's the craziest thing. I know we're different in many ways, but she makes me so damn happy. She does the cutest shit. The girl makes sweet tea by the gallon that could rot your teeth. She has a sweet tooth like you, but worse.

"She's obsessed with Justin Bieber and has never been to a concert, so I want to take her to meet him backstage, but I worry he'll like her. What kind of messed-up shit is that? I fear having my girl stolen by the Bieber."

Ellis laughs.

"She's a slob, too, whereas I'm neat. I'm up at five, and she'd sleep until noon, but all the ways she's different make her fucking adorable. I love that she eats purple popsicles and wears shirts that have unicorns and rainbows on them."

My foot taps fast from the adrenaline rush. "She's not trying to be someone she's not, and she only wants me. I guarantee it wouldn't matter if I was broke. She'd be right by my side, telling me everything will be OK and to have a Skittle."

Ellis's eyebrows lift, and I feel my face heat.

"Yeah, I hear myself. I can't help it; I'm lovesick, cuz."

The door opens, and a man wearing scrubs walks in and heads over to Camilla. He looks to be in his thirties, and I'm guessing he's the surgeon.

"Ms. Rose is out of surgery. She's going to be fine, but she's lost a lot of blood, so she'll be admitted for a few days. Someone will come get you once she's out of recovery. She's a lucky woman. If the bullet had been any lower, this wouldn't be the outcome."

"Thank you so much for saving her." Smiling, he nods and leaves the room, and I blow out a weighted breath.

"She's going to be OK," Ellis says. "You get to be lovesick together."

Sasha

"Good morning," Camilla says.

"Morning," I croak. I notice the irritation from my dry throat, but it doesn't compare to the pain in my chest and shoulder.

"You're in pain. I should call the nurse."

"No. I told them in recovery not to give me any narcotics. They said you told them I was an addict before surgery, so they asked."

Getting out of the reclining chair, she walks over and clutches my hand.

"I hope you realize your strength."

"Yeah, and I'm wondering where it came from."

"Sasha, what you did yesterday was reckless, but I'll forever be indebted to you for saving our lives."

I shake my head. "You kept me alive for years, so I was more than willing to repay you. My way was just faster and lazier." Camilla snickers, and I begin to laugh, but the pain radiating from my chest stops me. "Ugh, this sucks. Where is Liam? Is he OK?"

"Yes, he's home with Ellis. I came back about an hour ago, but you weren't alone last night."

"Who was here?"

"Greyson. He stayed so I could be with Liam. He ran home to shower when I got here, but he's coming right back."

Turning my head, I look out the window.

"I vaguely recall him being in the ambulance with me. I screwed up his party."

"He left there before you were shot, and even if he'd left for this reason, it wouldn't be your fault."

I look back at her. "Was he coming to see me?"

"Yes."

"What does that mean?"

"I think you need to wait to talk to him about it."

I frown. "Seeing him will only make getting over him that much harder. I do believe he misses the fun we were having, but I think deep down he wants someone like Whitney. Well, maybe he doesn't want a bitch like her, but he wants someone who fits in their world."

"I want someone smart, funny, kind and gorgeous," Greyson says. I turn my head toward the doorway. "And you possess all those qualities."

"That's my cue to leave," Camilla says. "I'll be in the waiting room."

She's out the door lickety-split, and Greyson strolls over to me. I'm gazing up at him and breathing in his intoxicating post-shower scent. His hair is slightly damp, and his jeans are hanging loose on his tapered hips. I know this because his t-shirt is snug on his torso the way I love.

He brushes my hair with his fingers. "I was supposed to be the daring one last night, not you. You're such a weirdo."

"I'm shot, and you're calling me weird?"

"Yes, because only a weirdo would step in front of a moving bullet."

"Don't make me laugh. It hurts." I wince. "I heard you stayed here with me last night. Thank you."

"It was where I belonged."

"Why? Why did you leave your party?" Dragging over a chair, he sits next to me and places my hand between his, resting them on the bed.

"I ended things with Whitney for good. I want to be with you, Sasha. Can you forgive me for being a coward?"

"You've been doing this dance with her for years. Are you sure you can stop?"

"You're right. I've been dancing with her for years, and none of it means shit to me. I danced with you one night, and I'll remember it for the rest of my life."

Lifting my hand, he kisses it. "She wants a fairy tale. I want forever."

"Those are exceptionally sweet words, but I don't know." I crack a smile, letting on that ultimately, I'll cave, but he must work for it first.

"I want popsicles in my freezer and Skittles in my new couch cushions. I want an excuse to watch zombie shows, and I don't want to sleep in my cabin alone ever again. Oh, and I sure as hell don't want to do *this* alone." He pulls out a folded-up paper from his pants pocket.

"What's that?" Opening it up, he hands it to me. I skim over the words, and my eyes bulge when I see that he ordered concert tickets. "You're taking me to see Justin Bieber? These are front row seats."

"Move back in with me. I'll even let you hit the snooze button in my bedroom."

"OK."

His eyes light up. "That's a yes?"

"Yes, and I won't even abuse the snooze button." I hold up the paper in my hand. "You spent too much money on these tickets. I'm not worth hundreds of dollars." Greyson's sudden laughter echoes in the room. He holds his stomach and shakes his head. "What's so funny?"

"You're worth way more than those concert tickets." His dimples make their grand entrance, and I can't believe I get to look at them forever. "Trust me, Ladybug, you have no idea the amount of money you're worth."

Ellis

"How is he?" Camilla asks as she strolls into the family room.

"He's good. We built an airplane out of Legos, and I took him outside to play before lunch. I can't believe how resilient he is, but we're taking him to counseling regardless."

"I agree."

"I talked to my FBI contact. He assured me Christopher is never getting out of prison. The case will be a headache, but once he's convicted, we can put it behind us. Anyway, I thought you'd be gone longer today." I glide my fingers through Liam's hair as he naps with his head on my lap.

"I felt like the third wheel. Greyson won't leave Sasha's side, and they're adorable together. You'd never know she was shot yesterday since she's by far the happiest I've ever seen her."

"Good. I'm glad they worked it out." Camilla squeezes inside the small space between me and the arm of the sofa and rests her head on my shoulder.

"It seems like the drama never ends, but I have a feeling it's only up from here."

"I agree, and we need to discuss the wedding again."

Lifting her head, she looks at me. "I told you I don't want an elaborate wedding. I thought we agreed on this."

"Weddings are typically a big deal for the bride, so I want to be sure you're OK with having only our family present."

"I have almost no one to invite, and I don't wish to see you miserable on our wedding day. You'd be the center of attention in front of hundreds of people your mother would insist on inviting."

"I couldn't be miserable at my wedding, and you'd be the center of attention, not me."

"We want the same thing, so let's set a date soon and make it happen."

I lean my head against hers. "I can't wait to make you mine. In the meantime, can you take my place here? I have something I need to do."

"Absolutely. I've been missing him like crazy." Camilla slides in under Liam, and as if he knows, he curls his body against hers. The nausea over yesterday washes over me again. To think I could've lost them both, and our future, too, is still a fresh wound.

After walking upstairs to my office, I sit at my desk. I look for a phone number on the thumb drive Lawson gave me and dial it.

"Ciao," I say to Camilla's grandmother. It's time to tell her a story about her beautiful granddaughters....

EPILOGUE

Three Weeks Later

Camilla

I clasp Sasha's hand at the dinner table.

"I'm glad you're healing up and feeling better."

"Me, too." Snickering, she leans over to my ear. "Greyson is happy about it, as well. We're finally spending *quality* time together, if you know what I mean."

"Ewww, I don't want to think about it." She giggles, and I could burst with joy over her happiness and from having us all here for dinner as a family. Ellis is to my left at the head of the table, and Greyson and Sasha are to my right.

To the other side of Ellis is Liam, who's trying to build something with his long green beans. Estella and James are seated next to him, and Irene's at the other end of the table. Ellis said he had some exciting news that involved her, too.

He taps his glass with his fork. "I want to make a toast." Everyone picks up their glasses, and I watch Liam look around. Grinning, he holds his cup up, too. "Over the last several months, I've become a richer man. No monetary value could ever be placed on the happiness I've acquired."

Ellis clears his throat, his admission making him uncomfortable and nervous.

"I'm blessed to have found an amazing woman to share my life with, who gave me the greatest gift a man could receive, my Liam here." Our kiddo glances around at everyone staring. "I never dreamed daddy would become my favorite word, but it has.

"I'm grateful for my soon-to-be sister-in-law, who helped save my family. As a bonus, she's making my cousin be a less pain in the ass." Everyone chuckles, and Greyson rolls his eyes. "In all seriousness, cousin, my life is richer with you in it, too."

"You said a bad word, Boss-Daddy."

"I'll put money in your piggy bank later."

"It's getting so, so full." Laughter fills the room again.

"I'm thankful for my parents, who I've grown to know and understand. You raised me to be an honest, decent man, and I'm grateful for that.

"Irene, I want to thank you for putting up with me all these years and for treating my family like they're your own. I hope you'll stick around for many years to come."

Ellis's eyes become glassy. "I also want to toast the family who are no longer with us. Through their flaws, we were brought together, and the good in them they lost sight of is what we'll keep in our hearts. Cheers, everyone."

With each one of us emotional, we clink our glasses together. "OK, now for my big announcement." Grinning with pride, Ellis reaches inside his blazer and pulls out a stack of envelopes.

"I hate to disappoint you, Mom and Dad, but Camilla and I have decided against a formal wedding, but with that said, we want everyone at this table by our side as we say our vows." Walking around the table, Ellis passes out the envelopes.

"What's this, dear?" Estella asks.

"Everyone, open them." Even Liam has one, and Ellis helps him so he doesn't tear what's inside.

"Ellis," I say before I cover my mouth.

"You bought us plane tickets to Italy?" Sasha asks excitedly.

"Yes. I'd like for all of you to join us in Italy for our wedding."

Jumping from my chair, I throw my arms around his neck.

"Thank you. This is incredible." He kisses my head. "I was hoping you wouldn't mind."

"Are you kidding?"

"Irene, I'd like you to join us in Venice. Then, I've arranged for you to fly to Florence to stay with your family for a vacation."

Covering her chest with her hand, she begins to weep.

"Oh, thank you, Mr. Burke."

"I have one more surprise for Camilla and Sasha." Ellis pushes buttons on his phone and hands it to me.

It rings a few times before a woman says, "Ciao." I cover my face, stunned by the voice I hear.

"Nonna, is that you?"

"Si, my nipotina." I sob into the phone, and she cries, too. "I hear you're coming to see me. I go to your wedding." Her English is broken, but I understand her words and can't believe them. It's a dream I've had for over a decade.

I look at Ellis. "My grandmother is going to be at our wedding?"

"Yes, baby."

"I'm going to let you talk to Sasha." I hand the phone to my sister, and she cries, as well, when she hears her grandmother for the first time since she was a little girl.

Grabbing Ellis, I hug him like my life depends on it.

"How will I ever thank you?"

"You already did, my Rose—twice." Releasing me, he places his palm over my belly. "And I'm certain this one will be as beautiful as her mother."

The End

END NOTES

Thank you for reading *The Terms Duet*.

Keep up with release information at
http://www.rubyrowe.com. You can also follow Ruby on
Amazon, Goodreads, Facebook, Twitter, Instagram,
Pinterest, and BookBub.

If you enjoy Ruby Rowe's writing, you may like romance
stories under her other pen name, Scarlet Wolfe.

Lastly, if you enjoy my writing, I'd greatly appreciate it if you
would leave me ratings or reviews. Thank you!

ACKNOWLEDGMENTS

Thank you to my amazing husband, Patrick, who didn't hesitate to support my desire to write under an additional pen name.

Like always, he wanted to support my dream, even if it added more work to my hectic schedule. I am so blessed to have such a patient man by my side.

Family and friends, I love you, and I appreciate you lending me an ear to blab to about my books.

Readers, thank you for taking a chance on *The Terms Duet*. I couldn't write full-time if it weren't for passionate book lovers like yourselves! I feel blessed anytime someone reads a story of mine. I hope you'll check out my future books and my first release, *Summer Trouble*.

Rosa Sharon, my MA/PA, thank you for your help! Your marketing knowledge is invaluable, and I appreciate how you're always there for me.

Samantha Wiley, I can never thank you enough for all you do. You're a great editor and a wonderful friend. I'm happy "Ruby Rowe" gives me another excuse to talk with you every day.

If you need editing or proofreading, Samantha and Rachel can help you at Proofreading by the Page!

I want to give a big shout out to Jo-Anna at Just Write. Creations for creating the sexy cover. She always produces fantastic work!

Thank you to Meg Estey and Melissa Gartland for helping me with my Denver, Colorado, research.

Thank you to my beta readers, Jennifer Balmer, Angela Evans, Dana Gallie, Amanda Hill, Rachael Leissner, Rachel Pugh, Karina Wade and Samantha Wiley. Your feedback is invaluable.

Bloggers, authors and readers who are sharing *The Terms Duet* with your followers and friends, I'm so appreciative. You have busy work schedules and personal lives, yet you use a portion of your precious time to help me succeed.

I can't thank you enough. Thank you, as well, for leaving reviews. Good or bad, they're important for both readers and authors.

Happy Reading!
Ruby

Made in the USA
Columbia, SC
05 January 2018